"O'Ban...
bidden...
Reader...
the hai...

"In the...
alive in this fourth book set in Egypt during the rule
of the powerful Roman Caesars."

DAUGHTER OF EGYPT

"The heroine is a smart, strong woman, a perfect
match for the warrior hero. Their sexual tension
permeates the novel, and the culmination of their
love is hot and sweet."

SWORD OF ROME

"O'Banyon continues the tale she began in *Lord of
the Nile* by introducing Adhaniá. The historical facts
are intriguing, and the effort of the characters to
foil the plot against Caesar is heartwarming. The
sensual scenes are sparse but tender and hot."

LORD OF THE NILE

"Fans of Egyptian lore and facts will find O'Banyon's
historical right up their alley. She sprinkles politi-
cal intrigue and love throughout the pages of this
enjoyable book."

HAWK'S PURSUIT

"O'Banyon's third book in her Hawk series is possibly the best yet, with a regular little spitfire heroine, great verbal sparring and some very emotional scenes."

THE MOON AND THE STARS

"Fast-paced and filled with adventure, this is a great read . . . O'Banyon has created some wonderful characters, an interesting plot and an entertaining book."

HEART OF TEXAS

"O'Banyon excels at bringing the grit and harsh beauty of the West and its brave pioneers to life . . . *Heart of Texas* gets at the heart of the West and its readers."

HALF MOON RANCH: MOON RACER

"Kudos to Constance O'Banyon!"

RIDE THE WIND

"Ms. O'Banyon's story is well written with well-developed characters."

TYKOTA'S WOMAN

"Constance O'Banyon delivers a gripping and emotionally charged tale of love, honor and betrayal."

TEXAS PROUD

"*Texas Proud* is another good read from Ms. O'Banyon."

The Captive's Choice

"Our spirits speak to each other. Have you not realized this?"

Her eyes widened and she shook her head. "We are nothing alike. Besides my father, you are the most important man in the tribe. I am merely a white captive."

"You are much more than that. Come," he said encouragingly, "we will walk this way." Clutching her hands in desperation, she glanced around for some means of escape. Slowly she turned back to Wind Warrior. "You could have any woman you want."

His mouth settled in a firm line. "I have made my choice. Your father is waiting for your answer. As am I."

She was so small, so delicate, with a face so beautiful it haunted him day and night. Her green eyes were even now drawing him in, and he wanted to loosen her golden hair and run his fingers through it. He wanted to find out if it was as soft as he had imagined.

His eyes hardened; his voice was deep and forceful and fierce. "My brother or me."

CONSTANCE O'BANYON

Wind Warrior

LEISURE BOOKS NEW YORK CITY

A LEISURE BOOK®

February 2010

Published by

Dorchester Publishing Co., Inc.
200 Madison Avenue
New York, NY 10016

ISBN 10: 0-8439-6301-8
ISBN 13: 978-0-8439-6301-4
E-ISBN: 978-1-4285-0811-8

Visit us online at www.dorchesterpub.com.

This is for you, Jim, because you asked for another poem.

Pathways

When the pathway of life does not lead you in the
direction you would choose,
Do not abandon hope.
Instead, establish an alternate direction.
Follow your heart,
And walk that path with me.

Wind Warrior

Chapter One

Montana Wilderness, 1859

Snow whipped down the gully in great gusts, its strength tearing at the bearskin robe draped about the young Blackfoot's shoulders. He-Who-Waits shivered from uncertainty as well as from the icy fingers of winter that stung his cheeks.

Word had spread throughout the village that the council of elders was meeting to settle an important matter, and even though he was in his sixteenth year, and a warrior in training, He-Who-Waits approached the lodge with heavy misgiving. He, who had never been allowed inside the council lodge, had been summoned to appear before the elders.

What could they want with him? he wondered.

What had he done that would require their attention?

Pausing at the lodge opening, He-Who-Waits drew in a deep breath, summoning his courage and trying to ignore the knot that had tightened in his stomach.

As a member of the Blood Blackfoot tribe, he had been taught from birth never to show fear. Swallowing hard, he could feel the rhythm of his own heartbeat thudding in his veins.

He-Who-Waits was aware he was considered a

loner by the rest of the tribe. Even his boyhood companions did not understand his need for solitude. While they looked forward to the camaraderie of a hunt, he would much rather climb into the mountains and study the sky, the rock formations, and the rich green pine forests. When his friends happily clamored to practice with bow and lance, he was often found walking along the riverbank, listening to the wind as if he heard something no one else could.

Suddenly the lodge flap was thrown open and He-Who-Waits stepped back a pace when he saw his father standing before him. He flinched—if his own father had been called to the meeting, something serious was transpiring.

White Owl swept his hand forward, indicating his son should enter. "You must not keep the elders waiting," he said in a gruff voice. "Already they have asked what has delayed you."

Feeling the weight of his father's rebuke, He-Who-Waits experienced great shame. "I ask your forgiveness, Father. I found an injured hawk, and tried to heal its broken wing. I believe it will survive."

White Owl frowned as he looked at his son. The young warrior's mother had died giving him birth, and White Owl had allowed his son too much freedom. "Nothing should have been as important to you as attending this meeting."

The young man sobered. "It will not happen again."

"Go inside," White Owl said, with an edge to his tone.

He-Who-Waits was taller than most young warriors his age, so he was forced to duck his head to enter. The only illumination came from the fire in the middle of the lodge, and it took a moment for his eyes to adjust to the faint light. Shields, bows, and lances covered the leather interior, reminders of successful battles of the past. He recognized his family's mark on one of the shields and wondered which of his ancestors had been honored by having his shield displayed.

A war lance with three crow feathers caught his attention and he knew it had once belonged to his grandfather, Black Feather, who had died in a fierce battle against the Arapaho. The tales of his grandfather's daring deeds were still told around the campfires.

White Owl cleared his throat, bringing his son's attention back to the matter at hand. He-Who-Waits was startled when he noticed everyone's attention centered on him. He glanced at the chief, Broken Lance, who appeared to be watching him closely. Dipping his head, he respectfully acknowledged the great leader, who was seated to the right of the three elders.

He-Who-Waits was surprised to see his brother, Dull Knife, also seated at the council fire.

Lowering himself onto a buffalo robe beside his brother, He-Who-Waits met the unflinching stare of each elder. His gaze halted on Lean Bear, the eldest and most respected member of the council. It seemed to him the old man's eyes darkened with disapproval, so he quickly looked away.

He-Who-Waits feared he was in real trouble.

Broken Lance spoke, "It has been decided that in

the spring, a war party will raid along the Missouri River, striking at the heart of our enemy, the white soldiers from Fort Benton." The chief looked at Dull Knife. "I expect you to lead our warriors and bloody your tomahawks to avenge the females who were killed at berry-picking season last spring."

Dull Knife nodded.

"You will make certain," Broken Lance continued, "that the white man learns he cannot come to our lands and kill our people without reprisal."

Dull Knife raised his head to a proud tilt. It was a great honor to be asked to lead a war party. "I will do as you say. I will slay as many enemies as cross my path."

The chief agreed with a nod. "My woman still weeps for the daughter we lost. Though Tall Woman does not ask for revenge, I ask it for her." The chief shook his head. "Nothing can soothe her grief, but your raids will help put out the fire of revenge that burns inside me."

Dull Knife's eyes hardened. "I will slay two for every tribe member we lost that day. And as special revenge on the white race, I shall take one of their girl children to replace the daughter you lost in that raid."

He-Who-Waits frowned, his gaze settling on his brother's face. Dull Knife seemed eager to please the chief, but unaware of the trouble that taking a child from the white soldiers could bring upon their people. Something stirred in his mind—a warning. It had something to do with the raid, but the thought was gone before he could grasp it.

"Many of us lost family that day," Broken Lance

stated. "Though my woman still grieves for her loss, no white child can replace the daughter she loved. Still, bring all the young white females you can."

He-Who-Waits had lost a sister in the same raid that had claimed the daughter of the chief. The white soldiers had come upon the women as they picked berries. It had been a senseless massacre because the women had had no weapons to defend themselves. The soldiers had spared no one, and many innocents had died that day.

Still, He-Who-Waits wondered why he had been asked to attend this council—surely the elders did not expect him to join the raiding party.

He was inexperienced—not a trained warrior like his brother, who had fought in many battles. He-Who-Waits was suddenly startled out of his musings when he heard the chief speak his father's name.

"White Owl, my friend, I have chosen you to lead those tribe members who wish to live in Canada, far from the threat of the white soldiers. You will leave in the spring and be away for two turnings of the seasons, until they are settled in their new land. The elders have called this meeting so you can say what needs to be said before you depart."

"I accept the task of taking our people to Canada," White Owl said.

"Now is the time," Lean Bear intoned, "for you to speak of that which was foretold many summers ago." His voice cracked with emotion. His gaze rested briefly on White Owl. "Is that not so?"

"It is so," White Owl answered. "This is the day that I saw in my vision quest when I was in my twelfth summer, the time when most young boys seek their true name. Instead I was given a name to pass to my son."

He-Who-Waits glanced at his father with growing interest. White Owl had never spoken of his quest, although He-Who-Waits had asked him about it many times. His father had always said he would tell his sons when the time was right.

"Speak to us of the quest," prodded Black Bear, the youngest member of the council. "Let us know of the new name your son will receive here today."

White Owl nodded. "At the time of my quest, I went into the sweat lodge and lay upon my robe while my father poured water over hot stones. The steam was so thick, I could not even see my father when he left the lodge. I closed my eyes, waiting for my vision. For two days and one night I waited, thinking I must be unworthy to receive a new name. When my vision finally came to me, it was like nothing I had expected." White Owl paused for a moment as if he was reliving the experience. "A voice in my head whispered that I would have a son who would be a great warrior, and many would follow him in a time of great tribulation for our tribe. I was further told that this son would hear messages on the wind, and even the animals would speak to him. I was told this son must have a special name to signify his importance to the tribe."

He-Who-Waits glanced at his brother, awed by the unheard-of honor that was being bestowed upon Dull Knife. He had always been proud of his brother's achievements and was glad to be there to witness this great occasion.

"We will hear more of this vision," Lean Bear

croaked, pulling his buffalo robe tighter about his frail body. "Have we not waited years to be told of it?"

White Owl took a deep breath and closed his eyes for a moment. When he spoke, his voice trembled. "The wind whipped past the lodge flap, stealing my breath. At first I heard only a soft whisper . . . it was like nothing I had ever felt before or since." He paused for a moment, trying to find the right words. "It felt as if the wind was moving through my entire body."

Surprised murmurs rumbled through the lodge. Everyone looked amazed except for Broken Lance, who seemed to know what White Owl was about to say. The chief held his hand up to silence the others. "Let him speak."

White Owl seemed reluctant to continue, and his voice was low as he said, "The voice spoke not for me, but for my son. Of course I was confused. I was told I would have two sons and one daughter. I was told my eldest son would be a mighty warrior."

White Owl glanced at Dull Knife with a slight smile. "You have accomplished that."

Dull Knife raised his head proudly. However, the pleased expression froze on his face at his father's next words.

"But my vision was not meant for you, my son." White Owl's gaze dropped to his younger son. "My vision was for you."

He-Who-Waits whipped his head toward his father, not comprehending his words. "It must be a mistake," he whispered, turning to look at his brother. "I do not understand."

"Nor did I at first," White Owl answered. "You must put yourself in my place; I was but a boy when this vision came to me. I was confused as to its true meaning—but through the years I began to understand what the voice meant. Have you never wondered why I kept you from going on your own vision quest, my son?"

He-Who-Waits nodded, feeling shame creep into the deepest parts of his mind. "I have always thought I was unworthy."

White Owl laid his hand on the young man's shoulder. "Nay, my son. You are most worthy. Have I not watched your kindness to others, your generosity to those in need? Have I not seen you help those who could not help themselves? I was told to wait until your sixteenth winter, and that I have done. Now the time is right for you to have the name that belongs to you."

He-Who-Waits could not answer past the lump in his throat. In truth he was confused, and even a little concerned.

White Owl turned his attention to the council, but his words were for his younger son. "After this day, my son shall no longer be known as He-Who-Waits— his waiting is over. I was told he would be called 'Wind Warrior.'" White Owl smiled down at his younger son. "From this day forward, let no man call you He-Who-Waits."

Wind Warrior's mind was filled with questions that he dared not ask in the presence of this honored body of warriors. He thought of the name his father had just bestowed on him, and wondered at it.

His father motioned for him to stand. "Go now

to each of the elders and listen to their words of wisdom."

Wind Warrior stood, reluctant to look at his brother, who had been passed over in favor of himself. In truth, he wished his father's vision had been for Dull Knife instead of him.

As he passed before the council members, they touched his arm and called him by his new name. Some told him to look to the future, others warned him to remember the past. When he finally turned to face his brother, he saw dark anger in Dull Knife's eyes, and from somewhere inside a warning of danger swept through Wind Warrior's mind.

But why should he fear the brother he had always revered?

Wind Warrior's thoughts took a curious path—with a suddenness that surprised him, all pretense was stripped away and he saw Dull Knife as he really was; his brother was eaten up with jealously and filled with hate and resentment, and it was all directed at him—it always had been.

Why had he not seen that before?

Dull Knife's face was cast in harsh shadows, but his eyes gleamed with hatred. When he spoke, his tone was callous and threatening, and he did not care who heard him. "Today the honor is yours, little brother. But do not think you will ever be as good as me. Be wary about what the future brings. Look to your back, for I will be there." Dull Knife nodded curtly at his chief, ignored his father, then stalked across the lodge, forcefully thrusting the flap aside and departing without taking leave of the elders.

For a moment there was silence. White Owl

glanced at Wind Warrior, seeing the confusion in his eyes. "If all that I saw the night of my vision comes to pass, Dull Knife will covet everything that is yours, my son," he warned, his dark eyes filled with pain "I tell you this with a heavy heart, for I love you both. Respect your brother, but do not trust him."

"Your father speaks with wisdom," Broken Lance said, nodding at the young warrior in dismissal. "But there is always a fog over the future, and we cannot know all that is to come. Allow your instincts to guide you."

Wind Warrior followed his father outside. He hardly noticed it had stopped snowing and the sun had poked through the clouds—his mind was occupied with troubled thoughts.

How could he become a mighty warrior?

How could he save the tribe from disaster?

He raised his face to the sky as the wind rifled through his hair. He had to find out the meaning of his new name. He would seek the high country for answers.

Word spread quickly through the village about what had occurred at the council meeting. As Wind Warrior rode across the river on his way to the mountains, many curious gazes followed him.

With rage in his heart, Dull Knife stood in the shadow of a pine tree, watching his brother ride up the opposite embankment. Was he not the eldest son? Should not the honor bestowed on his brother have been his?

With anger still boiling inside him, Dull Knife turned away. He would recapture his glory in the spring; he would tie feathers in his hair, and paint his face. He would lead the warriors to victory over the white soldiers, and everyone would praise him.

His father's vision might belong to his brother, but come spring, the honor would be his. Staring across the river, Dull Knife was determined to make his own future.

Chapter Two

Evening shadows crept across the land as the sun sank low in the west. Wind Warrior halted his horse, glancing down at the river that snaked through the green valley below.

Dismounting, he ran his hand over his horse's mane. "Go home."

As if the animal understood Wind Warrior's words, it turned and galloped back toward the village.

Wind Warrior realized he was losing the light and hurriedly began the ascent up the steep incline. He needed solace for his troubled thoughts and hoped he might find it in the mountains that were so familiar to him.

Pausing beside a crystal stream that spilled over a rock cliff face, he dipped his hands in the cold water and drank thirstily.

There was a chill in the air, but Wind Warrior did not feel it; his mind was too busy recalling his brother's angry threats and his father's admonitions.

He shook off the feeling of tragedy that clung to him like a second skin. Here in the serenity of this secluded place he felt more at home than he did in his own village. Since he had been old enough to climb the mountain, he had sought the peacefulness he found here. Often he would linger for days in solitude, until hunger drove him back to the village. His father had never questioned his absences, nor had he allowed anyone else to.

Now that Wind Warrior thought about his life, it seemed strange that no one minded his spending so much time in the mountains. None of his friends were allowed such liberties. Many things he had once taken for granted, he now questioned.

Then Wind Warrior caught a sound that made him smile. Turning, he observed a mountain goat dart up the cliff and disappear through a thicket of cedar bushes. A lone hawk spread its wings and circled above him, its cry echoing in the silence.

He was surrounded by peacefulness, but Wind Warrior could find no comfort; his heart was pounding like a drum. Despite the cold wind, he felt sweat gathering between his shoulder blades.

Many questions troubled his mind, but Wind Warrior could find no answers.

He climbed the last few steps that took him to the very peak of the mountain. He was never to know how long he stood there lost in thought, but the sun had already dropped behind a nearby mountain and darkness enveloped him when he became aware of the chill of the night wind.

In the soft glow of moonlight, he raised his arms to the sky and closed his eyes, seeking clarity. Slowly he turned in the directions of the four winds, paying them homage. "How can I do what is expected of me?" he cried in a voice that echoed across the deep valley. "I am not this Wind Warrior my people expect me to be."

Nothing happened.

Still he waited in hope.

At first he felt a gentle tug at his mind, barely in his consciousness. As he raised his head and opened his arms wider, he felt the chilling touch of the wind against his mouth. Then with a suddenness that took Wind Warrior by surprise, the force of the wind gathered, sweeping across his face and increasing in intensity until it seemed to whip through his entire body.

Without warning, a push of the wind drove Wind Warrior to his knees. He gasped and struggled for breath. It felt as if he was caught in the middle of a whirlwind. He could not move, could not take in air.

Blackness was beckoning to him and he fell forward into a bottomless pit of darkness.

Later, much later, he blinked his eyes to the first light of morning. The wind was still whirling around him and it took all his strength just to stand. His throat was burning with thirst, yet he knew he would not seek water until he understood what was happening to him.

Closing his eyes, Wind Warrior felt a consuming consciousness stirring within him. The wind scattered his hair across his face and then released him so suddenly he fell to his knees, taking big gulps of air.

Now the wind gentled to a breeze, caressing his cheek, and a strong feeling of peace settled over him. When he opened his eyes, it seemed to him that the sky was brighter, his hearing keener, and the aroma of the pine trees was overwhelming.

How could such a thing be?

With a suddenness that filled his heart with joy, he watched a hawk ride the currents of the wind. When the bird broke away, it circled above him and landed on the branch of a nearby pine tree, watching him.

Wind Warrior heard no sound, but there was understanding in his mind: *Brother of the wind, we are of one spirit.*

Wind Warrior had been on the verge of manhood when he climbed the mountain, but two weeks later as he descended the rocky cliff, he felt old beyond his years.

When he reached the village, he went directly to his father's tipi.

"Tonight I sleep under the stars, my father. Tomorrow I build my own tipi."

White Owl nodded, examining his son's face and seeing newly acquired wisdom in Wind Warrior's eyes. "It will be as you say," he answered with understanding. "I knew this time would come for you. Embrace the gift that has been given to you."

As Wind Warrior erected his tipi, his thoughts were deep, his mind open to finding the answers that still eluded him.

The future reached out to him, beckoning.

He needed time to seek what was hidden from him.

He needed time to discover who he was.

Chapter Three

Although it was early afternoon, dewdrops still clung to the wild daisies the young girl gathered as she walked beside the grassy bank of the Missouri River. Thirteen-year-old Marianna Bryant had decided since her aunt Cora had been having one of her headaches, and didn't feel well enough to attend the annual picnic, it would be nice to take her a bouquet of wildflowers. Spotting a wide variety of flowers in glorious colors growing in a nearby ditch, she walked in that direction.

Aunt Cora had been hesitant to allow Marianna to attend the picnic without her. But she finally gave in when Marianna promised she would remain in sight of the others and not wander off and get lost in the woods, as she had on other occasions. Marianna didn't like to remember the time most of the troops from Fort Benton had been pulled off their usual duty to join in a search party to find her. For the first time, Aunt Cora had yelled at her that day when her uncle Matt had brought her home, looking frightened and bedraggled.

Pushing those unpleasant memories to the back of her mind, Marianna watched the women setting out the food, while the men lay back on the grass, talking and laughing. She caught the delicious aroma of meat roasting on the spit, and it made her hungry. Marianna hoped Mrs. Post had brought her mincemeat pie again this year—it was her favorite. But she also liked fresh corn on the cob, dripping with butter.

She was diverted from thoughts of food when she heard Susan Worthington's infectious laughter drifting on the wind. Susan had arrived three months before to marry Lieutenant Worthington. Although Marianna didn't know Susan very well, the young married woman always greeted her with a smile and a kind word. Aunt Cora had told Marianna that Susan and Lieutenant Worthington had grown up together in Philadelphia. Marianna had heard the older girls grumble because an outsider had captured the heart of Fort Benton's most eligible bachelor. She glanced around for Susan's husband, but did not see him. No doubt he was on patrol duty today.

Tightening the ribbons of her red and white bonnet beneath her chin, Marianna saw seventeen-year-old Lillian Baskin, the daughter of the folks that ran the trading post.

It was too late to escape—Lillian had already spotted her, and was hurrying in her direction. Marianna had only spoken to Lillian on a few occasions, and she didn't really like her, although Aunt Cora said she must like everyone. Perhaps if Aunt Cora heard the hateful way Lillian gossiped about other people, she would understand why Marianna didn't like the girl.

Marianna took a deep breath and braced herself for the intrusion.

"Those are mighty fancy shoes to be wearing on a picnic. 'Specially since it's muddy," Lillian said, dropping down beside Marianna. "You trying to impress someone?"

"No. Why should I?"

"Well, you're off here by yourself like you thought you was too good for the rest of us poor folks."

Marianna's lips tightened at the older girl's spiteful remarks. "That's not so."

Lillian was a large-boned girl, with bright red hair and freckles sprinkled across her nose. Although she was not considered pretty, there were plenty of young men who seemed to admire her. Marianna glanced down at her new red leather shoes and scowled. "I don't want to impress anyone." Then she said worriedly, "I hope Aunt Cora won't be mad at me when she finds out I wore these today. She sent all the way to St. Louis for them."

"She always orders your clothing from St. Louis instead of buying at Pa's store like most everyone else does. Ma says your aunt thinks too much of herself just because she was once a famous singer before she married Lieutenant West. She says your aunt's voice must have failed her and she married the first man who would have her."

Marianna clamped her lips together, trying to control her temper. She stared at Lillian as if she'd lost her mind. "Your mother is wrong. Aunt Cora was performing in England when she got word that my parents had died in a landslide in the Sangre de Cristo Mountains, just outside Santa Fe in New Mexico Territory. Aunt Cora was my father's sister and the only family I had left. She left England so she could take care of me. She met Uncle Matt at the army post in Santa Fe and they were married a year later." Marianna's frown deepened. "My aunt still has a beautiful voice, and everyone knows it."

Lillian shrugged. "I didn't say I agreed with my ma." She pulled a blade of grass and chewed on the end of it. "How come you weren't hurt in the landslide that killed your folks?"

"My parents' ranch was near the base of the mountains. The day they were killed, they left me home with the cook."

"Don't you miss 'em?"

Marianna didn't really want to talk about herself with Lillian, but she couldn't think of a way to leave without seeming rude. "I don't remember them. Aunt Cora and Uncle Matt are the only parents I've ever known."

"So you think of them as your ma and pa?"

Marianna had never thought about it. "My first memory is of Aunt Cora singing me to sleep at night. Her voice was so pure and beautiful, I tried to stay awake to listen."

"Ma says she's nothing but an opera singer."

Marianna's eyes narrowed with annoyance. "A very famous one."

"You must take after her. I've seen Parson Rincon glaring at you when you sing so loud you drown out the rest of us. "

Her face reddening, Marianna nodded her head in agreement. "I know, I know. I just get so filled up with happiness when I sing, I forget where I am. Aunt Cora always warns me to tone my voice down. I do try."

"Ma says you're just showing off."

Marianna stood and glared down at Lillian. "It seems your mother has a lot to say about other people's business."

"Well, you don't have to get snippy about it. Most everyone else thinks like Ma does. I heard tell your aunt teaches you to read and write herself, instead of sending you to the post school with the rest of the soldiers' children."

Marianna decided to leave before she really lost her temper and told Lillian what people said about her mother's gossiping. In an attempt to jump across a ditch, Marianna landed short of the other side and wound up on the bottom. She felt mud ooze into her shoes, and drew in a deep breath.

Aunt Cora was not going to be happy that she had ruined her new shoes.

Lillian's laughter was tinged with malice, and she hollered loud enough for Marianna to hear, "I wonder what your aunt Cora's going to say when she sees those fancy shoes she ordered all the way from St. Louis."

Ignoring Lillian's jab, Marianna grabbed up a twig and attempted to scrape some of the mud away. But she only managed to smear it onto the buckles and straps. She paused to glance at Fort Benton, wishing she had stayed home. There were no girls her age at the picnic, and she surely didn't want to spend any more time with Lillian.

Flopping against the side of the ditch, which was so deep it came to her waist, she considered walking back to the fort, but decided against it since the settlement was over a mile away.

It had been a long time since she had thought about her folks, or wondered what they had been like. It was difficult to miss someone she couldn't remember. She couldn't imagine loving anyone more than she loved Aunt Cora and Uncle Matt. It had been Aunt Cora who had nursed her through sickness and Uncle Matt who put her on her first horse, and soothed her when she fell and skinned her knees.

As far as school was concerned, Marianna always looked forward to her daily lessons with Aunt Cora, who had a way of making history come alive. Most of all, Marianna loved geography, because Aunt Cora had been to many of the countries she told her about, and shared her experiences.

Marianna's gaze swept across the distance toward the river. She stood motionless as she watched a paddlewheel boat making its voyage back to Independence, Missouri. The boat would no doubt be loaded with fine furs and trade goods. She lost interest when the boat disappeared around a bend in the river.

The sound of happy laughter floated on the air, and Marianna smiled as she watched several small children dart behind trees and thick bushes, playing a game of tag. Deciding not to join the picnickers just yet, Marianna climbed out of the ditch, laying her flowers on the embankment. There were thickets near the river and huckleberries would soon be in season. Uncle Matt loved huckleberry pie.

Suddenly Marianna's attention was drawn to muffled sounds coming from the river. Curious, she climbed up high enough to see over the embankment and noticed about a dozen canoes.

Her heart froze.

Indians!

She tried not to panic because there were always Indians hanging around the fort.

But these Indians looked different somehow—they were taller, leaner. Lifting her hand, she shaded her eyes against the glare of the sun—it looked to her as though their faces were painted! Uncle Matt had told her that when Indians went on a raid, they usually painted their faces.

Frozen in horror, Marianna watched them paddle toward the shore. It appeared that they were deliberately staying within the shadows of the trees to avoid being seen. Her first instinct was to run, to hide. She slid back down the embankment into the ditch, huddling close to the side, her body quaking.

Closing her eyes tightly, she hoped the Indians would paddle on by. Since this part of the woods was on a high incline, surely the Indians could not see the picnickers from the river. At least Marianna hoped they couldn't.

Dread filled her heart when she heard the Indians pulling the canoes onto the riverbank. She hunched lower in the ditch, hoping they wouldn't discover her hiding place.

But what about the others?

She must warn them of the danger.

Marianna rose up enough to peer past a clump of pine trees where the unsuspecting picnickers were still playing tag, unaware of the danger. She attempted to call out to warn them, but her throat was clogged with fear, and only a shuddering moan slipped past her trembling lips.

Glancing hopefully toward the fort, Marianna

realized it was too far away for help to reach them in time. With her heart pounding, Marianna heard a shout and saw some of the men grabbing up their rifles and herding the women and children toward the wagons. She was thankful they were aware of the danger.

That's when Marianna realized her own plight. If she attempted to run to the others, the Indians would see her.

Hide!

That was her only hope.

It was as if her body were frozen in place and she couldn't move. Burying her face in the spindly grass that grew alongside the ditch, she clamped her hands over her ears, flattening her body against the muddy embankment. A sob was building inside her throat and she swallowed twice, trying not to make any sound that would draw the Indians' attention.

Suddenly screams filled the air, followed by the sound of gunfire. Above the fray she heard Widow Harkin's voice as she directed the others to the wagons. Why were the Indians raiding so near the fort? No one had considered it dangerous to picnic so near Fort Benton.

Tremors shook Marianna's slight body and she clamped her hands over her mouth to keep from screaming when she heard the clatter of wagons and realized that she was being left behind. If only she had stayed at home today as Aunt Cora had wanted her to, she'd be safe.

What must she do?

Run!

Reacting on instinct, Marianna leaped to her feet,

deciding to follow the ditch until she came to the thickest part of the woods. Then she might be able to follow the old trail home. With her heart beating so tumultuously it felt as if it would burst through her chest, Marianna ran as fast as her legs would take her. There would be a wide-open space before she reached the thickest part of the woods, but she had to take the chance—the Indians would surely find her if she stayed where she was.

Hearing a scream, and then a gurgling sound, Marianna paused, tears blinding her. Should she try to help whoever was in trouble? But what could she do?

Guilt lay heavy on her shoulders. If only she had called out to the others in time, all of them might have made it to safety. She had been cowardly. Taking a deep breath, she moved cautiously through the mud. Just ahead the ditch curved toward the woods. If she could make it that far, she might be safe.

Turning to gaze back at the picnic area, Marianna managed to gather the courage to raise her head just enough to peek over the embankment—and she wished she hadn't. Shivering with horror, she saw Lillian's mother lying sprawled on bloodstained grass; Widow Harkin was slumped against a tree, her mouth open, her eyes staring at nothing. If there were any other bodies, Marianna didn't see them. But she knew that those who hadn't made it to the wagons must all be dead.

Fear and guilt mingled with heavy grief, but what could she have done against an enemy bent on killing innocent people?

Nothing.

Fighting a wave of dizziness, she slumped onto the muddy ground, shaking so hard her teeth rattled. Where was Lillian? Marianna hadn't seen her. She clamped her hands over her ears when she recognized Susan Worthington's scream. Whimpering, she whispered a quick prayer that the Indians wouldn't kill her.

When rational thought finally returned, Marianna realized the Indians would surely see her if she remained where she was.

It was already too late.

Marianna froze in terror as one of the Indians jumped into the ditch, waving a bloody tomahawk in her face. The upper part of his face was hideously streaked with black paint. She tried to look away, but those black eyes held her gaze, and she saw her own death.

In that moment Marianna knew she wanted very badly to live.

The Indian reached out his bloodstained hand to her, and she backed away. He grabbed her by the wrist and yanked her toward him with such force that pain tore through her arm. But pain could not compete with the fear that roared in her mind. Her chest burned, and she finally gasped, realizing she'd been holding her breath.

The savage climbed out of the ditch and pulled her up beside him with such force that she heard the bone in her arm snap. Biting her lip to keep from screaming, she staggered, falling to the ground in agony.

The Indian muttered something to one of the others, then half carried and half dragged Marianna toward the waiting canoes. In the distance, she heard the sound of riders, and knew the solders were pouring out of the fort toward them. Glancing back over her shoulder, Marianna realized they would not arrive in time to save her.

Marianna's tormentor shoved her into one of the canoes and leaped in beside her as the current pulled them to the middle of the river. She cried out when she saw Susan Worthington and Lillian in other canoes. Hot tears blinded her and she reached out to Susan when the canoe she was in passed so close she could have touched Susan's hand.

Her captor's black eyes narrowed as he hit Marianna a stunning blow with the blunt end of his tomahawk. Pain exploded in her head.

Everything around her reeled and blackness rolled over her, stealing the light.

Chapter Four

Marianna awoke slowly, wondering why she felt motion beneath her, and why she felt sick. It took her only a moment to recall what had happened.

Panicked, she realized she was still in the canoe. A deep sob built inside her—the Indians were taking her far into the wilderness where Uncle Matt would never find her. There wasn't a part of her body that didn't hurt. She was so heartsick and lonely she felt like weeping, but she didn't dare.

When she saw her captor staring at her, terror took over her reasoning. She could not control her quivering body, and she clamped her hand over her mouth, hoping the queasiness would pass. She felt feverish and the pain in her arm was agonizing, making her think it was broken. In an attempt to ease the pain, Marianna tried to cradle her arm, but it didn't help.

Anguish and fear battled for possession of her mind. She struggled to sit up, while averting her eyes so she wouldn't have to look at the Indian who had captured her. She felt disoriented and fell back weakly against the bottom of the canoe. There was a huge lump on her forehead where the savage had hit her, and it throbbed painfully.

Glancing up, she met the Indian's gaze, and was sorry she had—those eyes were like black holes, sharp and cutting, and devoid of human feeling. She would receive no mercy from him.

Marianna cringed when he drew the paddle out of the water and hit her a stunning blow to the stomach.

She lay in the bottom of the canoe, unable to move, lost in utter pain and dread. She felt bile rise in her throat and swallowed it back down. Slowly the world tilted and she closed her eyes, trying to right it.

Then she pitched forward into darkness once more.

When Marianna regained consciousness, her first thoughts were of Lillian and Susan. Easing herself upward, she fought against another bout of nausea. Reaching into the water, she splashed her face and then cupped her hands and took a drink. When she could focus, Marianna turned to the canoe beside her and saw Lillian huddled in the bottom.

Moving her head was an effort for Marianna because the movement shot pain through her. But she had to know Susan was all right. Slowly looking over her shoulder, she was relieved to see Susan in the third canoe back.

They were all still alive—at least for the moment.

Marianna didn't want to think about the people who had died in the raid, but she couldn't help herself. Widow Harkin and Lillian's mother were the only bodies she'd seen. She felt pity for Lillian's loss. But then, perhaps those who had died were the fortunate ones.

Hopelessness overwhelmed her. There was very little chance that they would be rescued. The Indians would expect to be followed, and had probably made plans to mislead anyone trying to overtake them.

In despair, Marianna closed her eyes and finally fell asleep. Sometime later the roar of the Great Falls awakened her, and she realized the Indians were rowing toward shore.

Marianna was ruthlessly jerked to her feet and yanked out of the canoe. Trying to stifle a cry of pain, she stood trembling as several of the Indians smashed the canoes and sank them to the bottom of the river. Any thought of rescue plummeted when other Indians emerged from the woods leading horses.

Susan suddenly appeared beside Marianna, and clasped her hand. There was a deep gash on Susan's forehead and one eye was swollen shut. "Are you all right?" Marianna asked.

Lillian inched toward the other two. "None of us are," she said woefully. "They are going to kill us all."

"I don't think so," Susan remarked in a quiet tone, but Marianna guessed she was merely trying to ease their fears. "Otherwise why would they have brought us this far? It doesn't make sense."

"Then they'll rape us all, which would be worse," Lillian whined.

"Lillian, I'm so sorry about your mother," Marianna said, reaching toward the young woman.

Lillian's chin quivered. "Why should you care? Your aunt and uncle are still alive."

Susan shook her head. "This morning I was sorry

my husband had to go out on patrol and couldn't attend the picnic. Now I'm happy he wasn't there or he'd . . . probably be dead."

Marianna saw blood was dripping into Susan's eyes and fumbled with her one good arm to tear a strip from her petticoat. "Let me help you." She dabbed at the blood. "I could do this better if I had water."

Susan looked at Marianna with gratitude and with pity. "I can see that your arm's broken. You're the one who needs help." Susan ripped a wide strip from the bottom of her own petticoat and fashioned a sling, quickly helping Marianna slip her arm into it and tying it about her neck. "Try to keep your arm close to your body. It'll hurt less that way."

Lillian was shaking so badly, she could hardly speak. Clutching Susan's hand, she started weeping. "We're as good as dead." Her sobs rose to a high-pitched wail. "I want my ma and pa. But Ma's dead and maybe Pa is too."

"Stop it!" Marianna warned Lillian, noticing she was drawing the attention of several of the Indians. "They'll hurt you if you carry on like this."

There was no time to say anything more because the Indians were beginning to mount their horses. The one who'd captured Marianna mounted his horse and reached down, pulling her on behind him.

Riding behind the man made Marianna shiver with revulsion, especially since she had to slide her good arm around his waist to keep from falling. The jostling of the horse made her head ache more, and her arm throbbed so much she could hardly stand the pain. Marianna dared not complain—she had learned that her captor retaliated swiftly and mercilessly.

She saw Lillian just ahead of her, and Susan was riding behind another Indian a few horses back. If only they could rest for a while, maybe her arm would stop throbbing.

But the Indians rode on, rarely pausing to rest the horses. Marianna finally reached the point where she could no longer hold her head up. Despite her dislike for the Indian, she was forced to lean her head against his shoulder.

Dull Knife was pleased that the raid had gone so well. There was no chance that the white soldiers would be able to catch up to them; still, he issued the order for Wild Feather to backtrack to make certain they'd left no trail.

He nudged his horse forward. Glancing at the now overcast sky, Dull Knife smiled. Everything had gone in his favor—it would rain before the day was over, washing away any tracks they might leave behind.

Looking down at the small grimy hand clutching his side, he knew the white girl hated touching him, and he found satisfaction that she was forced to bend to his will. If a man did not mind her strange yellow hair, or her odd green eyes, she looked well enough. The important thing was that she was about the age of the chief's dead daughter. If Broken Lance chose to take this child, he might feel indebted to Dull Knife, and that was just what Dull Knife intended.

The hand that clutched his side trembled and he heard the young girl sigh. She was in pain; he knew that. But so far she had not given him much trouble. If she did, he would see that she regretted it.

Charging Bull rode beside Dull Knife, respect in his gaze. Most of the warriors admired Dull Knife for his bravery, though several of them had voiced their disapproval of how harshly he had treated his young captive. But what did he care what they thought, as long as they followed his orders?

After a moment Charging Bull spoke. "What will you do with the yellow hair?"

Turning his dark gaze on the warrior, Dull Knife glared at him. "I have not yet decided. But why should you care?"

"I would buy her from you."

Dull Knife's eyes narrowed. "No. I will offer her to the chief and his woman."

Charging Bull tightened the reins to control his spirited mount. "What about the older one?" He nodded at Susan. "What of her?"

Dull Knife turned to glance back at his second captive. "She is too advanced in age to take to our way of life. I have no use for her."

"Then perhaps you would trade her to me?"

"What do you have that I could possibly want?"

"My captive with the red hair, and two fine horses."

Dull Knife shook his head. "I do not want your toothless horses, and I certainly do not want the one with red hair."

Charging Bull's temper flared, but he had learned to guard his tongue around Dull Knife. "I like the looks of your older captive. She would do very well for my second wife. What if I offer you the red-headed one and three horses?"

"Do not speak to me about either of my captives. I will do with them as I please."

Still Charging Bull persisted. "I have thought *I* might present *my* captive to Broken Lance." He met Dull Knife's gaze. "I have not injured her, as you have this younger one. Perhaps Broken Lance will choose my white captive over yours."

Snorting, Dull Knife glanced back at the red-headed girl, whose eyes were swollen and puffy from crying. "Broken Lance will never choose that one—she cries too much, and she is older than the yellow-haired one, who is wise enough not to complain too much. If that one was my captive," he said contemptuously, "she would already be dead."

Dull Knife was thoughtful for a moment. He was beginning to think he should not have been so rough with the yellow-haired one. The chief's woman probably wouldn't want an injured captive. He would refrain from harming her further if the girl did not provoke him.

Frowning, he thought back to the day of the council meeting when his brother had stolen his glory. Jealousy still burned through him. Let his brother be the favored one for now. Dull Knife had other plans.

Thunder rolled through the valley and lightning streaked across the sky. The heavens opened and rain fell in heavy drops. He felt the girl shiver with cold. If she became ill, she would be no good to him or to Broken Lance.

* * *

Tears mixed with the rain. Marianna was wet and miserable. The pounding of the horse's hooves continued to jar her body, shooting pain through her arm. She was so weary she could hardly lift her head from where it rested on the Indian's back—even with the rain the smell of blood still clung to him, and her stomach churned. She wasn't sure how much longer she could endure the pain.

One thing Marianna did know—if she got the chance, she would escape. She would rather be lost in the woods and devoured by wild animals than remain this savage's prisoner. But at the moment she was just too bone weary to do anything. It was only moments later that they stopped to rest the horses and Marianna was lifted to the ground with a gentleness she had not expected.

Struggling to keep from falling, she watched Lillian and Susan being led in her direction. Lillian was still crying, and Susan was white-faced. All three of them dropped down on the wet grass in total misery.

"How is your arm?" Susan inquired, reaching forward to straighten the rain-soaked sling. "Does it pain you much?"

Marianna knew that Susan was trying to be strong for them. And the woman's matter-of-fact manner was comforting amidst the uncertainty of their situation. Marianna was determined to be brave too. She forced a smile. "It feels better since you made me the sling. Thank you, Susan."

"Neither of you asks about me," Lillian whined.

"What about what I'm suffering? Has either of you thought of my pain?"

"You don't have a broken arm," Susan told her gently. "Try to control yourself, or those savages *will* break your arm, and you'll find out what Marianna is suffering." Susan gazed at the Indians, who were huddled about a fire they had just built. "I wanted to urge both of you to escape if you get the chance. Take any opportunity to run."

Marianna met the married woman's eyes, seeing acceptance in their brown depths. "What about you?"

"Marianna, you are young, but I am finding you to be levelheaded, so I'm going to be honest with you—" She softly touched Marianna's cheek. "Should anything happen to me, you will have to be the strong one."

Shaking her head because she didn't understand what Susan was telling her, Marianna said, "But you will be with us."

"Marianna, promise me something," Susan said, lowering her voice, but still speaking with urgency. "If you ever do escape and find your way home, tell Cullen for me . . . that I was not afraid. Tell him I am taking his love with me wherever I go. Tell him . . . tell him to find another woman to love. I do not want him to spend his life in loneliness."

Lillian broke out in fresh tears. "We all are going to die! That's what you think, isn't it?"

With gut-wrenching clarity, Marianna realized what Susan was telling them, even if Lillian didn't. "If I ever make it back to the fort, I will tell your husband what you said," Marianna vowed. "I promise I will. But let us hold on to hope—we need that." She brushed a tear away with a grimy hand and looked at Lillian. "Aunt Cora always told me when things look the stormiest, that is the time to look for a rainbow."

Lillian glared at her. "What's that supposed to mean? It's raining, but there ain't any rainbow."

Susan nodded. "I believe what Marianna's aunt meant is we must look for the good in any bad situation."

"There-ain't-nothing-good-to-think-about," Lillian stated, enunciating every word. She glared at Marianna. "You're just a silly little girl, and we aren't listening to you anyway."

Marianna's nerves were frayed from Lillian's constant complaining. Of course they were in a horrible situation, but they had to depend on each other to get through it. "I may be silly, but there is always something good to think about," Marianna said, cradling her aching arm. Somehow she had to find something to take Lillian's mind off her fear.

"For the first rainbow," Marianna volunteered, "we are still alive. And for the second . . ." Her voice trailed off—she could think of nothing else to call a rainbow, so she glanced at Susan for help.

"We have each other," Susan added guardedly. "Surely that's worth a rainbow."

Silently Marianna nodded her head as she thought about her aunt. In truth, there was no real rainbow in their present situation. She met Susan's gaze and knew she felt the same.

What tomorrow would bring, she could not guess.

But whatever it was, it wouldn't be good.

"I want to rest and the ground's cold and wet," Lillian whined.

Susan looked at Marianna and shrugged, both of them silently agreeing that hard wet ground was the least of their worries.

Chapter Five

Wind Warrior ran across the shallow stream in pursuit of a large buck with twelve points on its antlers. He strung his bow as he ran, never losing sight of his prey.

He placed his arrow in the bow and took aim without slowing his pace. The arrow flew true and brought the animal crashing down.

Bending down beside the dead buck, Wind Warrior gently touched each velvety point. "You will feed those who are hungry, my brother. I will take your knowledge and be better for it." Suddenly Wind Warrior rose to his feet. He listened to the wind and raised his head skyward.

His eyes widened, and he grabbed up his bow and quiver of arrows and ran toward the village, leaving the buck where it lay.

Quickly he crossed the river, heading for the other side of the village and into the forest beyond. Once again he placed an arrow in his bow and ran up a small incline, watchful.

Lean Bear was walking with his young grandson, Small Tree, regaling him with stories of his youth, when an enormous puma appeared on the cliff above them and started following them.

For long moments, the cat stealthily stalked its prey, its yellow gaze fixed intently on the young boy.

When gravel rolled down the bluff, Lean Bear looked up and saw the predator. He lunged for his grandson, but the child, unaware of the danger, thought Lean Bear was playing a game with him and ran ahead, his path taking him nearer the puma. Lean Bear called out frantically for the boy to stop, but it was too late. He saw no way he could reach his grandson before the puma leaped.

Suddenly the old man heard an arrow whiz past him and watched it strike the big cat right in the heart. Hurrying forward, Lean Bear drew his now frightened grandson away from the dead animal, which had tumbled off the cliff and landed at the boy's feet.

The old man turned as Wind Warrior appeared beside him.

"Is the boy unharmed?" the younger man asked.

Lean Bear nodded, too overcome to speak.

Wind Warrior bent down so he was eye level with the wide-eyed Small Tree. "You are brave," he said, "but also foolish. Never run ahead unless you know what is waiting for you."

"You saved my grandson's life," Lean Bear said as his heartbeat finally returned to normal. "I will always honor you for this deed."

Wind Warrior shook his head, his eyes on the dead cat. "Somehow I sensed you were in trouble. I do not know how."

Lean Bear placed his hand on the young warrior's shoulder. "You knew because the animal spoke to you, as it was foretold."

Wind Warrior would not believe that—did not want it to be true. He did not want to be set apart from others any more than he already was. He just wanted to be like everyone else. "No. That is not so," he insisted.

"Then you were walking nearby and saw the danger?" the elder questioned.

"I had just slain a deer, on the other side of the village, and something . . . told me to come here with all haste," Wind Warrior admitted reluctantly, knowing Lean Bear would think that "something" had been the puma.

Lean Bear's eyes widened with awe. "You are truly the great warrior your father saw in his vision quest. From this day forward, we will honor you—you shall become adviser to the council."

"I do not deserve such an honor," Wind Warrior protested. "I do not want it. Surely I am too young."

Lean Bear took his grandson's hand. "Look upon this great warrior and remember he saved you from death this day. When you are grown and have a grandson of your own, tell him your life was granted to you by Wind Warrior himself."

That night around the campfires of the Blackfoot village, the story of the puma was told and retold, and the legend of Wind Warrior began.

Chapter Six

A heavy gray mist hung over the land at sundown, but Marianna was glad it had stopped raining. Her head was throbbing, the pain in her arm was almost unbearable, and the world spun sickeningly. Her captor had made her walk the last few miles, taking Susan up on the horse with him instead. Now as they drew to a halt, Marianna staggered, trying to keep her footing, and he merely laughed at her.

Glaring into cold hard eyes that made her shiver, she said pleadingly, "I'm hungry, and cold, and tired, and my arm hurts."

When the Indian slid off the horse, he grabbed Marianna by her good arm and tilted her head upward, scrutinizing her closely. She flinched, wanting to push his hand away, but she dared not for fear of what he would do to her. He touched a lock of her hair, studying it with a curious expression.

The rain had washed the gruesome paint from his face, and she was surprised to find he was handsome, or he would have been if not for those angry black eyes. He saw her studying him, and his eyes narrowed.

Unable to stand his hands on her for a moment longer, Marianna cringed and stepped back. "Don't touch me," she said, her chin going up at a stubborn angle. "I don't like you." She didn't know if he understood her words, but her tone was clear.

To Marianna's surprise, instead of reacting with anger, the Indian actually smiled. But it wasn't a friendly smile; it was more of a sneer.

When she stepped back another pace, he frowned and shoved her so hard, she slammed into the trunk of a pine tree. Gasping to catch her breath, Marianna quickly cradled her injured arm. Even though the pain was excruciating, she would not give him the satisfaction of seeing her cry.

He pointed, indicating that she should join Lillian and Susan, who were huddled at the edge of a thick forest. Marianna lost no time in joining her friends. She was relieved to see Susan's wound was no longer bleeding.

"We are going to die of hunger," Lillian moaned, as Marianna sat down beside her. "Aren't they ever gonna feed us?"

Susan shushed her. "Lillian, don't call attention to yourself."

"Well, I'm starving. And you can't tell me you and Marianna aren't hungry too. I'll die if I don't get something to eat."

"The tall Indian seems to be the leader and I wouldn't count on anything from him," Marianna said, nodding at her tormentor. "I don't think he understands English. And I don't think he cares anything about our comfort."

Marianna noticed a fresh cut on Lillian's face and dabbed at the blood with the sleeve of her gown.

"Your captor has already hurt you. Don't give him cause to do it again," she cautioned.

Lillian met Marianna's gaze. "He hits me if I say anything. I've learned to keep my mouth shut."

Fighting against tears, Marianna turned her gaze on Susan. "I guess they are taking us to their village." Looking at the soles of her red slippers, which now had holes in the bottoms, she wiped away blood where stones had cut her feet.

With tears rolling down her cheeks, Lillian slumped forward. "I keep seeing my ma bleeding, and my pa . . . I don't even know what happened to him." A deep sob tore from her lips. "One of the Indians—I think it was the tall one who captured you—took Mrs. Truckles into the forest, and didn't bring her back. He must have raped and killed her."

Susan, who had been trying to be strong for the two younger girls, closed her eyes. "I don't think they will be taking me to their village. That brute that captured you and me, Marianna, watches me all the time. He . . . t . . . touches me."

Marianna understood and tears gathered in her eyes. She laid her hand on Susan's shoulder. "Then you must run into the woods and hide. Go now. They aren't watching us at the moment."

"I can't leave you and Lillian."

"Susan, if we went with you, we'd only slow you down, and Lillian would . . . they would hear her crying. Go! Run while you can!"

Susan drew in a deep breath and rose, leaning against the tree trunk. Nodding at Marianna, she took several cautious steps backward. Then she turned, running as fast as she could toward the thickest part of the woods.

With her heart in her mouth Marianna watched Susan until she was out of sight, and prayed as hard as she could that she would be able to hide where the Indians couldn't find her.

Lillian dropped her face in her hands and sobbed. "Why did you tell her to leave? We'll be punished when they find her missing. They'll take it out on us."

Becoming weary of Lillian's constant complaints, Marianna turned to her. "Stop it! Don't you ever think of anyone but yourself?"

Lillian jerked her head up, her anger boiling. "I've got reason to complain. And don't you ever speak to me that way again. You're just a child."

Marianna was only half listening to Lillian—her gaze was glued to the place where Susan had disappeared. Turning to watch the tall Indian, she knew the very moment he realized Susan had escaped. She swallowed her fear as he ran toward the woods. She held her breath, praying harder that God would give wings to Susan's feet so she could outrun the Indian. Her blood turned to ice when she heard Susan scream, and scream, and scream.

Without thinking, Marianna jumped to her feet, running into the woods, not knowing what she could do to help Susan, but certain she had to try. "Susan," she cried. "Susan, where are you?"

Suddenly Marianna came to a halt. The Indian had Susan on the ground with her gown above her waist and he was laboring over her. Marianna was an innocent and she didn't know what he was doing to Susan but she knew it was something bad.

"No!" Marianna cried, running toward them. "What are you doing to her? Let her go!"

The Indian turned his malevolent gaze on Marianna and although she did not understand his words, she knew he'd ordered her to leave. She flinched when he withdrew his knife and held it at Susan's throat.

Susan looked at Marianna and shook her head, saying forcefully, "You can't help me. Go away!"

The Indian ran the blade down one of Susan's cheeks, cutting her. Glaring at Marianna, he moved the knife back to Susan's throat. Marianna knew as well as if he had said it in English, he would cut Susan again if she didn't leave. With despair in her heart, she turned away, knowing there was nothing she could do to help her friend.

Just as she reached Lillian, they both heard a shrill scream, followed by an eerie silence.

Marianna and Lillian stared at each other in horror.

"She's dead and it's your fault," Lillian accused. "You told her to run. If you hadn't, she'd still be alive."

Guilt lay heavily on Marianna's shoulders. For all she knew, the tall Indian would have allowed Susan to live if she hadn't interfered. More than likely it *was* her fault that dear sweet Susan was dead. Sobbing, she dropped her head, whispering a prayer that Susan had died a quick death.

"You know what he did to her," Lillian said, reaching out and giving Marianna's hair a yank. "I hope you remember this forever."

Shivering, Marianna wiped tears on the back of

her hand. "I will never forget the sight of Susan—" She broke off, shivering. "I just hope I can be as brave as she was if he—" Tears washed down her face, and she grieved for Susan. The hurt was so deep she would carry the scar forever.

"I hope he takes you into the woods and does the same thing to you," Lillian spat. "You deserve it."

Marianna stared into the gathering darkness with growing apprehension. Moments later, the tall Indian stalked out of the woods, wiping his bloody knife on his leggings.

Marianna hated him with such passion, she wanted to run at him and pound him with her fists, to drive his knife into his black heart. But all she could do was shiver with fright and feel cowardly because she was completely at the savage's mercy, just as Susan had been.

Marianna flinched when her captor stopped in front of her. She closed her eyes, waiting for him to strike her, but nothing happened. She heard him walk away and was overcome with relief.

Lillian trembled. "He raped her, didn't he, and now he's killed her?" Sobs shook the older girl's shoulders. "I don't want to die like that!"

Marianna couldn't find the right words to comfort Lillian, so she wept with her. She wept for the young woman who had been a bride for only such a short time and had been so brutally slain, and she wept for the sorrow Susan's husband would feel at the loss of his wife. Marianna tried to think of something to say that would give Lillian hope, but there was no hope.

"Lillian, they will be coming for us shortly. Don't let them see you crying. You know they don't like it."

Glowering at Marianna, Lillian shook her fist at her. "Don't you dare tell me what to do."

"Listen to me, Lillian," Marianna said forcefully, knowing they didn't have much time. "I've been thinking about something. Do you remember that white woman a French fur trapper brought to the fort last year—the one who had been kidnapped by the Shoshoni when she was a child?"

Lillian wiped her eyes. "I didn't see her, but I heard about her."

"I saw her." Marianna closed her eyes to gather her strength. "She was half crazed and didn't even remember her real name or how to speak English. Her hair was dirty and tangled, and she wore buckskin and moccasins. The day after the trapper brought her in, when no one was watching, she shoved a knife into her own heart."

Lillian nodded. "I remember. What's that got to do with us?"

"I'll never forget who I am, or how to speak English. The very first chance I get, I'm going back home, and I'm taking you with me."

Lillian shook her head, her face a mask of rage. "It's not possible, Marianna. Even if we did manage to escape, we couldn't find our way home. We'd end up being supper for a bear, or a mountain lion. Or the Indians would catch us and do to us what they did to Susan."

Grabbing Lillian's chin, Marianna looked her squarely in the eye. "You can't think like that. Every night whisper your name over and over. Remember your folks, and talk to them like they were with you."

"I . . . I'll try. But we don't know what those devils are going to do with us."

"You have to try to remember, or you'll become like that woman who lost her mind."

"I want my ma," Lillian said, her body shaking with fear.

Marianna held Lillian's hand, trying to comfort her. The poor girl's face was so dirty it was difficult to see her freckles. Marianna knew she was just as dirty. She was weak from hunger and exhaustion, in constant pain from her arm, and uncertain what action of hers might anger her brutal captor and cause him to lash out at her. She wondered how much longer she could endure this torture. Then she remembered that Susan had expected her to take care of Lillian. She set her jaw stubbornly. Susan had been so brave; could she do any less?

Marianna felt a hand on her arm as someone abruptly shook her awake. Needing more sleep, she shoved the hand away.

Whoever it was became more persistent; fingers dug into her arm. Her eyes flew open, and she blinked awake. It wasn't a nightmare—she hadn't been dreaming. Cautiously rising from the grass where she'd been sleeping, she watched the Indian with dread in her heart. She moved back, shaking her head when she saw the leather rope in his hand. Marianna understood that she would pay for what had happened the day before.

Terror stabbed into her mind like thorns, and she bit her lip to keep from crying out as he made a noose and slipped it over her head, tightening it just enough to make her choke. Then just as suddenly, he released her, handing her a chunk of dried meat. She gobbled it down, all the while watching the Indian with suspicion.

Marianna was relieved when he muttered something and pushed her toward the horse. It looked as if she was going to live another day. She tripped on a root and would have fallen if she hadn't reached out to steady herself against a tree trunk.

The Indian smiled cunningly and yanked on the rope. She would receive no mercy from this man. What else could he do to torture her? she wondered. Then she thought of what Susan had suffered and knew there was much more he could do to her if he wished.

As she stood by the horse waiting for the Indian, he pulled the rope, tightening it so she could barely breathe. Marianna had never imagined anyone could derive such pleasure from torturing another. She clawed at the robe, trying to loosen it. The world around her darkened and she had difficulty focusing.

Gasping for air, she slid to her knees. Everything was spinning and she truly believed she was going to die.

Suddenly her tormentor loosened the rope and laughed when she gasped, filling her lungs with air.

"You are a monster," she said, her voice coming out in a painful croak. "I despise you."

His eyes suddenly became dark and dangerous. Using the rope to yank her to her feet, he mounted his horse and swung her up behind him.

Marianna worked her fingers between her neck and the rope, loosening it a bit so she could breathe.

Later in the day the clouds moved away and Marianna could see tall mountains in the distance. She guessed they must be nearing the border of Canada.

She doubted that any white man had ever left footprints on this pristine wilderness. Low-hanging branches tangled in her hair, while thornbushes dug into her skin. Misery settled on her young shoulders—how would she ever find her way home?

Marianna lost track of the days they had been traveling. Had it been two weeks or three?

Maybe more.

Would this journey never end?

When would they reach their destination, and when they did, what would happen to her and Lillian?

For torturous days they traveled deeper into the wilderness. The only thing that kept Marianna sane was the thought that she might one day escape and find her way back to Aunt Cora and Uncle Matt.

She had not seen the sun for days, but one afternoon it broke through the clouds and a warming breeze touched her cheek.

Marianna's heart stopped and all hope died. In the distance she saw an Indian village.

As they crossed a river, laughing children dove into the water, swimming to meet them. When they rode through the village, many Indians came out of their tipis to greet the returning warriors.

They rode past brightly painted tipis that were scattered along the riverbank, each with its own unique markings.

As the Indian halted before one of the tipis,

Marianna was yanked off the horse and grabbed by the scuff of her neck and propelled forward. She struggled and struck out at her tormenter, even knowing he would probably retaliate.

He shook Marianna, and she closed her eyes when he raised his hand to strike her. Cringing, she waited for the blow.

But the blow did not fall.

Chapter Seven

Marianna's eyes snapped open and she saw the struggle between the two Indians. They were both using such force she saw their muscles bulge. To Marianna's amazement, she saw that the Indian who held her tormenter's wrist was much younger than he. Heated words were exchanged between the two, and it was her tormentor who backed down.

She didn't know why the younger Indian had interfered. When she looked into the dark eyes of the younger warrior, it was obvious he was angry, and that anger seemed to be directed at her.

Marianna was at the mercy of both men, and she feared she was lost forever.

As soon as Wind Warrior saw the smallest white captive and realized how his brother had brutalized her, anger exploded in his brain. The wind rifled through his hair as if speaking to him, and he knew instantly that his future was somehow tied to the girl, though he did not know how.

He was not yet a man and she was a mere child— how could their futures come together? For the first time he questioned his instincts. She was young and frightened, and had been terribly hurt. Wind Warrior did not know why he should care what happened to the white girl, but he did.

His gut wrenched when he saw how pathetic the poor creature was. She had been so ill-used by his brother, she could hardly stand on her own. He could not understand why Dull Knife had taken such a pitiful girl as his captive.

"Do not strike this girl," Wind Warrior commanded, tightening his grip on Dull Knife's arm and baring his teeth. Wind Warrior had become strong climbing in the mountains. It surprised him that he was now stronger than his brother. "Do not!"

Dull Knife's eyes widened and he jerked against his brother's grip, but he could not pull loose. "Do you dare speak to me in such a way?"

Wind Warrior's gaze dropped to the girl, who looked more dead than alive. Her yellow hair was plastered to her head, and her face was covered with a mixture of mud and blood. It was easy to see by the angle at which she held her left arm that it was either broken or dislocated. Either way, she must be in excruciating pain.

"Have you not already damaged her enough?"

Dull Knife met his brother's gaze. "It seems you have grown bold since last I saw you."

"And you have grown more ruthless."

Dull Knife sneered. "It is not your place to question me."

Pity welled inside Wind Warrior as he looked into green eyes that were dulled with pain. "You will not raise a hand to her again."

Dull Knife finally managed to jerk his arm free. "Command those you capture, little brother. This captive is mine to do with as I will."

Others were beginning to gather, watching with interest the confrontation between the brothers. White Owl had always known the day would come when his sons would have a serious conflict. He had not expected the fight to be over a white girl.

"The young cub challenges the older wolf," Lean Bear said, smiling. "The cub seems to be winning."

White Owl met the elder's gaze. "It is dangerous for my younger to humiliate his brother in public. I fear reprisal."

At that moment, Wind Warrior stepped in front of the girl, his gaze hardening. "What do you intend to do with her?"

"It is no concern of yours," Dull Knife said, his anger flaring. He would not forget that his brother had shamed him in front of others, when this should have been his time of triumph. Wind Warrior would regret what he'd said and done here today.

Wind Warrior gave no sign of relenting.

"This girl is meant for Broken Lance," Dull Knife ground out savagely.

"No," Charging Bull put in, pushing Lillian forward. "I mean *this* girl for the chief and his woman."

Dull Knife's anger shifted from his brother to Charging Bull. "As I told you before, that one is too old, and she complains too much. The chief will not want her in his tipi."

Frowning, Wind Warrior watched the yellow-haired child raise her chin to a stubborn tilt. He felt a rush of respect for her—although she must be in agony, she seemed proud, trying not to show her pain. There was a sudden stirring within his chest; this white girl seemed familiar to him, although he could not have said why. The only white people Wind Warrior had ever met were the occasional French trappers who came to the village to trade for furs. And they were nothing like her.

He studied the yellow hair that was snarled about her face.

Why did he feel they were tied together in some way?

The girl must have felt his gaze because her head turned in his direction and she stared back at him as if challenging him in some way. Wind Warrior's eyes widened in amazement, and he was struck to the heart. Never had he seen such eyes—they were as green as the spring grasses. There was defiance sparkling in those green eyes, and his admiration for her grew.

Wind Warrior's gaze shifted to the older, red-headed girl whose head hung down in defeat as if she dared not look any of them in the eye. He found himself hoping Broken Lance would choose the younger girl. She would be safe then and free from his brother's cruelty.

Then it occurred to Wind Warrior that the chief's wife, Tall Woman, would be the one to choose. The pitiful little one might strike a chord of sympathy in her kind heart, or she might choose the older, stronger girl, who would be more help to her.

Wind Warrior watched tensely with the others when Tall Woman came out of her tipi. She first scrutinized the redheaded girl, lifting her chin and looking into her eyes. Shortly she turned her full attention on the yellow-haired one. For some reason it was agony waiting for the chief's wife to make her choice. Of course she might choose neither girl. She had long mourned her dead daughter, and might not want to replace her with a white girl.

Tall Woman motioned for her husband to come near. "This child is in pain. Her arm is broken and she is in need of nourishment. We will take her into our tipi and give her care."

Broken Lance nodded. "If that is your wish," he said reluctantly, staring into sparkling green eyes that were too defiant for his taste. "But if you want one of the girls, should you not choose the older one? She seems strong enough to work hard, while the other is sickly and weak."

Tall Woman raised Marianna's chin and looked her over carefully. "This one needs care, but she has spirit. It is doubtful that I will ever think of her as my daughter, but I would like to see her health restored."

Frowning, Broken Lance turned to Dull Knife. "What do you want for the girl?"

Dull Knife could hardly keep from smiling. "She is a gift."

"Is it agreed that if this white girl does not suit my wife, I will return her to you?"

Dull Knife looked at his brother with a smirk on his face, though his words were for the chief. "Yes. If she does not suit, I will take her back."

"Rest from your journey. Come to the elder's lodge at dusk tonight. I will hear of your raid," Broken Lance remarked. "It would seem you have done well."

Turning to Wind Warrior, Dull Knife said, "Follow me, brother. I would have a word with you."

Reluctantly Wind Warrior fell into step with Dull Knife, still thinking about the young captive. "The girl is sickly. She might die."

"That is possible. But her fate is not in your hands. Do not waste my time with your concern for the white girl. It is about you I wish to speak."

Wind Warrior met his brother's dark gaze. "There was a time when I admired you more than any other warrior. Now I see your cruelty and disregard for others, and I no longer respect you."

Dull Knife snorted in disgust. "Do you believe I care what you think of me? I will give you this warning only once. Do not again attempt to get in my way as you did today. If you value your life, stay out of my reach."

Wind Warrior stepped away from his brother, his gaze never wavering. "The time will come when we will face each other as enemies. It is not my wish, but it will happen."

Dull Knife shook his head, loathing gleaming in his eyes. "Do not pretend to me that you can see the future."

"I do not claim to be able to see the future," Wind Warrior responded. "I only know you and I are walking different paths, and our roads will one day bring us to a collision."

If that is so, then beware," Dull Knife warned. "Think on this—Broken Lance has no sons. Therefore, when the white girl is of an age and I take her for my woman, Broken Lance will look to me as his son."

The thought of Dull Knife taking the young captive to wife was disturbing to Wind Warrior. "I will be watching you," he warned.

Dull Knife swung onto his horse. "One day I will have to kill you." He dug his heels into the horse's flanks and shot forward, forcing Wind Warrior to step out of the way or be trampled.

Wind Warrior watched his brother until he disappeared across the river. In some way a girl he had not even known existed before today had sparked something dangerous between him and Dull Knife. How had he gone so quickly from admiring to loathing his brother? It pained him that he had searched his brother's heart and found only cruelty and greed.

Marianna didn't understand what was happening. She watched helplessly as Lillian was led away. "No!" Marianna cried, reaching out to the other girl, who was sobbing. "Do not separate us."

But her plea went unheeded. As the Indian woman led her toward the tipi, Marianna called out, "Be brave, Lillian. Remember what I told you. Remember who you are."

Despite the encouragement she had called out to Lillian, Marianna didn't feel very brave herself. If she were to look for a rainbow, it could only be that both she and Lillian had survived another day.

Fear fluttered in Marianna's stomach—what was to become of them?

The inside of the tipi was larger than Marianna had expected from looking at it outside. War clubs, bows, and lances hung on the leather walls. There was a stack of cooking pots and clay bowls near the cook fire. But what really caught Marianna's attention was the wonderful smell of something cooking among the hot stones, and although she didn't know what it was, her mouth watered.

Raising her gaze to the Indian woman, Marianna saw that she was striking in appearance. Her black hair was pulled away from her face in one long braid that hung down her back. Marianna felt hope when she read compassion in the large brown eyes that rested on her injured arm.

Although Marianna could not understand the woman's words, she was able to interpret her hand motions—she wanted her to sit on the reed mat, so Marianna sank to her knees.

Marianna's head jerked toward the opening when she heard someone entering. The old woman who stepped inside was stooped with age; her mouth was crabbed with wrinkles and she looked frightful. Marianna cringed against the tipi wall as the two Indian women conversed, nodding at her.

Finally the two of them came toward her. The white-headed woman bent to examine Marianna's arm. She was surprisingly gentle. Then the two women talked some more.

At last the dark-headed woman knelt beside Marianna and spoke softly, gesturing at Marianna's arm. She didn't want them to touch her because of the pain. The elder woman held on to Marianna while the younger grasped Marianna's arm and yanked it hard.

Stabbing pain ripped through Marianna, and she could not keep from screaming; then blackness swallowed her.

* * *

When Marianna's eyes opened, she had no idea how much time had passed. When she tried to sit up, she was hindered because her arm had been bound to her body with wide leather strips—it ached and throbbed, but she didn't feel the sharp pain she had known before.

Her gaze swept the tipi and she found she was alone with the younger Indian woman. When she saw Marianna was awake, she knelt beside her and forced her to drink a nasty-tasting herbal concoction. There must have been something in the drink that dulled her pain, and soon she sighed with relief.

Smiling, the woman handed her a wooden bowl of meat. Marianna forgot all the manners her aunt had taught her. Aunt Cora would have been appalled if she had witnessed the way Marianna gobbled down a piece of meat and reached for another.

By the time Marianna had eaten her fill, she could hardly hold her eyes open. As she lay back against the buffalo robe, her eyes fluttered shut and she realized the herbal drink had not only helped her pain, but it had also made her sleepy.

Forcing her eyes open, she tried to fight against the drowsiness. She stared through the opening above her and saw night was falling, and that was all she remembered before sleep took her once more.

Lillian's captor was not a young man. If she was any judge, he was in his late forties. His neck was thick, his nose hooked at the end, and the last day before they reached the village, he had begun brushing his hands against her breasts, and once slid his hand down her belly and clamped it between her legs.

She understood that he had offered her to the Indian couple who'd taken Marianna into their tipi. But she had not been chosen, and now she knew her fate was in his hands.

Lillian had been thrust into a tipi and left alone, crying on a buffalo robe. As soon as darkness descended, the Indian returned. Lillian heard him speak to someone, a female who had entered at the same time. Surely he wouldn't rape her if there was another woman present.

Raising her head, she watched the two of them argue. The woman was thick-waisted, her face round, her arms and legs like tree stumps. It soon became clear to Lillian that the woman didn't want her there. It was also clear that the woman was losing the argument.

Lillian sat up quickly, her hand going to her mouth when the woman hurried out of the tipi and the man turned his attention to her.

Dropping to all fours, she scrambled to the back of the tipi, knowing very well what the Indian's look meant. Soldiers at the fort had often looked at her that same way, and she had flirted with some of them, welcoming the touch of those she liked. She'd frequently slipped off into the woods with different men to have her body caressed and give them what they wanted. Willingly she had tasted their kisses and trembled with pleasure as they had stroked her naked flesh.

But this was different. This would be rape by a

dirty savage. She didn't want him to touch her in any way.

She felt his hands on her waist and he flipped her to her back, hovering over her. Lillian's eyes widened. "Please don't." She shoved against him. "I beg you not to do this."

The Indian jerked Lillian's gown up to her waist, his hands seeking and finding her most intimate places. It hurt when he jammed his finger into her, and Lillian would have cried out in protest, but she knew it would do no good.

Squeezing her eyes together tightly, she swallowed a sob. She tried to think of home and of the life that had been ripped from her, but it was hard when the Indian jerked her head around and forced her to look at him.

When he drove into her body, she quivered with revulsion. He pumped into her hard and fast, not caring if he hurt her.

When he finally shuddered and fell forward, his weight pressing into her, Lillian thought she was going to be sick. She didn't dare move, hoping he would leave her alone.

But he was not finished with her.

"No. Not again," she moaned, as he took her again, and still again.

Later, when he left and the woman had returned, Lillian huddled in a ball, wishing she had died like Susan.

Her body ached and her spirit was crushed. She thought of Marianna and wondered if she had suffered the same fate.

Dark thoughts took over her reasoning. No, precious Marianna had not been raped. That woman had taken her to tend her wounds.

She despised Marianna because she was everything Lillian wanted to be. Crying quietly because she knew she would be beaten if the woman heard her, she rolled her head back and forth, writhing in misery.

She was sore and hungry. Her mouth was dry because she had not had a drink of water since the day before.

Trembling with fear, Lillian heard the man return. Closing her eyes, she hoped he would go to his wife, or whoever the woman was to him.

But he didn't.

He came to her, ripping what was left of her soiled gown, and plunged his hardness into her. Grunting and sweating, he pumped harder in a dance she thought would never end. Her humiliation was twofold because Lillian knew the other woman could hear everything that was happening to her.

Tears ran down her cheeks and she tried to think of something to take her mind away from what was happening to her body.

Again her anger against Marianna raged through her. At this moment Marianna was probably being shown every kindness, while she was being denigrated and misused.

In Lillian's twisted way of thinking, everything that had happened to her was Marianna's fault. The seeds of hatred had been planted in Lillian's mind, and they now festered and grew.

"I despise you, Marianna," she whispered. "I'll make you pay for what you've done."

* * *

Marianna awoke during the night to find herself wrapped in a warm buffalo robe. She was too weary to dwell on what might happen to her at sunrise. All she knew was that she had escaped the horrible savage who had captured her.

At least for now.

She felt the roughness of the buffalo hide and thought of the softness of Aunt Cora's sheets, which always smelled faintly of lavender. She was still drowsy, and tried to focus on conscious thought.

Why had she been placed with these people?

What if the cruel and evil Indian who captured her came back for her?

Hearing the mournful howl of a wolf pierce the night air, Marianna closed her eyes, wondering what had happened to Lillian. She tried to picture the faces of her aunt Cora and uncle Matt.

In her mind Marianna hummed the song Aunt Cora had always sung to her as a small child. But it didn't help much.

Aunt Cora had always bragged to anyone who would listen that her niece, Marianna, was a happy child, always laughing or smiling.

Well, she wasn't happy now. And she doubted she ever would be again.

She prayed silently that Aunt Cora and Uncle Matt would find her and take her home, even though in her heart she knew that was not possible.

How would she endure living with these savages for the rest of her life, however short that turned out to be?

What would happen if she snuck out of the tipi and made her way across the river and into the woods?

That was foolish thinking—she could never make it to freedom in her condition. But later, when she wasn't being watched so closely, she would look for a chance to escape.

If she didn't believe she would one day escape and find her way back home, Marianna would lose all hope.

She remembered the crazy white woman who had been brought to Fort Benton, and shook her head.

"My name is Marianna," she whispered over and over, determined to repeat her name every night before she went to sleep. "My name is Marianna Bryant. My home is Fort Benton."

Chapter Eight

Several months later, Marianna stood in the frosted air, watching wild geese on their migratory flight, their numbers stretching endlessly across the bluest sky she had ever seen. There were clouds gathering in the north, and she thought it might rain before long.

She was beginning to pick up threads of the Blackfoot language, so she could at least communicate. She had found life hard in the Blackfoot village, but there was also companionship and loyalty—joy in the children who played in the shadows of the vast mountains.

The young girls worked beside their mothers, learning crafts that had been handed down through unknown ages. It was the women who really sustained the family units; they toiled from morning until night, their hands never idle. The warriors spent most of their time hunting and providing food, while young boys were given freedom to practice and learn how to use weapons.

Marianna wore a soft doeskin gown and moccasins, and found them to be quite comfortable—certainly more suited to the weather than her own gown, which had been in tatters when she'd arrived in the village.

Chief Broken Lance frightened Marianna when he turned his dark gaze on her. But he hardly noticed her at all, even though they shared the same tipi. Marianna noticed how loving he was to his wife, Tall Woman, so he must be a good man. She'd never thought of Indians showing affection, but in many ways Broken Lance and Tall Woman reminded her of Aunt Cora and Uncle Matt.

The biggest surprise to Marianna came the day she understood enough of the Blackfoot language to discover she was considered their daughter. The old woman who had treated Marianna's broken arm told her that white army troopers had killed Tall Woman's own daughter, and that she had been captured as a replacement for that dead child. Marianna wondered how anyone could take children away from their own families and expect them to learn a new way of life.

Marianna also didn't understand how Tall Woman could accept her so easily when she was white, like the men responsible for her daughter's death.

Tall Woman placed her hand on Marianna's shoulder. "You have toiled enough for one day. Go to the other maidens and speak to them. Try to make friends with them."

"Lillian—"

"Daughter, your friend's name is now Spotted Flower. Charging Bull insists she be called by that name, and he has that right."

"But it is not her real name."

Tall Woman's eyes grew sad. "You must let the past go. I have seen how the others turn away from you because you do not make an effort to know them.

I want you to be accepted for who you are. But those young maidens do not know you as I do. Let them see the person you are and they will acknowledge you."

Ducking her head, Marianna was overcome by strong feelings for the kind woman who called her daughter. It would be hard to explain to Tall Woman that she was standoffish with the other girls because she did not know how to act around them—their customs were new to her, and she was always afraid she would make a mistake. In avoiding the others, Marianna understood she had made enemies.

"I will try for your sake."

Tall Woman smiled as she sliced meat into long strips, preparing to let it dry on a wooden rack. "Succeed for your own sake."

Broken Lance chose that moment to approach them. He immediately turned his dark gaze on Marianna, but his words were for his wife.

"Woman, see that the white girl does not cause trouble today. She angers many of our people because you allow her to keep her white name, and she brings shame on us because she will not accept our ways."

"She will soon earn a name worthy of the daughter of the chief," Tall Woman said slowly, choosing each word. "You will see."

Broken Lance looked doubtful. For himself he would let the girl go, but in the time she had been with them, his wife had quit grieving for their dead daughter. The white girl did labor hard at her tasks without being asked to, and she never complained.

"She is undisciplined," Broken Lance said pointedly. "No one likes her except Dull Knife, who has asked that he be considered for her husband when she is of age." His brow knitted when he looked at Marianna. "I cannot think why such a powerful warrior would want this white girl for his wife. He should take a lesson from Charging Bull's troubles with the redheaded one. Dull Knife would be wise to look elsewhere."

Fear struck Marianna, but she dared not say anything.

Tall Woman knew she was terrified of Dull Knife. Pausing in her work, she looked at her husband. "Marianna is too young to be considered for anyone's wife. And I do not like Dull Knife." She looked at her husband, expecting him to object to her dislike of the warrior—when he said nothing she went a bit further. "I know how Dull Knife treats women."

"Dull Knife is a great warrior, and he has many fine horses," Broken Lance said. "When the time comes, I will be the one who will consider whether he is a worthy husband for your daughter."

Marianna bit her lip. Even now she sometimes woke up in the middle of the night, her heart pounding, sweat pouring off her body as she relived that moment when Dull Knife came back from killing Susan, his bloody knife testament to what he'd done.

Tall Woman gently touched her husband's arm. "If we are to follow the elders' decision to make the younger brother adviser to the council, we must not appear to favor the elder, who undermines Wind Warrior at every turn. Besides, my husband, Marianna is afraid of him."

"Since when does a maiden have any choice in

who will walk the path of life with her?" he grumbled.

Tall Woman laughed. "If I had not been given a choice in the matter, I would not now be your wife, I would have been forced to marry Thin Beaver."

He touched Tall Woman's cheek lovingly. "See that she does not disrupt the whole village." His critical gaze swept Marianna's face. "And see that she is given a proper Blackfoot name. If you do not, I will."

Broken Lance stalked away, not liking to be reminded that he had almost lost Tall Woman to another warrior. Then he stopped in his tracks and smiled. She had always been too much woman for Thin Beaver. It took a strong man, like him, to control her.

Tall Woman turned to Marianna. "Do not worry about what was said here. Go out and enjoy this beautiful day."

Spotted Flower saw none of the beauty that surrounded her as she paced along the riverbank toward several other women and young maidens who had gathered to talk. If anyone had looked into her eyes, the anger that ate away at her would have been obvious. As a second wife, she had to obey the commands of the first wife, Yellow Bird. She resented being Charging Bull's lesser wife, because the jealous Yellow Bird made her life miserable.

She spotted Marianna casually walking toward her, and resentment almost choked her. The hatred that had hatched on their first night in the village had now grown into rage. As far as she could tell, Marianna was comfortable in the chief's tipi, without having to endure a man's probing hands on her body, while she found only cruelty and abuse.

At night she would pray that Charging Bull would choose to lie with his first wife, but he always came to her mat, forcing her to endure his lust. In the daytime Yellow Bird punished her for stealing her husband's attention.

When Marianna approached the group of women, Spotted Flower pulled the younger ones into a huddle and whispered, "Ignore her. She believes she is superior because she was chosen as daughter of the chief. Do they not allow her to keep her white name just to please her? Is it not wrong for her to be so indulged?"

Marianna smiled down at a small child who tugged at her gown, then offered her the clump of wildflowers she clasped in her tiny hand. The child had become attached to her, and usually tagged along after her whenever she could.

"For me, Little Bird?" Marianna exclaimed, taking the offered gift. "They are beautiful, but not as pretty as you."

The child laughed delightedly, and Marianna's heart swelled with love for the small girl, so far her only friend.

White Wing, granddaughter to one of the council elders, watched the exchange and glared at Marianna. "I believe you speak the truth, Spotted Flower. That white girl never offered us friendship." White Wing nodded speculatively. "It is up to one of us to teach her a lesson on how to be a woman of our tribe." White Wing looked at each maiden. "Who will take her to task?"

"It should be you, since you are the daughter of an elder," Spotted Flower told White Wing, and the others nodded in agreement.

With satisfaction growing in her heart, White Wing spoke. "Watch and learn," she told the other young women.

With Little Bird's hand clasped in hers, Marianna hesitantly approached the maidens. She expected to be rebuffed as she usually was. For reasons Marianna didn't understand, Lillian took pleasure in making her life miserable.

Marianna saw the confrontational expressions on all the maidens' faces and decided today was not a good time to try to engage them in conversation. Gripping Little Bird's hand tighter, she hurried past them with quick measured steps. Sometimes the girls followed her, taunting and pulling her hair— she hoped they wouldn't today. Since she had Little Bird with her, maybe they would keep their distance.

The four-year-old Little Bird was always fascinated by the color of Marianna's hair, and she liked to cuddle in Marianna's lap and stroke the blond braids.

"I like to walk with you," Marianna told her. "You are the one who helped me learn to speak Blackfoot." Marianna tucked the wildflowers the child had given her into the sleeve of her gown. "There is nothing I like better than to spend time with you."

"Away from those mean ones," the child said, pointing at the group of maidens watching them with hostile expressions.

"Little Bird, did you know you are my first friend here in the village?"

The girl smiled up at Marianna, her soft brown eyes dancing with joy. "You are my first friend too."

White Wing stepped in front of Marianna, blocking her path. "Where are you going with one of our children? And why do you ignore the rest of us for the company of a mere child?" she asked, malice dripping from every word.

Marianna moved Little Bird to the other side so she would be away from White Wing. White Wing was a pretty Indian maiden with high cheekbones and large, dark eyes, but the frown that twisted her lips downward was not attractive.

Watching her carefully, Marianna sensed danger. "I am merely taking a walk with Little Bird."

White Wing tapped Marianna on the shoulder. "She would rather go for a walk with me."

"No. I would not," the child said, her hand tightening on Marianna's. "You cannot sing like she does. She always sings to me."

"Sing! What does she sing?" White Wing wanted to know.

"It's pretty, and I like to hear it," the child said with a pout on her small lips.

Marianna's gaze shifted to Lillian. "Why don't you explain to your friend about my singing, Lillian? And while you're at it, tell them I told Little Bird she could walk with me and I don't intend to break my word to her."

Lillian's eyes narrowed, and she answered in the Blackfoot language. "You dare speak to me in English and call me by a name that no longer belongs to me? You know very well I am Spotted Flower," Lillian replied in a sugary tone. "While you cling to the old ways, I have found a better life here," she said mockingly.

For the first two months in the Blackfoot village, Marianna and Lillian had not been allowed to see each other—probably it was the Blackfoot way of bringing them into the tribe. Now, Marianna knew Lillian was denying her old life for the benefit of the other maidens, and not saying what she really felt. Lillian couldn't be happy living with the brute who had kidnapped her.

Lillian had always been unpleasant, but now she was even worse. Why was she trying to stir up trouble?

"You have a very short memory," Marianna said to her in English. "Have you forgotten Susan?" Marianna looked into Lillian's blue eyes and saw the shadow of pain reflected there. Turning away, she guided Little Bird toward the river path with anger driving her footsteps.

Glancing back at the other girls, Little Bird asked, "Why is she so mean?"

"Sometimes when people are unhappy, they strike out at others."

"Why?"

"I do not know, Little Bird."

Becoming aware that they were being followed, Marianna whipped her head around in time to see White Wing just behind her. Before Marianna could even react or defend herself, the Indian maiden gave her a powerful shove that sent her flying. Not wanting Little Bird to go down with her, Marianna released her grip on the child's hand before she fell. It angered her when she heard the other girls laughing.

White Wing towered above Marianna, scowling. "You offend me by breathing the same air I breathe."

Marianna scrambled to her knees, examining Little Bird, who was in tears. When pain ripped through her side she tried to ignore it for the child's sake. "Do not cry, Little Bird. I am unhurt," Marianna assured her.

Marianna's anger soared when she turned her attention to White Wing. "Do not ever do that again. If you do, you will regret it."

"I am not afraid of a puny white girl. What do you think you can do to me?" White Wing taunted as if she was trying to goad Marianna into a fight. "Can you not see that none of us like you?"

"I care little what you or your friends think of me. But if you had hurt Little Bird, I would teach you to fear me."

For a moment shame flashed in White Wing's eyes before she shook her hair so her long dark tresses swept her shoulders. "My contempt for you is such that I forgot about the child. I would not harm her."

A shadow fell between them, and both girls looked up in astonishment. "What did you say to White Wing that would warrant such anger?" a husky male voice asked Marianna.

She faced Wind Warrior, her onetime savior, and the most mysterious and honored warrior of the tribe. "I . . . do . . . not know why she is angry. You will have to ask her."

White Wing backed up a step as Wind Warrior turned to her. "If you had hurt the child, White Wing, you would have been brought before the elders,"

Wind Warrior remarked. "Why would you chance hurting Two Moons's little daughter?"

White Wing shook her head. "I was not—I was just—"

Wind Warrior held his hand up to silence her, the look in his dark eyes sharp and dangerous.

"Think on what you did and said here today. I have known you all your life without realizing you were capable of such an unwarranted act."

The child, in awe of the noble warrior, made a dive for Marianna, tugging on her gown, her eyes round with fright. Marianna clasped her hand, stepping back a pace, wondering why Wind Warrior had intervened. Of course, she told herself, it was for the child's sake.

Then Marianna remembered Wind Warrior protecting her from his brother, Dull Knife, her first day in the village. Of course she had not known who he was at that time. Now she was in awe of him, as was everyone else in the tribe.

"Return to your friends," Wind Warrior told White Wing. "I would speak to Marianna alone."

With her heart beating like a drum, Marianna watched White Wing pull back.

Wind Warrior surely wanted to chastise her. Worse still, he might tell Broken Lance about the heated exchange between her and White Wing.

She was in so much trouble.

Words caught in her throat and she could not speak when Wind Warrior turned his marvelous gaze on her. All she could think about at the moment was how beautiful his eyes were—how his ebony hair shone in the sun, and how handsome he was.

"Do you mind if I walk with you?" Wind Warrior asked, breaking into her thoughts.

She drew Little Bird closer to her, needing something to do with her hands because they were trembling and she didn't want Wind Warrior to notice.

The other girls were watching her as if she had just sprouted two heads. She was sure they were wondering what Wind Warrior had to say to her—she was wondering that herself. With her heart thundering inside her, she glanced up at Wind Warrior, who was patiently waiting for her response.

She lowered her head in a show of subservience, since she thought he would expect it of her.

"Marianna," he commanded, "Raise your head. Let no one make you feel less than who you are."

Her head came up slowly, and she met his gaze. It was difficult to find her voice, and when she did, it came out no more than a whisper. "I would not have allowed them to hurt the child."

He looked deeply into her eyes for a long moment. "I know that."

She began to walk and Wind Warrior fell into step with her. He moved with such an easy grace, Marianna felt awkward beside him. Her mind was muddled and useless. She expected him to chastise her as he had White Wing, and she dreaded it.

For a time they walked in silence. Suddenly they veered into a narrow path and Marianna's hand brushed against Wind Warrior's arm. He quickly jerked away and turned his dark gaze on her.

Even he did not want to touch her, she thought sadly, as a new longing was born inside her, though Marianna did not know what it was.

After another long moment of silence, Marianna gathered enough courage to glance back into his face. His brow was furrowed as if he were deep in thought. She watched the breeze lift his ebony hair from honey-colored shoulders. His dark eyes held depths she could not begin to understand. Wind Warrior was the most striking man she had ever seen. In any race he would be called handsome. The white eagle feathers he wore in his hair were a sharp contrast to its dark color. He wore leggings and a beaded porcupine quill vest that left his shoulders and upper back bare.

He glanced up and caught her watching him, and his eyes became even more intense. Again Marianna lowered her head, concentrating on the beadwork of her moccasins.

Wind Warrior spoke at last. "I saw what happened between you and White Wing."

Marianna couldn't seem to look any higher than his mouth, fearing those all-knowing eyes. "It is my understanding that an unmarried maiden is not allowed to speak to a warrior without permission." She closed her eyes, berating herself for daring to instruct Wind Warrior on tribal laws. Was he not the one many people sought out for advice? He needed no instructions from her.

A smile curved Wind Warrior's mouth. "That would be so had I not first asked permission from your father." He nodded forward. "Let us walk toward the woods. There are things I would say to you."

While the other maidens watched in amazement, Marianna accompanied him. She took a misstep and would have stumbled had Wind Warrior's hand not shot out to steady her.

Marianna was sure he must think she was not only tongue-tied, but clumsy as well. As soon as she was steady on her feet, she pulled away from him.

Wind Warrior guided them down the riverbank and eventually around the bend, and out of sight of the gawking females. Little Bird yawned, and Marianna reached down and took the child in her arms, glad the little girl was with her so she wouldn't have to be alone with Wind Warrior.

Smiling, Little Bird snuggled into Marianna's arms.

"She seems sleepy," Marianna said. "Perhaps I should return her to her mother."

"In a while. As I said, I have things to say to you."

Suddenly it occurred to Marianna why Wind Warrior had asked to see her. Was he not the brother of Dull Knife? Had she not heard that Dull Knife was claiming she would one day be his woman?

Fear and anger battled in her mind, and anger won, giving her courage to speak her mind. "If you have come to speak to me about your brother, I know he expects me to be his woman. That I will never agree to. I will not listen to anything you have to say. I despise him."

Wind Warrior's eyes widened and he seemed startled by her words. He halted beneath the branches of a spreading pine tree, giving Marianna his full attention. "I do not come on behalf of my brother. Rather I asked to speak to you for your sake."

Marianna dropped down on the grass because

she feared her legs would buckle beneath her. "For my sake?"

Wind Warrior settled a little way from her, bracing his back against a tree trunk, his arms folded over his broad chest. He was silent for a long moment, seeming to listen to sounds she could not hear. "Why do you refuse to accept our ways?" he asked at last.

Marianna looked up to find his gaze lingering on her face. "I am not always clear about what is expected of me. I am not a Blackfoot, and this is not my home."

"Will you not accept us as you find us?"

"If you want an answer, I will say this to you: I have learned your language, I have worked beside Tall Woman, doing all she asks of me. I tan hides to make clothing for Broken Lance, and I give him my respect—beyond that, I do not know what more I can do."

"Tell me about your parents."

She was startled by his request. "They died when I was a baby, so my aunt and uncle took me in and I became like a daughter to them. Should I accept a third set of parents just because your people demand it? I never shall!"

Glancing up at the overhead branches, Wind Warrior spoke softly. "Life does not always take us down the path we would choose for ourselves. When there are circumstances beyond our control, should we not accept them?" He turned his gaze back to her. "Should you not?"

Marianna turned his question back to him. "Would you?"

His chest rose as he took a deep breath. "Probably

not. But let us speak of the way you are treated by the other maidens. I have seen how they torment you. This cannot be pleasant for you, and it cannot be allowed to continue."

Suddenly Marianna lost her temper. "They treat me the way I expect to be treated by your people. I was kidnapped, beaten, almost starved, and forced to stand by while my friend was brutally killed. I did not choose to come here, and I will never forget who I am. The only kindness I have received since I was forced to live among you is from Tall Woman, and at times Broken Lance." She glanced down at the child, who had closed her eyes. "And Little Bird is my friend."

He was frustrated. "Then do something about the ones like White Wing who torment you. It is the only way you will make them stop."

Marianna looked at him, trying to understand what he meant. "You want me to stop them by being cruel in return?"

"No. Not cruel. By being strong and making them respect you."

Marianna shook her head. "Do you expect me to be unkind to prove how strong I am?"

Wind Warrior smiled down at her, stealing her breath. "Little one, I have often observed you. I do not believe you know how to be unkind."

Chapter Nine

Wind Warrior studied Marianna as she gazed across the river. He could see that she was wondering if she could trust him.

Her vulnerability touched him. Small of stature, she was delicate with the soft beauty of a young girl who was on the edge of becoming a woman. Her hair was as golden as an early spring sunrise; her mouth was beautifully shaped. When she spoke, small dimples danced in her cheeks enticingly. But sadness clung to her, and she had no hope.

She had been judged and found unworthy by some of the maidens. If they did not accept her, she would never find happiness among the Blackfoot. She was totally alone, cut off from everything familiar to her. Wind Warrior wanted to see her smile, to laugh. But what he must say to her now would not make her smile—it would confuse her even more.

When he saw her chin quiver, her hurt was like an arrow piercing his own heart.

"You must challenge White Wing, and you must beat her," he said at last. "Otherwise you will have no peace and the other maidens will never accept you."

Marianna's mouth fell open and she frantically searched his eyes. "You . . . want me to fight her?"

Again he was struck by how small she was, and how defenseless against the other maidens.

"I see no other solution. But do it in this way—the next time White Wing tries to antagonize you, do not allow her to succeed. In life there are those who take pleasure in tormenting others, especially those who do not fight back."

"Why must that be?"

"It is the way of the world," he said enigmatically. "I have known White Wing all her life, and I have never seen her be unkind until she became friends with Spotted Flower."

Marianna nodded. "I wanted to hit White Wing today," she admitted. "But I have never struck a person in my life." She glanced down at Little Bird, who was half asleep. "I do not know if I can cause pain to anyone."

Wind Warrior smiled. "No. I did not suppose you could. There is gentleness in your heart. But there is a time to fight."

She raised her gaze to his. "When is that?"

"When the cause is just."

Little Bird cuddled closer to Marianna's body as a gentle rain began to fall. Unaware of what she was doing, she unconsciously began humming a lullaby that her aunt had always sung to her.

Wind Warrior's eyes widened and he stilled. "What is that you are singing?" he asked, leaning toward her, his dark eyes wide with astonishment.

Marianna immediately stopped humming, feeling embarrassed. "It is a—I do not know the word for it in Blackfoot." She lapsed into English. "It is a lullaby—a song."

"A . . . song." He reached out his hand to her and then pulled it back. "When the Blackfoot dance and sing about the campfire, it has a meaning. What does your lull . . . aby mean?"

"Singing in the white world is not so much a ceremony as it is for pleasure. The songs have words, but I do not know how to say them in your language."

"Then sing the . . . lullaby in white man's words."

"It would embarrass me."

"No one will hear you but me and the child." His voice deepened. "Do this for us."

Feeling somewhat disconcerted by his request, Marianna nodded. At Fort Benton she had sung in church and even while going about her work with Aunt Cora. But here in the Blackfoot village she had hidden her need to sing, fearing she would be punished for it.

"I will try." At first she was shy and Wind Warrior had to lean forward to hear. She hit the low notes and reached easily for the high ones. Suddenly Marianna felt a rush of happiness. She put all her loneliness and pent-up emotions in her song, and her voice seemed to float on the wind.

For the moment Marianna was back home with her family; she had even forgotten Wind Warrior was there.

When the last note of the song faded, Little Bird sat up and glanced at her. "Do that again," she said, tugging on Marianna's sleeve. "I want to hear it."

Marianna glanced at Wind Warrior, who was staring at her with a strange expression on his face. "Will you do as the child asked? I too would like to hear it again."

Marianna ducked her head, her face reddening. "I would be in trouble if Broken Lance found out I sang in English."

Wind Warrior shook his head. "Have no fear that you will be punished. I will tell your father I asked it of you."

She glanced down into Little Bird's shining eyes. "It is a children's song really. First I will tell you what it means, although it loses something when I say it in Blackfoot." She reached in her mind, trying to translate the words. "When evening falls, let not your heart be troubled, little one lying in my arms . . . I will protect you and keep you from all harm." She paused and frowned, trying to interpret the rest of the song. "It says something like, your mother is near, so be not troubled and never fear. Evening brings you sleep, sleep." She shook her head. "My translation is not exact."

"What is this . . . song called?" Wind Warrior wanted to know.

" 'Night Lullaby,' " she told him.

"Sing it for me again," he urged.

Marianna watched how raindrops glistened on his dark hair. He had asked her to sing, and she would. With the confidence she had had when singing with her aunt, she let her voice grow in volume. She was soon lost in the melody and the familiar words she loved so dearly, words that for the moment took her back home.

The music she sang was like nothing Wind Warrior had ever heard—it touched his soul, wound its way through his heart. Her voice was so strong and clear, his chest swelled at the beauty of it. He wanted

to hold on to the sound, keep it in his heart, and take
for his own the girl who had introduced him to . . .
such beauty.

Marianna was unaware others had gathered about
her, listening to her sing. None of them except Spotted Flower had ever heard this kind of melody before and they were stunned by her beautiful voice.

When she sang the last note, Marianna became
aware of her audience. She looked into Spotted Flower's angry eyes and then at White Wing, who stared
back at her in amazement.

"It is just Marianna showing off," Spotted Flower
said in disgust.

Tall Woman came striding through and the crowd
parted. "Bring the child. We will leave now," she told
Marianna.

Marianna rose slowly, ashamed that she had drawn
so much attention to herself. "I am sorry," she said,
looking about her. "I never meant to—"

Wind Warrior watched her hang her head, and he
was angry that she had been made to feel shame.
"You will sing as often as you wish. I saw it gave you
joy and it brought me joy to hear you." He turned to
Tall Woman. "I believe you should now call Marianna 'Rain Song.' No longer will she be known by
her white name."

"It is fitting," Tall Woman agreed.

Without another word, Wind Warrior walked away,
soon to be lost from sight in the now hard-driving
rain.

Confused, Marianna brushed past the others with
Little Bird in her arms. She had to quicken her steps
to keep up with Tall Woman. She heard Lillian com-

ment that no one liked a show-off, and White Wing remark that she had never heard such horrible screeching.

She returned Little Bird to her own mother and followed Tall Woman into the tipi, wondering what her punishment would be.

But Tall Woman said nothing to Marianna that night, nor did Broken Lance mention the incident when he returned from hunting, although Marianna was certain someone must have told him.

Marianna lay upon her robe watching the light fade and the inside of the tipi darken. It seemed as though hours passed as she relived the strange events of the day. Later, as her eyelids grew heavy, she became afraid.

Today she had been given an Indian name, and lost another piece of herself.

In spite of her uncertainty, she felt honored that Wind Warrior had been the one to name her. When she had told him about those who had been kind to her since she had come to the Blackfoot village, she should have mentioned him, since he had been kindest of all. She mouthed her new name—Rain Song. It was a beautiful name.

Her mind drifted back to Wind Warrior. He was not like any man she had ever known. She wished she had not been so shy and awkward around him. She still did not know why he had wanted to help her. Was it perhaps to atone for what his brother, Dull Knife, had done to her? Or was he just kind to everyone? She supposed she would never know. But he had given her back the gift of song, and she would always be grateful for that.

Rain Song? Was that the way it happened with those captured by Indians—the way they forgot who they were and where they came from?

She must not allow that to happen to her.

"My name is Marianna Bryant," she whispered to herself. "I have a family that misses me. My home is at Fort Benton." Her eyes drifted shut. "I am Marianna . . . Bryant." Sleep beckoned to her. ". . . I am Marianna . . . Bryant. I . . ."

Three days later Rain Song had another confrontation with White Wing.

She had bent down, cupping her hands to drink, when she felt a hand in the middle of her back. A sharp shove sent her flying into the river. Earlier in the morning it had rained in the nearby mountains, and the runoff had caused the river to rise and the water to run swiftly.

The current was powerful and carried Rain Song to the middle of the river. She was glad Uncle Matt had taught her to swim. Her strokes were strong and sure as she made her way back to the riverbank. Without pausing to consider the consequences, she remembered what Wind Warrior had told her to do the next time White Wing tormented her.

Several people had gathered about, watching to see what would happen. Rain Song saw Broken Lance among them and knew he would probably have her punished for what she was about to do—but that would not stop her.

As Rain Song stood dripping before White Wing, the girl looked at her with a sneer on her face, but the sneer disappeared when Rain Song grabbed her by the arm and flung her into the river.

Murmurs arose from the people watching and soon tipis emptied as others ran forward to see what the commotion was about.

Rain Song paid no attention to what was going on around her. She was watching White Wing, who was being swept away by the current. From the way the Indian girl splashed and sank into the churning water, Rain Song realized she could not swim. White Wing resurfaced in the middle of the river, but went under once again and disappeared.

Running, Rain Song dove into the water, swimming toward White Wing. When she reached the girl, she grabbed for her, trying to bring her up, but White Wing, in a panic, fought her, taking them both down.

When they finally surfaced, Rain Song wrapped her arms around White Wing's shoulders. "If you continue to struggle, we will both drown. If you will relax, I can get us safely to shore."

White Wing immediately stopped struggling and Rain Song's strong strokes soon moved them out of the swift current to the shallow water along the bank.

Panting with exertion, Rain Song helped the frightened girl ashore. "You will be all right," she said. Then she jerked White Wing's chin up and stared into her eyes. "If you ever touch me again, I will not rescue you the next time I throw you into the river."

Turning away, Rain Song hurried toward the tipi, looking neither right nor left. The crowd parted to allow her to pass. She did not see White Wing watching her with confusion, or the smile that lingered on Broken Lance's lips.

"Your white daughter is brave," Lean Bear said. "You have every reason to be proud of her."

"I am," Broken Lance replied. "She brings her mother joy, and though I was late to recognize her worth, I see it now."

"Would this have anything to do with Wind Warrior's interest in your daughter?" the elder asked.

"In part. But mostly because she is a gentle spirit."

Lean Bear laughed. "She did not look gentle to me," he said, teasing his old friend. "But perhaps we should ask White Wing what she thinks."

Rain Song entered the tipi, her wet gown flapping against her legs, and her moccasins making a squishing sound every time she took a step.

Tall Woman looked at her, startled. "What has happened to you?"

"I'm wet."

"I can see that for myself. Why are you wet?"

Rain Song removed one moccasin and shook the water out if it. "White Wing pushed me in the water and I had to go back in to keep her from drowning."

Tall Woman's brow furrowed. "You saved her life?"

"Yes. After I pushed her in the river."

Tall Woman's mouth opened in astonishment, then she smiled before laughing aloud. "She deserved what you did to her. It is past time for you to take action against her. I only wish I had been there to see it."

Rain Song nodded as a smile crept over her lips. "I admit it felt good."

"Sometimes, my daughter, you can look the other way, and other times you must fight."

"That is what Wind Warrior said."

Looking pensive, Tall Woman agreed with a nod. "It seems Wind Warrior has taken an interest in you. I have never known him to single out any other maiden in the village." She shook her head regretfully. "But I would not put too much significance on it. He saw a wrong and wanted to right it. That is how he is."

Tall Woman's words troubled Rain Song, though she could not have said why.

Chapter Ten

The seasons passed swiftly in the Blackfoot village. Once again it was summer, though there was a chill in the air. Several women and young girls were picking huckleberries in contented companionship. Rain Song raised her head, feeling the sun on her face. It was times like this when she missed home the most.

For some reason Wind Warrior had uncharacteristically remained in the village throughout the winter and spring seasons, and Rain Song saw him frequently, although he usually ignored her. Dull Knife was often in the village too, and invariably he tried to catch her attention, but she ignored him.

She stared down at her fingers, which were stained by the berry juice. She popped a plump huckleberry into her mouth and dropped a handful into the doeskin bag she wore about her neck. The berry picking season lasted for but a short while and Rain Song found this task a welcome break from the tedious work of curing hides.

She did love the beadwork Tall Woman was teaching her. It had taken a while to become accustomed to using a porcupine quill instead of a needle. If she had her sewing basket from home, she would give it to Tall Woman as a gift.

Her pouch was almost full; she just needed to pick a few more berries, and then she could quit for the day. Her search took her close to the cliffs, which she usually avoided because the drop-off was so steep, and it was a long way to the bottom.

Going down on her knees, Rain Song looked under the bush and saw several plump ripe berries near the cliff's edge. Moving forward cautiously, she reached as far as she could. She was within inches of her goal when she felt someone come up behind her.

"Here," Spotted Flower said, bending down beside her, "let me help you reach those. My arms are longer than yours."

Rain Song was surprised Spotted Flower would offer to help her. She felt the other girl's hand against the middle of her back, and was unprepared when Spotted Flower gave her a hard shove. Berries scattered everywhere and Rain Song fell forward, her face hanging over the cliff. She clawed at the vines that hung over the edge, trying to save herself, but a second shove sent her careening over the side.

It had happened so suddenly, Rain Song had no time to save herself. The face that flashed through her mind was that of Tall Woman, who would grieve terribly if she lost a second daughter. In that moment, Rain Song knew she thought of Tall Woman as her mother.

Suddenly her foot caught on a protruding root and it slowed her descent. She grabbed for a bush growing on a thin ledge, praying it was strong enough to stop her fall.

It did, but the sudden jolt painfully wrenched her arms.

Feeling the bush coming out by its roots, she clung to a small sapling, but it tore out of the ground too, so she grabbed another thick bush.

Slowly Rain Song moved her body forward and placed one foot on a small ledge, taking some of the pressure off the bush. Drawing in a deep breath, she eased her other foot forward. The ledge was just wide enough for her to stand on, and she prayed her weight would not cause it to give way.

Trembling with fear, she pressed her face against the cliff, fearing to move, yet fearing to remain. After a moment she grew brave enough to glance down and wished she hadn't. It was at least twenty feet to the bottom, and there were jagged rocks below. If she had not caught herself, she would be dead.

Voices called down to her and she heard Tall Woman's frantic cry. "My daughter, stay where you are. Do not move until I get someone to help us."

"Please hurry, my mother."

Rain Song felt a piece of the cliff crumble beneath her feet, so she leaned heavily against the cliff face, hoping to take some of her weight off the ledge.

The wind stopped blowing and the sun beat down on her unmercifully. Seeing blood on her hands, Rain Song realized the shrub that had saved her life had thorns as sharp as needles.

She felt so alone. So frightened.

"My mother?" she called out in a shaky voice.

"I am here. I will not leave you. Help is on the way."

In a short time she heard a man's voice, and a braided rope was tossed over the side. "Rain Song, I am coming down to you. Remain calm. I will save you."

Tears filled her eyes. It was Wind Warrior. She was going to live.

As he descended, she began to panic. "Wind Warrior, the cliff will not hold us both. You must be careful. I do not want you to fall."

By now he was even with her and gave her an encouraging smile. "That is not a concern. Two Moons's horse is on the other end of this rope. Come to me and he will gradually lower us to the bottom of the canyon."

"I . . . am afraid."

His dark eyes perused her face. "Do you think I would allow anything to happen to you?" He shook his head. "I would give my life to save you."

She looked into those intense eyes and knew he spoke the truth.

Wind Warrior held one arm out to her. "Come toward me slowly."

She would have to let go her hold on the bush to reach out to him, and that took a lot of courage.

He saw her hesitate. "Trust me, Rain Song."

Closing her eyes, she reached out to him. She felt his strong arm clasp her about the waist, and he brought her against his body. Looking into his eyes, she knew she was safe.

"Lower us slowly," he called up to his friend.

Rain Song buried her face against Wind Warrior's shoulder and closed her eyes. In no time at all, her feet touched solid ground, and Wind Warrior released the rope, but he did not let go of her immediately. Both arms tightened about her and he said close to her ear, "Never frighten me like that again, my soul." His lips skimmed her ear. "When I heard what had happened, I was afraid I wouldn't reach you in time."

A sensation like warm honey poured through Rain Song's body. She wanted to remain in Wind Warrior's arms forever, and she pressed her innocent body against his.

He released her abruptly and stepped back. "No, I cannot let this happen," he said, taking a deep, ragged breath.

Rain Song's cheeks flushed at his rejection of her, and she was ashamed of her bold actions.

Wind Warrior frowned when he saw the blood on her doeskin gown. "Where are you hurt?"

She clasped her hands behind her and tilted her chin at a proud angle. "It is nothing that need concern you."

He took her arm and pulled her resisting hands forward. "Everything about you concerns me." He clasped her hands in his, unmindful of the blood. "I regret I have nothing to wrap them with," he said, studying her wounds. "You have been brave, Rain Song."

She did not see it that way. "I was terrified."

"Even the bravest warrior knows fear, little one."

Wind Warrior had already learned that Spotted Flower had shoved Rain Song over the cliff. But he now tested Rain Song to see if she would accuse the other girl. "Why did you venture so near the edge of the cliff?" he asked, watching her carefully.

Rain Song paused for a moment, her jaw jutting out stubbornly and her eyes sparkling with anger. Spotted Flower had deliberately shoved her, but she would deal with the girl in her own way. "It was careless of me," she said, not meeting his eyes. "I will be more careful in the future."

His heart softened. She was so easy for him to read—she would rather make herself look careless than place the blame where it belonged. Gently, he took her by the elbow. "Do you feel like climbing back up the cliff? I know of a path and it is not too steep."

"I can do it."

Wind Warrior stared at her for a moment, and Rain Song felt her cheeks flush.

"Rain Song, I want you to know if you are ever in trouble, you must come to me."

Her eyes widened in surprise and then she smiled. "If I ever fall off a cliff again, I will call out for you."

He shook his head. "I cannot take another scare like this one. I feared that the ledge would crumble before I could reach you, and you would be lost to me forever."

She ducked her head in confusion. What did he mean? Wind Warrior had already turned away, so she followed him up the steep path that twisted and turned along the sides of the canyon. When the terrain became rough, he took her arm to guide her.

As they reached the top, Tall Woman hurried to Rain Song. "I was so afraid for you."

Wind Warrior nodded to the chief's wife and then moved toward the village, but turned back to say, "Your daughter has courage." He noticed Spotted Flower cringing behind a tree trunk, and she moved away quickly when she saw he was staring at her.

Rain Song watched Wind Warrior leave. He carried himself straight and tall, and he was so very appealing. Once more he had come to her rescue.

As if he sensed her gaze on him, he turned and stopped. For a long moment, he looked at her. Even after he had gone, her heart still thundered inside her.

Rain Song waited until the village was quiet before she went to Spotted Flower's tipi. She was still shaking with anger as she called out. "May I enter?" she asked, determined to end this trouble that had been building between them for a very long time.

"Go away. I have nothing to say to you."

Rain Song shoved the tipi flap aside and entered. She was glad Charging Bull was not there, but his first wife, Yellow Bird, was, and the woman watched her with interest as she stalked directly to Spotted Flower, her anger apparent in her quick steps.

"You pushed me."

Spotted Flower's eyes opened in surprise, and she took a step backward, coming up against the lodge pole. "You do not know that for sure."

"I know and you know."

"What does it matter?" Spotted Flower said furiously, her gaze slyly sliding toward the tipi opening. "Did not Wind Warrior himself rescue you? Nothing goes wrong for you, while nothing goes right for me."

"That does not excuse what you did. If you ever touch me again, I will speak of your treachery to anyone who will listen and you will know shame. I have tried to be your friend, but you do not know how to accept friendship."

Rain Song stepped closer to Spotted Flower and slammed her fist into the woman's stomach. When

Spotted Flower moaned and dropped to the ground, Rain Song stared at her. "You are a miserable person. I do not want you for my friend."

Yellow Bird giggled. "Hit her again. I always do."

Turning, Rain Song stalked out of the tipi and headed toward home.

Home?

When had Tall Woman's tipi become home?

That thought frightened her. She was falling into the trap she had promised herself she would avoid.

I am not Blackfoot!

I am white!

That night as Rain Song lay on her mat, she remembered the feel of Wind Warrior's arms around her. She shivered with delight as she remembered the words he had said to her. No different from the other maidens in the village, she had fallen under Wind Warrior's spell.

Her young heart yearned for him. And her mind fought against it. "I am Marianna Bryant. My home is Fort Benton."

The next morning the sun peeked out from behind dark clouds and bathed the land in its warmth. By midmorning a heady breeze scattered the clouds toward the mountains.

Rain Song bent to fill a water jug and hoisted it on her shoulders. She hadn't slept well because she couldn't stop thinking about Wind Warrior, and when she did fall asleep, she dreamed about him.

"I see you have no lasting ill effects from your fall."

She whirled around to find Wind Warrior standing behind her. Rain Song found she was shy with him and was having trouble meeting his gaze. Her eyes widened when she saw he carried a small pup in his arms.

She melted when she looked into the animal's soft golden eyes. Reaching out, she gently rubbed the puppy's ear. "Is this your dog?" She met Wind Warrior's dark gaze. "He is not very old, is he?"

He took the water jug from Rain Song with one hand while he handed the animal to her. "It is a female, and not a dog, but a wolf cub. The mother died, as did her other cubs."

Rain Song's heart ached for the motherless animal. She nestled it in her arms and it seemed to press against her. "Oh, what a sweet creature you are." She rubbed its padded foot. "And all alone in the world."

"She is not alone if you will accept her."

Rain Song's mouth flew open and there was hope in her voice. "If only I could." She shook her head. "I do not think Broken Lance would allow me to have a wolf cub," she said wistfully.

Wind Warrior watched her gentleness with the cub. "I have already spoken to Broken Lance and he has agreed you may keep her."

"Oh!" Hot tears sprang to her eyes and she buried her face in the soft fur, cuddling the cub close. "Sweet little orphan—we are both without parents. We will have to look after each other."

Wind Warrior watched her smiling, glad that she liked his gift. He nodded, indicating that they should walk together.

"There are some things you must understand. A wolf is a wild animal, and belongs to nature. You can be her custodian for a while, but the time may come when she will leave you to seek her own kind."

Rain Song met his gaze and found him smiling at her—her heartbeat bumped up a notch. "For as long as she will remain with me, I shall love her."

Wind Warrior saw the bruises on her face caused by her mishap the day before. He wanted to touch her, to assure her he would be watching her enemies. But he did not.

"Wolves are known for their loyalty," he told her. "They mate for life, and care for their cubs for years after they are grown. When this one is a little older, she will become your protector—for now you must be hers."

Rain Song raised tear-bright eyes to him. "It seems I am always thanking you. Thank you for this precious gift."

Today she wore her golden hair loose and it shimmered in the sun. Her lovely young face was turned up to his, and there was such trust in her green eyes that he was overcome with tenderness and longing. She touched a place in him that no other had ever found. "I call her Chinook—she is one season old. You can give her another name if you would like."

"Chinook, strong wind. I like it."

Wind Warrior reached over and touched the wolf's head. "I left food for her with Tall Woman. Take care of Chinook and she will take care of you."

"Thank you."

He studied her face for a moment, with seemingly curious detachment, and then he looked away, his gaze tracing the far mountains.

"People say you most often live in the mountains, but since I have known you, you are usually here in the village. Will you soon be returning to the mountains?"

He thought of Dull Knife, who also was spending a lot of time in the village. Wind Warrior did not trust his brother around Rain Song, even though she had the protection of the chief. "No, I will not be returning just yet."

Chapter Eleven

Two Years Later

Unlike the white race, the Blackfoot calculated the passing of time by the changing seasons. They did not measure hours by a clock, but by the amount of work accomplished in one day.

Since Rain Song had been a captive, spring had come around three times; she was now in her sixteenth year. She had no knowledge of calendar dates, and her birthdays had passed without her knowing. By her calculations, the year was 1863.

Rumors reached them that a great war had erupted in the white man's world; only this time they were fighting each other. But that world seemed far away to Rain Song. Certainly the Blackfoot took no interest in the white man's squabbles.

Rain Song tried to imagine what her aunt and uncle were doing. She realized they would have long ago given her up for dead.

Glancing at her stained hands, she shrugged and continued to grind the berries that she would later mix with nuts and dried meat to make pemmican. She worked silently beside Tall Woman, whose belly was swollen with child. Rain Song noticed Tall Woman tired easily these days and she tried to do most of the heavy work so her mother could rest.

She had grown to love Tall Woman, and had even developed respect for Broken Lance, although he still made her nervous. He seldom spoke to her, and that was fine with her. On the occasions that he turned his dark gaze on Rain Song, she cringed inside, thinking he still disapproved of her.

"Would you like a son or daughter?" Rain Song asked, pausing in her work.

Tall Woman touched her belly. "I would like to give my husband a son, I already have a daughter."

"What was she like, your daughter who died?"

"Although she was nothing like you in appearance, you remind me of Blue Dawn. She was kind and gentle and I loved her."

Chinook lay at Rain Song's feet, contented to be near her. No longer did Rain Song feel the deep-seated loneliness that had marked her early days with the Blackfoot. The wolf was like her shadow—Chinook was always at her side, even sleeping beside her at night.

At first Broken Lance had grumbled about sharing his tipi with a wolf, but he soon accepted Chinook. Rain Song had once seen him lay his hand on the wolf's head, but he removed it and left the tipi when he saw she was watching him.

"I always wanted a brother or sister."

"Rain Song, this child will be a gift to us all." Tall Woman gently touched Rain Song's cheek. "As a daughter you are a great joy to me, and you have brought happiness back into the chief's tipi." Tall Woman pushed a damp strand of hair off Rain Song's forehead. "I do not know what I would do without your help. This child I carry drains my energy. You have assumed the bulk of the work, and I am grateful, and although your father has not said so, I know he appreciates your easing my burdens."

For reasons Rain Song didn't understand, she wanted to win Broken Lance's approval. But somehow she never seemed to do the right thing as far as he was concerned. In all the time she had lived in his tipi, Broken Lance had not once smiled at her, or called her by name.

Returning to her work, she wondered what Aunt Cora was doing at the moment. Had Uncle Matt gone to war? Despite her determination not to forget her old life, many things were becoming distant memories. In the beginning Rain Song had stayed true to her vow to remember details about her life before she had become a captive. But lately she often forgot her nightly ritual of repeating her white name. The past was slipping away from her as she became more immersed in the Blackfoot way of life.

"I have heard Spotted Flower is expecting her second child," Tall Woman observed. "I have also heard she is not happy about it."

"She has reason to be unhappy. Everyone knows Charging Bull beats her," Rain Song said, looking into Tall Woman's eyes. "I would not want to live with a man like him."

"Daughter, not all Blackfoot men are like Charging Bull, just as not all white men are like the ones who killed my daughter. Spotted Flower brings much of the harm on herself. It is said she complains and rebels against her husband. I have seen for myself that she neglects her baby daughter, and Yellow Bird has taken the child as her own."

Rain Song scooped up the crushed berries and added them to the meat mixture. "In many ways I pity her—she saw her mother die, and she does not know if the rest of her family escaped the day we were taken captive. Then she was forced to be the wife of a man she fears and despises. I would act no differently if I were in her place."

"Yes, you would, daughter. You are nothing like her."

"Do you think . . . will I . . . be forced to wed a man I do not like?"

Tall Woman looked pensive. "If it is within my power, you will only be given to a man you admire."

"Whenever Dull Knife is in the village, he watches me, and it frightens me."

"I like him no more than you do," Tall Woman admitted. "Just make certain you are never alone with him," she warned.

Feeling relieved, Rain Song took more dried berries from her doeskin bag and began pounding them into powder. She was startled when Broken Lance entered the tipi, took his bow from a hook, and paused to speak to his wife.

"There is trouble. Wind Warrior has warned that we will be flooded and lives will be lost if we do not move the village away from the river."

Tall Woman looked puzzled. "Why is there trouble? Wind Warrior's advice is always sound."

The chief was silent for a moment, gathering his thoughts. "Dull Knife has challenged his brother and called him a coward. He says anyone who follows Wind Warrior is also a coward. I must try to keep the brothers from disturbing the peace of the village. People are divided in their loyalties. Most of them will follow Wind Warrior, but some have decided to remain behind with Dull Knife."

"Which brother will we follow, my husband?"

"My concern is for the people," he said, his eyes dropping to his wife's extended waistline. "I will heed Wind Warrior's warning."

"We always knew the day would come when those two brothers would go head to head."

Broken Lance nodded. "That day is here. I go now to speak to the elders." He turned his attention to Rain Song. "Help your mother break camp and load the travois. We depart at sunup tomorrow."

Tall Woman watched her husband leave. "I had thought to have my baby here in this place, where I was born."

Quickly mixing the last of the pemmican so she could pack up the tipi, Rain Song asked, "Do you believe Wind Warrior?"

"I do. He would not have us move the village unless there was a good reason. The difference between the two brothers is Dull Knife runs among the buffalo to show the other warriors his courage so he can boast about it—Wind Warrior helps our warriors find the herds so we will not starve."

"Why would anyone trust Dull Knife?"

Tall Woman bent to fold a robe. "Trust him or not, he is a great warrior. His friends, who are also strong warriors, accept his opinion. I fear for the safety of their families."

Though Wind Warrior was only nineteen winters old, his strength and wisdom were already legendary, and his name was spoken with reverence among the Blackfoot. When he came striding through the village, his dark hair hanging down his muscled shoulders, every maiden stared at him with her heart in her eyes, and so did Rain Song. But Wind Warrior had chosen a solitary life in service to his tribe. There were times when Rain Song felt he had burdens that lay heavily on his mind. She had seen it in his eyes and wished she could help him.

She touched Chinook's head, as she often did when she thought of Wind Warrior. Through her connection to the wolf, she somehow felt she had a part of him with her.

Rain Song took a heavy cooking pot from Tall Woman and set it outside the tipi to be loaded on the travois. They must be ready to leave by morning.

Later in the afternoon, when the tipi had been taken down and all their possessions packed, Tall Woman and Rain Song walked through the village to see if any of the other women needed help. Rain Song counted five tipis that had not been struck—they belonged to the people who had decided to remain with Dull Knife.

They passed Charging Bull's tipi. Rain Song was relieved to see Spotted Flower packing their belongings.

"Would you like us to help you?" Tall Woman asked.

Spotted Flower did not even look up. "I do not need *your* help."

Mother and daughter looked at each other and walked away.

"How can Wind Warrior know there will be a flood?" Rain Song asked.

Tall Woman paused to gaze at the sunset. "There are those who say he sees things before they happen, although he denies he has that power." She took Rain Song's arm and led her toward a group of men. "Let us find out for ourselves."

Broken Lance stood among the warriors, as did Wind Warrior and Dull Knife. Dull Knife was speaking loudly, waving his arms about, stabbing a finger against Wind Warrior's chest.

"Why do you foolish people listen to the ravings of my *younger* brother? Have I not proved my worthiness? Those of you who follow him will endure the scalding heat of the prairie while the rest of us will be situated here beside the Milk River, where it is cooler. Do not come complaining to me when you discover my brother has misled you. Do you believe he can see tomorrow? I know he cannot."

Murmurs of dissent echoed through the crowd. Broken Lance held up his hand, calling for silence. "Let us hear what Wind Warrior has to say."

Rain Song fixed her gaze on the young warrior, and her heart pounded inside her. She would follow him anywhere he led. For a moment, their eyes met, and then he looked away.

"I can no more see the future than any one of you. This I will tell you. I was climbing in the mountains when I saw a rock slide blocking the stream that brings the water to the river. I would have cleared the boulders away, but they were too heavy for six men to lift. Not even in a full season could the rocks be removed. I watched the force of the stream building up behind the rock slide—it will not be many days before the force of the water is so great, it will break through the boulders and flood this entire area. I say this as the truth."

Dull Knife gripped his brother's arm. "Do not believe him. Stay with me. I will keep you all safe."

Stepping forward, Broken Lance shook his head. "As your chief, I can only advise you. As for me, I am taking my wife, daughter, and unborn child to the prairie. I advise the rest of you to do the same. If there was time, we would go into the mountains and see for ourselves what Wind Warrior has seen."

Rain Song stared at Broken Lance. It was the first time he had referred to her as his daughter, and her heart swelled with pride.

"I go with Wind Warrior," a strong voice called out. A tall man with long white hair pushed his way through the crowd. "If you want to live, you should also heed Wind Warrior's warnings."

"Father," Dull Knife said contemptuously.

Wind Warrior looked at his father sadly. For him to return from Canada at this moment was unfortunate. It hurt him that White Owl had so publicly chosen between his two sons. Wind Warrior knew that that choice had cost his father.

"As you all know," White Owl said, "I led some of our people to settle in Canada. At last I am home to stay." White Owl looked meaningfully at Broken Lance and then stepped between his two sons, looking first at the elder and then the younger. "What is happening here today is about much more than whether or not the river will flood."

"And just what do you think is happening?" Dull Knife wanted to know.

White Owl touched Dull Knife on the shoulder. "From what I just heard, you are attempting to cause division between our people."

"No, not I," Dull Knife stated forcefully. "It is Wind Warrior who wants to drive them to the prairie, where there is much greater danger than here."

"My father," Wind Warrior said. "No one expects you to choose between your sons, least of all me."

"Our father has already chosen," Dull Knife hissed.

His hate-filled gaze suddenly settled on Rain Song. She had seen that menacing look before, when he had killed Susan.

"You, white girl," Dull Knife called out, moving toward her. "Will you remain here with those of us who do not want to follow Wind Warrior? Do you want to spend the heat of the season on the dry prairie and die without water?"

Chinook pressed her body against Rain Song and stared into her face, as if she knew something was wrong. Then the wolf whipped her head around, her golden eyes fixed on Dull Knife—the bristles on her neck standing up, her teeth bared. Rain Song placed a calming hand on the wolf's head while she glared at Dull Knife and stepped closer to Tall Woman. "I do as my father commands," she answered coldly.

"So," Dull Knife said, anger reddening his face. "You go with those who believe my brother. I want you to remember I offered you the chance to remain safe."

Rain Song turned her head, wishing Dull Knife had not singled her out. She watched as two families who had chosen to stay by the river moved to stand with the ones who were going to the prairie. Tall Woman touched Rain Song's arm and motioned that the two of them should leave.

Rain Song felt drained from the hostility she had just witnessed. "I do not understand why anyone would remain with Dull Knife."

They had reached the river and both stood watching the calm water lapping against the bank. "Dull Knife is making an attempt to grab power. And he believes he will win. My fear is what he will do next to obtain that power."

"What do you mean?"

"I fear his first victim will be his brother." Tall Woman's brow furrowed. "Then he will come after my husband, because Broken Lance sided against him. I wonder if he will even seek revenge on his own father"

Chapter Twelve

Poised beside the Milk River, Wind Warrior stared into the star-strewn night in brooding silence. The moon was so big and bright it appeared to be a huge golden ball hanging in the sky. His eyes widened as he watched a shower of shooting stars streak across the heavens.

Something stirred deep in his mind, the meaning just out of reach.

He was troubled. The confrontation with Dull Knife had left him angry. His father was still trying to convince him to leave, but his brother would remain out of stubbornness, willing to sacrifice those who believed in him, rather than admit he was wrong.

A warm breeze touched his cheeks and he closed his eyes, freeing his mind of all thought.

Hearing footsteps behind him, Wind Warrior did not need to turn around to know who it was. He easily recognized Falling Thunder's footsteps. They had been friends for years—but he did not want to talk to the warrior tonight.

"You have been out here for a long time," Falling Thunder observed. "Is there something in the sky of particular interest?"

"If there is, it evades me," Wind Warrior absently responded, not yet ready to end his solitary musing.

His friend shook his head and laughed. "That is not an answer. You live behind a veil of secrecy and share your thoughts with no one."

Wind Warrior gazed in the distance as heavy sadness struck him to the heart. "I shared my thoughts with the village today and had a hand in dividing loyalties. That was not what I intended."

Falling Thunder gazed into the darkness. "Yet you were right to do so."

"I have no answers for myself. It is a lonely road I am destined to walk," Wind Warrior said solemnly.

"Lonely?"

"At least for now."

"It is said by many that you can see into the future."

Wind Warrior smiled. "People will believe what they want. I can no more see what the future holds than you can."

His friend looked up at the sky, wondering what Wind Warrior saw that others did not. "If you cannot foretell the future, how could you warn us that we would be hit by a flood if we remained here?"

"You heard me tell of the landslide."

"Yes."

Wind Warrior turned to study Falling Thunder. "It was not a matter of reading the stars to see the disaster that would strike the land along the Milk River. It was reasoning that I used."

Falling Thunder studied his friend for a long moment, his expression skeptical. "What are your special powers if not looking into the future?"

"I do not have any special powers." Wind Warrior was annoyed that his friend did not understand that. "I do feel our people are somehow my responsibility, and I must look out for them. But I have felt this for a long time—no doubt, because the thought was planted in my mind when I was given my name." He had rarely shared his thoughts with anyone, but tonight it was difficult to carry his burden alone. "For reasons I cannot say, I seem to sense when there is trouble, but I never know exactly what the trouble will be, and I am never guided to the complete truth."

"Last year you helped us find a large buffalo herd when our meat supply was growing sparse."

"I merely followed the trampled grass, and the buffalo droppings. It was no more than anyone else could have done."

"None of the others did."

Wind Warrior sighed. "I do not want to discuss this tonight."

His friend shrugged. "Will you lead us in the morning when we leave the village?"

"I will join you later," Wind Warrior said in a measured tone. "I have a need to be alone."

Falling Thunder understood and nodded. He was accustomed to his friend's dark moods and sought to divert him. "Then perhaps you would like to hear what troubles me?"

Wind Warrior looked at him knowingly. "You speak of White Wing. You want her for your wife, yet you think she does not see you."

Startled, Falling Thunder searched Wind Warrior's face. "You do see inside our minds; otherwise you would not have known how I feel about her." He glanced up at the sky. "Did you see this in the stars? Will she one day be mine?"

Wind Warrior laughed. "I see nothing in the stars. Like everyone else, I see the way your gaze follows White Wing, and the way you always lose your power to speak whenever she is nearby." He smiled. "And you stumble over your own two feet when she looks your way."

Smiling, Falling Thunder felt warmth wash through him just thinking of White Wing's soft brown eyes. "She is the woman I want to walk beside me through life."

Wind Warrior placed his hand on his friend's shoulder and clasped it. "Take heart, I have also seen her watching you. I wish you many fine sons."

They were both silent for a time and then Falling Thunder spoke again. "Has no woman interested you enough to cause you to lose your voice and stumble like a fool when she is about?"

"There is one, but she is not yet a woman, so I must wait for her. She is afraid of her own feelings. I will wait until she reaches marriageable age, and hope she loses that fear."

Falling Thunder shook his head and laughed aloud. "There is not a maiden in our village who would not agree to walk beside you. Who is this young maiden you speak of?"

Wind Warrior closed his eyes for a moment, reluctant to reveal too much of what he felt. But he trusted his friend with his life, and he would trust him with his secret yearning. "You will say nothing of what I tell you tonight."

"You know I will not."

"I know it makes no sense—I have told myself this. But in my mind, when I see a woman walking beside me, it is the chief's daughter, the white maiden with hair the color of gold." His expression hardened. "I do not like that I see this. I do not want to need her. But I do."

With his mouth gaping, Falling Thunder hesitated a moment before answering. "Now I know what troubles you. It would be better for you if you never looked in her direction. Look what Charging Bull suffers because he chose the crazed red hair."

"The red hair is devious and untrustworthy. My little golden hair has a heart of kindness. I have seen only goodness in her."

"Are you sure it is your heart that wants her, or are you misinterpreting your body's desire to possess her?"

"I have considered that and discounted it. She is too young to look at with lust. I want much more than to join with her body. I want her spirit to merge with mine. I find myself wanting to know everything about her life. I want to share her happiness—already I shared her pain when others were unkind to her. My name might as well still be He-Who-Waits. I must wait for her to grow into a woman."

Falling Thunder was stunned by Wind Warrior's admission. "She is not so young. She now has the body of a woman." He frowned. "It is said Tall Woman guards her white daughter against those who want to take her."

Wind Warrior nodded. "I know all this. I know every reason I should turn away from her. Perhaps with the passing of time, I will be able to do so."

"Think of her no more," Falling Thunder urged.

"She is all I can think about. Winning Rain Song's heart is my burden—and my joy. Before knowing her, I had not really lived. But loving her, without knowing how she feels about me, is like a thorn in my own heart."

When Wind Warrior spoke next, it was so quietly, Falling Thunder had to lean closer to hear his words.

"The day draws near when I will have to fight my brother."

"Because of the white girl?"

"Yes."

"And you say you do not see the future—how could you know that?"

"I know it because Dull Knife watches her as you watch White Wing. But his reasons are not as pure as yours."

Wind Warrior lifted his head to the stars and concentrated on a particularly bright one, and after a few moments of silence, his friend left him alone.

"Why, Rain Song?" he whispered. "Why must you haunt my thoughts?"

Chapter Thirteen

Twenty families had left the village by the Milk River and were now encamped in a desolate land with no trees for shade, and miles of nothing but tall grassland. Since the prairie was so open, Broken Lance had ordered the people to arrange their tipis in a tight circle so they could be more easily defended should trouble come upon them.

All of the warriors had ridden out that morning because an enormous herd of buffalo had been spotted near the craggy hills a day's ride from camp. Broken Lance had been hesitant to leave his wife since her time to deliver was near, and the warriors would be gone for several days, but it was his duty.

Chinook was curled up on a buffalo robe, ever watchful. Rain Song handed Tall Woman a bowl of meat. "The heat is oppressive. You must rest as much as you can."

"It is hot because there has been no rain."

"If it does not rain, the village by the river may not flood."

"Just because it is not raining here does not mean it is not raining in the mountains, Rain Song."

"I know that is true. It is just that the waiting is so hard."

"It is hard." Placing her hand on her stomach, Tall Woman sighed. "This child waits long to be born. You must not let your father know I am not feeling well. The others look to him for guidance in this troubled time. He does not need a wife clinging to him."

Rain Song was worried. "Are you feeling the birthing pain?"

"It comes and goes. Just when I think it is time to give birth, the pains stop."

Rain Song reached for a water skin and wet a cloth. "I will bathe your face so you feel cooler."

Tall Woman smiled. "There is such kindness in your heart, little one. I bless the day you came into my life."

Rain Song bit her lip. The day she had come into Tall Woman's life was one of the worst of her own existence. No matter that she'd learned the Blackfoot ways and taken up their customs, she was not one of them and never would be. "I love and honor you, my mother. But sometimes I yearn for that which I left behind."

"I know this. But I could not give you up."

The thought of leaving the Blackfoot stabbed at her heart. She loved Tall Woman, and even Broken Lance, who had given her a fine pinto just the day before. And to never see Wind Warrior—how would she bear it?

Tall Woman closed her eyes while Rain Song fanned her. "Sleep will be good for you. I will watch over you."

Her mother's lips curled into a smile. "You do that very well. You work hard, my daughter. Take time for yourself. I want to hear you laugh." She clasped Rain Song's hand. "It would fill my heart with joy if you could be happy."

Rain Song said nothing. She kept fanning Tall Woman until she fell asleep. From the occasional frown that fluttered across Tall Woman's face, Rain Song could tell she was in pain.

Yesterday she had heard some of the women talking, and they were worried that the baby was too late in coming. Rain Song wondered how much longer Tall Woman would suffer before this child was born.

It was afternoon when Rain Song stepped outside the tipi to find several women mounting their horses. With Chinook walking at her side, she approached them. "Are you leaving?" she asked Bird Woman, who would be the one to help Tall Woman deliver the child. The older woman's hair was white, and she was rail thin, with wrinkles falling in folds. But she was the one the women depended on when they were ready to give birth.

"Spotted Flower has brought word that the men found the buffalo and need us to help with the carcasses," Bird Woman said. "Let your mother know we will be away for two days."

Worriedly, Rain Song laid her hand on Bird Woman's horse. "My mother is feeling pain—should you not remain here? She might need you."

"Does she say it is the birthing pain?"

"She does not think so. But—"

"It is only right that you should worry about her. But be comforted by the fact that we will be in a nearby valley. Spotted Flower says she will remain with you. Should Tall Woman need me, send her and I will come."

Rain Song watched the women ride out of sight, feeling uneasy. Chinook laid her ears back against her head, and her neck hairs bristled. Rain Song turned to find Spotted Flower behind her, glaring at her.

"You must be feeling the heat as Tall Woman does, since you are with child," Rain Song said.

Watching the wolf warily, Spotted Flower answered angrily. "Yes, I am with child! Charging Bull rapes me repeatedly and takes delight that I do not fight back. But you have a life of ease. You know nothing of what I suffer."

Chinook did not like Spotted Flower's tone and placed herself between Rain Song and her.

"I am sorry he beats you. I have seen the bruises on your face and understand how you have suffered over the years. If only we had been friends, it might have been easier for us both."

"I do not need a friend. Certainly not you." She pointed at Chinook. "And keep that wolf away from me."

"She will not hurt you unless she thinks you are a danger to me."

"Let me test that." She reached forward and yanked Rain Song's braid.

Instantly, Chinook leaped toward Spotted Flower.

Rain Song reacted quickly, catching the wolf by the neck and clamping her hands around the animal's mouth. "No, Chinook. Do not!"

The wolf immediately pulled back, but her yellow eyes never left Spotted Flower's face.

"Do not make any sudden moves, Spotted Flower. Back away slowly. I do not know if I can control Chinook if you touch me again."

The woman stepped quickly back, her gaze on the wolf. "You do not suffer as I do. You are the daughter of the chief. No one would dare hit you or bruise your face."

"You dared, Spotted Flower. Do not think I forget that you pushed me off the cliff."

"Yes. I did. And look what happened. Wind Warrior rescued you and the very next day gave you this wolf. Everyone thinks he gave you the wolf to protect you from me."

"Your words are bitter. You are bitter. But I am warning you, if you attack me again, I will not need the wolf."

Spotted Flower merely smiled, taking another step away from Chinook, who still watched her every move. "The day will come when you will beg me to help you, and I will not lift a hand. I have watched you in your comfort while I am nothing but a slave to a man I hate. One day your comfortable world will crumble."

Warning bells went off in Rain Song's head. "That sounds like a threat to me."

"Maybe it is. Or maybe I know things you do not."

"I will not play games with you, Spotted Flower." She stared the woman in the eye. "I know what you are capable of."

Giving a half shrug, Spotted Flower frowned. "I did not say I was going to harm you. But I know those who might."

A growl rumbled in Chinook's throat and she flattened her body as if preparing to spring.

"Do not say any more," Rain Song ordered. "My wolf does not like your tone of voice. I am warning you to leave while I can still control her."

Cautiously Spotted Flower stepped back several more steps and then turned and walked away.

Troubled, Rain Song entered the tipi. Was Spotted Flower trying to warn her, or was it a threat? The woman was bitter, but her life was hard and Rain Song still pitied her.

Chinook watched Spotted Flower until she was at a safe distance, and then padded inside to lie beside Tall Woman.

Rain Song picked up the leather fan and fanned her mother. Something wasn't right. All the women except for the very young and the very old had left camp. She would be watchful and allow nothing to harm Tall Woman or her unborn baby.

Chapter Fourteen

As far as the eye could see, there was not one tree, just the vast prairie. The spiky grasses rose and fell with the whims of the wind, giving the appearance of waves upon a restless sea.

But the prairie was not devoid of life. Rain Song watched a deer mouse scamper among the grass while a watchful hawk glided overhead. Farther away a gopher burrowed into its hole.

Loneliness enveloped Rain Song as she stared into the distance. She craved the sight of Wind Warrior. Chinook buried her nose into Rain Song's hand, and she smiled down at the animal.

"Daughter," Tall Woman said, coming out of the tipi. "Come, sit beside me, and sing one of your songs."

Another day had passed, and still the baby had not come. Rain Song knew Tall Woman was uncomfortable although she would never admit it to anyone.

They both longed for the cool hills beside the Milk River.

Rain Song jerked awake.
Something was wrong.

Her heart was thundering inside her and she sat up quickly, shaking her head to clear her sleep-drugged mind. A bright moon shone through the opening at the top of the tipi and she could see Tall Woman sleeping peacefully nearby.

Had it been the howl of a wolf that awoke her?

Scrambling to her knees, she automatically reached for Chinook, only to discover the wolf was not beside her. Rising slowly, she quietly made her way outside, trying not to awaken Tall Woman.

The night sky was strewn with thousands of stars. A full moon lit the countryside and she watched the dried grass bend in the wind. It was desolate here on the prairie—the wind never seemed to stop blowing, and the heat was intense.

At first she hoped she might have heard some of the others returning from the hunt. But there was no sign of anyone—all was quiet.

Too quiet.

Suddenly Chinook came bounding out of the shadows, whining. The wolf bumped against her leg, and her golden eyes probed Rain Song's.

She bent down to Chinook, rubbing the stiff hair on her neck. "What is it? What is wrong?"

Chinook moved away from her, trotting to the horses, which were kept in a roped-off area. Then the wolf trotted back to Rain Song. There was no doubt; Chinook was trying to warn her of something.

Then she smelled it—smoke.

Twisting around, she froze in fear as she watched flames lick at Spotted Flower's tipi.

The fire must be extinguished before it spread to the other tipis. With the dried grass and the strong wind, it wouldn't take long for the fire to rage out of control and kill them all!

"Chinook, wake the others! Hurry!"

The wolf seemed to understand because she threw her head back and gave a fearful howl that would have awakened the deepest sleeper.

Rain Song ran through the camp shouting as loudly as she could, "*Fire!* Everyone wake. Bring your water skins. Help me put out the fire."

Racing across the distance, Rain Song knew she had to reach Charging Bull's tipi and make certain Spotted Flower got out safely.

Rain Song caught her breath and slid to a halt: It was too late—the tipi was engulfed in flames; no one could have survived. Driven by a strong wind, the fire was already spreading to the nearby dry grass. If she couldn't contain it, the fire would soon engulf the entire encampment.

Watching the tipi poles collapse, Rain Song was horrified to think of Spotted Flower being burned alive. Later she would grieve for Spotted Flower, but for now she must help the others. Utter mayhem broke out among the women and children as they saw the approaching flames. Realizing it was too late to save the remaining tipis, Rain Song and one of the older women tried to direct everyone to the horses.

She was learning about the strong ties within the Blackfoot tribe. They took care of each other in times of trouble.

Looking around, Rain Song noticed that Tall Woman was not with the women and children who had fled their tipis.

She gathered up the reins of two horses and quickly led them to the far end of the camp, where Tall Woman's tipi stood.

Chinook glanced up at Rain Song, whining. "Stay beside me, Chinook. The fire is spreading quickly." With Chinook running beside her, she reached the tipi. After she tied the horses to a stake so they would not run away, she rushed into the tipi and dropped down beside Tall Woman, who was stretched out on her mat. "There is a fire—we must leave this place at once."

Tall Woman groaned, grabbing her stomach. "The baby comes. I cannot go." She bit her lip against the next pain. "You must leave without me."

"Never! You are coming with me." Rain Song helped Tall Woman stand and watched her sway on her feet. "Can you make it to the horses?"

Tall Woman grimaced in pain. "I will try."

"I will put you on a horse—just hold on until we are free of the fire. The wind is coming out of the north, so we must ride south."

Tall Woman bent, gasping. "I do not know if I am able to sit a horse."

"You must think of the child. Lean on me, my mother, and I will lend you my strength."

At that moment another pain hit and Tall Woman doubled over. When it passed, Rain Song led her out of the tipi. By now she could feel heat from the rapidly approaching fire.

In that moment, a rider appeared in front of them,

the horse rearing, and Rain Song had to duck to keep from being struck by the flailing hooves.

"Spotted Flower," she cried out in relief. "I am glad you are safe." She saw Spotted Flower had untied their horses and held the reins in her hand. "Thank you for coming to help us. If you will assist my mother to mount, I will make certain everyone else got away safely."

"The others have gone," Spotted Flower said, her face distorted in the shadows of the dancing flames. "I think only two perished in the fire. Too bad you will not be among the survivors. Neither will Tall Woman."

Rain Song met Spotted Flower's eyes and she saw hatred reflected there. "At least help my mother— she could give birth at any time."

Shaking her head, Spotted Flower looked at the older woman and said with venom dripping from each word, "If you had chosen me for your daughter, I would save you. But you chose *her*, and today you pay the price for that choice."

Shaking her head, Tall Woman turned to Rain Song. "What is she saying?"

"She is saying she will not help us, and she is taking the only remaining horses with her."

"I started the fire," Spotted Flower boasted. "I planned everything and it worked even better than I imagined. I will tell the others I tried to help you both, but I was too late." Her expression hardened and her hands tightened on the reins of the other two horses. "Everyone will understand how sad I feel."

While Spotted Flower spoke to Tall Woman, Rain

Song took the opportunity to dart around her toward the horses. "You cannot do this."

Spotted Flower laughed, swinging the reins to strike Rain Song across the cheek, drawing blood. "I have waited a long time for this night. I am only sorry I cannot stay to watch you burn."

They were running out of time, so Rain Song gave the order, "Chinook, attack!"

The wolf was suddenly airborne, leaping at Spotted Flower and knocking her from her horse. Not wasting any time, Rain Song grabbed one of the horses' reins and turned to Tall Woman, helping her mount. "Leave now. I will help Spotted Flower and then follow you."

Knowing she had no choice, Tall Woman nodded, urging the horse forward. "Hurry. The fire advances swiftly."

"I will be right behind you." Hurriedly turning to Spotted Flower, she saw that Chinook was standing over the woman, growling low in her throat, her teeth bared in a menacing snarl. One word from Rain Song and the wolf would rip Spotted Flower to pieces.

"Help me before this beast devours me!"

Dark smoke was billowing in the air and Rain Song felt it clog her throat. "Let her up, Chinook."

The wolf immediately obeyed, going to Rain Song's side, her yellow eyes still on the woman. "Give me your hand. I will help you up, Spotted Flower."

Spotted Flower watched the wolf. "Keep her away from me."

"Chinook will only attack if she thinks I am in

danger. You had better get on your horse and leave now. Let me help you."

The redhead batted Rain Song's hand away. "I do not want your help. You were supposed to die and Wind Warrior was supposed to be discredited for exposing the tribe to the prairie fire."

"Why would you want to place blame on Wind Warrior?"

"Not I. I am not his enemy."

Rain Song could not believe anyone could hate as fiercely as Spotted Flower. She had involved innocent people in her need for vengeance, and that was unforgivable. "Stay or leave as you will. The fire is dangerously close—you should not hesitate."

"Is that all you have to say? Do you not want to tell me how evil I am?"

Rain Song struggled to lift the wolf in her arms, then mounted her horse, setting Chinook across her lap. "You do not need me to confirm what you already know. You must live with what you have done." Rain Song suddenly lapsed into English. "Lillian, you will face justice for what you have done here tonight. Because of you, people may have died."

Spotted Flower was crying as she mounted her horse. "I don't care. Being dead is better than living with Charging Bull."

The advancing fire had already devoured everything in its path, and Rain Song was having difficulty controlling her frantic horse. She was not sure either one of them could outrun the fire that was suddenly upon them. The wind had whipped up and the flames were advancing like a hungry pack of wolves. She jabbed her heels into the horse's flanks and the frightened animal shot forward. As she raced ahead of the fire, Rain Song knew she had to catch up with Tall Woman.

A frightened herd of elk darted around her, as they also ran from the fire. Antelopes stampeded past, racing against the flames that roared violently forward, consuming everything around them.

As Rain Song raced down a gully, she saw Tall Woman waiting for her. "We must hurry, daughter. The fire is spreading fast."

"Your pains?"

"They are coming close together. I hope to find a safe place to give birth."

Glancing behind her, Rain Song shook her head. "I do not know what happened to Spotted Flower."

"I saw her ride away in a different direction."

"Where should we go—where would be safe?"

Tall Woman slumped on her horse as another pain grabbed her. "If we can make it to the bluffs," she whispered, trying to catch her breath, "I do not believe the fire will follow inside the canyon."

They both pushed their horses in an all-out run. At times Rain Song smelled the smoke and knew the fire was not far behind them. On they raced until their poor horses were lathered and weary. Rain Song saw Tall Woman's horse stumble and she reached for the reins, but the animal managed to keep from falling, and Tall Woman hung on tightly.

"The horses . . . cannot run . . . much longer," Tall Woman gasped. "The canyon . . . just ahead."

When they finally reached the bluffs, Rain Song

released Chinook and leaped off her horse to help Tall Woman dismount.

The wall of smoke was so dense they could hardly see where they were going. Ash flew into their faces and singed their hair. Their throats were clogged and Tall Woman bent, coughing, while Rain Song took shallow breaths.

Somehow they made it to the cliff. "It is steep going down," her mother warned her. "And there is no trail, so we must release the horses and continue on foot."

"We will let Chinook lead us down," Rain Song said, slipping her arm around her mother. Glancing behind her, Rain Song saw the flames were so near, they still might not make it. "Let us hurry." She heard the frightened horses run away and hoped they would stay ahead of the fire.

Deep sobs shook Spotted Flower. Nothing had turned out the way she had planned. Pain hit her and stabbed into her abdomen, and then she felt a gush of wetness between her legs. She saw blood dripping down her leg and realized she was losing her baby. The miscarriage had probably been caused by the wolf knocking her off her horse.

Although she had not wanted the child, she blamed Rain Song for her loss.

If everything had gone as she'd planned, Rain Song would be dead now. Dull Knife had asked for her help. She was only supposed to start a fire, and then assist the others to escape. He had told her he especially wanted Rain Song to be safe, but she had taken it upon herself to alter the plan.

Spotted Flower turned to glance behind her and saw the wind had shifted, taking the fire in another direction. As she hated her horse, a slow smile curved her mouth. There was no sign of Rain Song or Tall Woman. They had not made it away from the fire after all.

A strong cramp hit her as she whipped her horse around and rode toward the buffalo camp. Everyone would feel sorry for her when they found out she had lost her baby trying to help Rain Song and Tall Woman.

She was in pain, but she had to go on. When she crossed a small stream, she dismounted and washed herself. She had lost the baby.

After Spotted Flower had washed the blood off her gown, she climbed back on her horse. If the Fates were with her tonight, and if there was any justice in the world, her most hated enemy would be dead.

Tall Woman fell to her knees. "I can go no farther. I do not think the fire will reach us here."

Chinook dropped down on the ground as if on guard. Rain Song knelt beside Tall Woman, knowing she was going to have to deliver the baby. Fear took over her reasoning—she knew nothing about childbirth. Trying to sound calm, she faced her fear and conquered it. "You will have to tell me what to do."

Tall Woman moaned, twisting in pain. When the pain subsided, she reached for Rain Song's hand. Running her tongue over her dry lips, she said, "Stay beside me. I will instruct you."

"We do not have water or a knife."

Tall Woman pointed to the doeskin bag that had

fallen beside her. "You will find a knife and a soft strip of deerskin. They will have to do."

Tall Woman labored through the night, and at times Rain Song was afraid she would die. When the pains came upon her and Tall Woman gripped her hand to keep from screaming, Rain Song looked away so her mother would not see her tears.

The sun had just broken across the canyon when the baby made its way into the world. Rain Song's heart leaped with joy as she held the incredible miracle in her hands. Against all odds, the child had been safely delivered. Laying the baby on Tall Woman's belly, she smiled at the lusty crying that bounced off the walls of the canyon. "You have a son."

Tall Woman was weak but happy. "And you have a brother. We would not have survived without your bravery, my daughter."

The two of them had shared an experience that would bind them together forever.

Tall Woman ran her hand over the child's dark hair. "Your father will think we are dead."

"I believe he will." Then a smile curved her lips. "Will he not be surprised when he finds us alive—especially when you present him with his son?"

They were still not out of danger. Tall Woman needed water and she needed food. Wrapping the child in the soft buckskin, Rain Song sat beside her mother. "What should we do now?"

"Send Chinook for help."

Rain Song handed the baby to its mother and went to the wolf, slipping the knife into her moccasin. There were cougars and bears in this place, and they were two helpless women. "I hope you can understand me, Chinook. We are in trouble." She leaned close to the wolf's face and made eye contact. "Find Broken Lance," she commanded.

Much to both women's surprise, Chinook scrambled to her feet and went bounding toward the cliff, soon to be lost from sight on the other side. "Do you think she understood me?"

"We will have to wait to see."

Rain Song thought of Wind Warrior, wishing he were there. Just thinking about him made her feel safe. A thought hit her that sent her mind reeling: she loved Wind Warrior! Closing her eyes, she could see his face in her mind, and she wished more than anything she could be in his arms.

Tall Woman had fallen asleep, so Rain Song walked the baby and sang to him. He was beautiful, the brother she had always wanted. She felt fiercely protective—she would give her life to protect this child. But they might all die if help did not come soon. Tall Woman had had a difficult time giving birth and she was too weak to walk anywhere. And of course the horses were gone.

Evening shadows fell before Tall Woman awoke. Rain Song handed her the baby, so she could nurse him.

"How are you feeling?" she asked.

"Proud," Tall Woman replied, smiling.

Rain Song touched the baby's face. "I am proud of him as well."

"Yes, but I was not speaking of my son. My precious daughter, it is you who fill me with pride. Without your help, the baby and I would have perished."

Tears gathered in Rain Song's eyes, and she brushed them away. "I love you and this child, my mother."

Tall Woman's eyes glistened with tears. "At last you have said the words I waited to hear. I love you, my daughter. I always have."

Chapter Fifteen

Rain Song awoke immediately when she felt something wet touch her face, and she opened her eyes to find Chinook's nose pressed against her. She smiled, her hands going through the wolf's thick hair.

"So you have returned."

A shadow fell across Rain Song's face and she stared into Wind Warrior's eyes. "The wolf brought us with her."

Rain Song scrambled to her feet. "Wind Warrior! I was . . . I was wishing for you, and you are here."

A smile curved his mouth. "Were you?"

He came to her side, looking her over, apparently to see if she had been injured. She was aware ashes must have smudged her face, her hair was tangled, and her gown was bloody from delivering the child. He seemed satisfied with what he saw, however, and offered his water skin to her.

Remembering her outburst when she first saw him, she wished she could take her rash words back. A blush climbed her face and she turned away so he would not see her confusion. "Please give my mother a drink first. She is in greater need."

Wind Warrior shook his head. "This water is for you. Broken Lance is seeing to Tall Woman's needs."

Seeing Broken Lance bending near his wife, Rain Song gratefully took the water skin and drank deeply, then wiped her mouth on the back of her hand. "How did you find us?"

"Chinook insisted we follow her." Wind Warrior removed a twig from Rain Song's golden hair. He could not tell her the despair he had felt when Spotted Flower came into the buffalo camp and said Rain Song and Tall Woman had perished in the fire. After the initial shock, he had known Rain Song was alive because if she had died, he would have felt it in his heart.

Broken Lance explained: "By the time we saw the fire, it had consumed everything in its path." So great was his relief that they were alive, he had to pause before he could continue. "I thought I had lost my family. Most certainly when Spotted Flower arrived, telling us of your deaths. Of course," he said grimly, "now that Tall Woman has told me of her misdeeds, she will be punished."

Taking his son in his arms, Broken Lance smiled. "Something good came from this." He glanced at Rain Song. "My heart swells with pride in you, my daughter. This all would have ended differently if not for you."

Rain Song felt tears in her eyes. It was the first time he had called her his daughter. When she took a step, she stumbled and Wind Warrior swept her into his arms.

"You are weak. I will help you."

"Let us leave this place," Broken Lance said, gazing about him. "We will carry the women up the path."

Wind Warrior started toward the cliff with Chinook trotting behind. "You will ride with me," he said to Rain Song.

"I must tell you," she said, looking into his eyes, "Spotted Flower admitted she started the fire to discredit you."

"I know. Tall Woman told us while you slept."

"She hates me so."

Wind Warrior's eyes hardened and he nodded. "Do not think about it."

When they reached the top of the cliff, Wind Warrior placed her on the horse in front of him. She closed her eyes, feeling as if she belonged in his arms. She was young, and so was he, but love knew no age, and she loved him desperately.

As they rode away, Rain Song snuggled in his arms.

"You are mine," he whispered. "I will always look after you, my soul."

But Rain Song had not heard him because she had fallen into an exhausted sleep.

Broken Lance looked at his woman. "What will we do about Spotted Flower?"

"She must be punished," Tall Woman replied.

"She is Charging Bull's wife and he is an important member of our tribe. Perhaps we should allow him to decide her fate."

"It would be justice to allow our daughter to decide her punishment."

He shook his head. "Rain Song's heart is too soft. I will decide. For our daughter's sake I will not have the woman killed, although she deserves it. I will banish her from our village, and everyone will be told of her shame."

"It is just, my husband. The penalty of shame is a powerful punishment. Spotted Flower will be too ashamed ever to show her face in a Blackfoot village, and no one will take her in."

They came to a halt, and Rain Song opened her eyes. In the morning light, there was nothing but devastation all about them. As far as she could see, the prairie was blackened by fire.

Wind Warrior handed her down and joined her. "It is a sad sight."

"Such destruction. I do not understand why Spotted Flower would do such an evil deed."

Wind Warrior studied her closely. "One with your honor will never be able to understand a person like your friend."

She turned to look at him. "She is not my friend, Wind Warrior. I do not believe she ever was."

He studied her, his eyes gleaming with an expression she did not understand. "Do you consider me your friend?"

Rain Song considered him so much more, but how could she tell him that? "Yes. I do." She smiled mischievously. "You gave me Chinook."

That was not exactly what he wanted to hear, but it would do for now. "I must speak with your father," he said, turning away.

Rain Song went to her mother, taking the baby in her arms and touching her lips to his cheek. "He seems to be thriving, my mother."

"He has a lusty cry," Tall Woman said with pride. "He will be like his father."

After they had rested the horses and Tall Woman

had fed the baby, they were once more on their way.

Rain Song felt Wind Warrior's breath against her cheek and went weak all over. He must have sensed her feelings, because his hand slid about her waist and he pulled her closer.

"Do you feel what I feel?" he whispered against her ear.

Not knowing what he felt or how to respond, she shook her head.

"I think you do." He laid his cheek against hers. "In that one moment when I thought you were dead, I felt as if someone had torn away pieces of my flesh."

She turned her head so she could see his eyes, trying to understand his meaning—he did suffer for others, she had come to understand that. "I do not know what you want to hear."

"Then I will wait."

She was befuddled. "Wait for what?"

"There are things I would say to you. But this is not the time."

By now they had reached the encampment and Wind Warrior handed her to the ground. Those who had been concerned about their safety quickly surrounded them. Everyone had to see the chief's new son, and many praised Rain Song for saving the lives of mother and baby.

"Until his vision quest," Broken Lance said, raising his son for all to see, "let this child be known as Fire Wolf because he survived the great fire and I was led to him by my daughter's wolf."

Rain Song glanced about her. Spotted Flower was nowhere in sight. Perhaps she had heard they had survived the fire and was afraid to face Broken Lance.

Her gaze went to Wind Warrior, who was still mounted. He dipped his head to her, whirled his horse around, and rode away.

Rain Song watched him race his horse across the blackened plain, his ebony hair flowing out behind him. Her feelings for him were more intense than she would have thought possible. She thought about him every day, and he visited her dreams at night.

Remembering the words he had said to her, she dared hope that he cared for her just a little.

Chinook nudged her nose against Rain Song's hand and she bent to hug the wolf. "You are amazing. You saved our lives."

Chinook turned her head to watch Wind Warrior disappear over the hill. "I believe you will miss him as much as I do," Rain Song said, rubbing the wolf's head. "He has a way of affecting a female in a most unusual way." She laughed aloud. "Especially you and me."

Chapter Sixteen

When the Blood Blackfoot finally reunited at their fall encampment beside the river, they were a bedraggled lot. With winter just a short time away, new tipis had to be quickly erected, robes cured, and supplies replenished. The people worked tirelessly, helping each other when they could.

Sadly, twelve members of the tribe had lost their lives when the stream burst through the rock barriers, flooding the village, just as Wind Warrior had predicted.

A touch of early winter was on the wind. Cool air settled over the land, bringing the first frost.

The village was unusually quiet as the people waited to hear the outcome of the meeting the elders had called. Dull Knife had been summoned, as had Tall Woman and Rain Song.

Wind Warrior approached the council lodge, reminded of that day years before when he had been given his name. Now he was a member of that honored council.

Many eyes watched Wind Warrior as he moved through the village with the lethal grace of a mountain lion. He did not seem to see the young maidens who tried to draw his attention or those who watched him longingly. His mind was set on a single purpose—to settle the matter of the prairie fire. On entering the lodge, he acknowledged each of the elders and Chief Broken Lance. He nodded toward his father, who seemed much frailer since the tragedies of the fire and flood. His gaze brushed over Dull Knife, and his eyes widened when he saw that Rain Song and Tall Woman were present.

Wind Warrior had not seen Rain Song since the summer season, and it seemed to him she was even more beautiful than before. Her golden hair was decorated with beads and hung down her back in a single braid. She wore a buff-colored fringed gown without ornaments. She looked into his eyes and dropped her head. In that brief moment he had read joy in her green gaze, as if she were happy to see him, and he felt a squeezing sensation around his heart.

"Join us," Broken Lance said, motioning for Wind Warrior to come forward. "We were discussing the flood that washed away the tipis of those who remained in the river camp. It took some time to recover the bodies that were washed down the river. Twelve are dead, three missing."

Wind Warrior dropped to his knees, waiting to be called upon to speak. Dull Knife, however, did not wait to be asked, but rose angrily to his feet. "The flood was not as bad as my brother predicted it would be. We have lost more people when our enemies raid the village."

"Yes," Broken Lance agreed. "We have lost many of our friends and families when the enemy came upon us unaware—but those who died in the flood were warned and could have survived. If the rest of us had not moved, we would have suffered untold loss of life."

Dull Knife held his temper with effort. "Two lives were lost in prairie fire, and all the tipis were burned as well. My brother did not foresee that."

Broken Lance glanced at his daughter. "I will ask Rain Song to tell us why there was a fire on the prairie. Stand up and come forward, daughter."

Rain Song was nervous but determined to speak of the events as they had occurred. She stood, clasping her hands, feeling everyone's attention centered on her.

Broken Lance smiled encouragingly. "Speak, daughter."

She wet her lips. "The fire did not begin spontaneously. Spotted Flower admitted to me and my mother that she was the one who started it."

"Why would she do such a thing, Rain Song?" asked Big Hand, the elder who had taken Lean Bear's place when he grew sick the previous winter and died.

Rain Song looked into the elder's earnest eyes and realized he wanted to hear her opinion, which surprised her. "I do not know why she did such a thing, but I do know she wanted to see me dead and Wind Warrior discredited." Her gaze moved to Tall Woman, who encouraged her with a nod. "Spotted Flower attempted to take the remaining horses so my mother and I would not have a way to escape the fire."

Dull Knife looked at her with anger. If what Rain Song said was true, then Spotted Flower had disregarded his orders. She was supposed to make certain

Rain Song escaped the fire unharmed. He wanted the council to believe the fire had been a natural occurrence. "You say this is true. Are we supposed to believe you?"

Seeing her daughter's trembling lips part, Tall Woman interceded. "May I speak?" she asked.

The elder nodded.

"What my daughter told you is the truth. For her part in the tragedy, Spotted Flower was banned from our midst. As I see it, the matter is over."

Dull Knife could hardly challenge the word of Chief Broken Lance's woman. His expression was sulky, and his face reddened as it always did when he was furious.

"Then let us bring this meeting to a close," Big Hand said. "Dull Knife, you were mistaken when you chose to remain near the river and convinced others to do the same. But I place no blame on you—you thought you were right, and Wind Warrior thought he was right. Now that we know the outcome, we can all draw our own conclusions. As for me, I believe you were wrong, Dull Knife. Let the matter rest there."

Rain Song remembered that Spotted Flower had said someone wanted to discredit Wind Warrior. Her gaze met Dull Knife's—she believed it was he, but she had no proof.

Should she say something to the council?

Ducking her head to break eye contact with Dull Knife, she decided to say nothing. Rain Song waited until her mother rose to leave, and then she did the same. Once she was out of the tipi, Rain Song wished she had voiced her suspicions of Dull Knife. But that was all they were, only suspicions.

Looking skyward, she watched the first snow-flakes of the season drift downward. There was cold-ness in her heart, and a fear that Dull Knife would do something to harm Wind Warrior. Not wanting to take the chance of running into Dull Knife, Rain Song hurried down the footpath into the woods, soon joined by her faithful Chinook. It had been difficult to relive the horrors of the prairie fire to-day, but it had been necessary to settle the matter.

Now she needed to be alone.

The wind whipped up and sent a chill through her body. Halfway down the path, she heard foot-steps coming from behind and she turned.

The bristles on Chinook's neck stood, and the wolf growled deep in her throat, dropping into an attack stance.

Dull Knife had followed her.

She wanted to run, but there was nowhere to go that he could not overtake her.

"You once walked with my brother—now walk with me," he demanded.

She glanced down at Chinook—the wolf was quiv-ering, ready to attack. "My father gave his permis-sion for Wind Warrior to walk with me. He did not give you permission."

Dull Knife grabbed her arm and shoved her be-hind a tree, and Chinook lunged, going for Dull Knife's throat. Before Rain Song knew what was happening, Dull Knife stabbed Chinook, and the wolf fell to the ground.

Crying out in horror, Rain Song broke away from Dull Knife and rushed to Chinook. Going down on her knees, she quickly examined the wolf to determine if the wound was life-threatening. Chinook was bleeding from her side, and Rain Song tried to stop the flow of blood by pressing her hand against the wound. When Chinook tried to get up, Rain Song ordered her to stay.

Her anger overruled her fear. Turning to Dull Knife, she narrowed her eyes. "You are evil."

Dull Knife yanked her up, slamming her against a tree. "Forget about the wolf. I do not believe you yet comprehend that you belong to me," he growled. "I will kill any man who comes near you. Do you understand that?"

He pressed his body against hers. She struggled and fought, trying to push him away. Bile rose in her throat and she willed herself not to be ill. She said forcefully through clenched teeth, "Let-me-go."

Ignoring her, Dull Knife tightened his hold, glancing down the path to make sure they were alone. "I will have you now, Rain Song. No man will want you after I've finished with you," he said, lifting her gown and shoving his hand underneath. His voice was deep and husky. "I *will* have you."

All Rain Song could think was that the hands touching her were the same as had touched Susan, murdered her. She felt a sob building up inside. "Leave me alone!"

He jerked her chin and made her look at him as his hand continued to climb higher up her leg. "I will leave you alone when I am finished with you."

Wind Warrior appeared so quietly, neither of them heard him approach. "You are finished. Take your hands off her."

Dull Knife released Rain Song and turned to his

brother with a sneer. "I knew you were watching me when I followed Rain Song. I have been expecting you, little brother."

"Move away from him, Rain Song," Wind Warrior said, all the while watching his brother.

Dull Knife gave Rain Song a vicious shove toward Wind Warrior, and at the same time, withdrew his still-bloody knife.

Wind Warrior quickly pushed Rain Song behind him.

She had never seen Wind Warrior so angry. Well, perhaps the day she arrived in the village, when he had stepped between her and his brother. In horror she watched him withdraw his own knife and face Dull Knife.

Wind Warrior circled his brother. "You will never again put your hands on Rain Song."

Dull Knife, so certain of his advantage over Wind Warrior, merely sneered. "Do you really want to challenge me, little brother?"

"It is time someone stopped you."

"I have waited for this day for a long time. You have been a thornbush scratching at my skin for too long."

"No, do not fight him!" Rain Song cried. "Not because of me."

Neither man paid her the slightest attention. They were circling each other, both filled with anger, both waiting for an opening.

"You can walk away, Dull Knife," Wind Warrior warned, "if you give your word not to come near Rain Song again."

Dull Knife gave a derisive laugh. "You only say this because you know I am stronger, and you do not want to test your blade against me. Today, little brother, you die."

When the two warriors came together, it was with such force that one of them, Rain Song did not know which, bumped into her and she went tumbling to the ground. Quickly rising, she watched with her heart beating in fear. Dull Knife was the larger of the two, the more experienced, and ruthless. She feared for Wind Warrior.

Dull Knife shoved Wind Warrior backward, but Wind Warrior caught himself and managed to remain on his feet. Once more the two of them circled each other. When Wind Warrior finally made his move, it was with such quickness it took Rain Song by surprise and Dull Knife as well. Wind Warrior slammed into his brother, taking them both to the ground. Locked in a life-and-death struggle, with muscles bulging, the strain showed on both their faces.

"You cannot have her," Dull Knife panted, attempting to throw his brother off.

"And I will not allow you to have her," Wind Warrior said.

Rain Song was shaking, unable to take her eyes off the two warriors. She moved to Chinook, and when the wolf tried to rise, Rain Song placed the animal's head in her lap, stroking her gently.

The two warriors were still struggling for supremacy. In no time at all, Wind Warrior had gained the advantage over his brother. He threw Dull Knife to the ground and pinned him there with the weight of his body. Dull Knife might be heftier, but Wind Warrior had superior strength.

Grabbing up a broken branch, he pressed it across Dull Knife's throat until his brother gagged and gasped for breath.

"Tell me you will no longer haunt Rain Song's steps. Say it!" Wind Warrior demanded.

In a last burst of defiance, Dull Knife tried to shove Wind Warrior away, but his brother was too strong for him. "It is not for you to tell me to leave her alone," he croaked. "She was my captive. She still belongs to me."

Wind Warrior pressed the branch tighter across his brother's throat. "You gave up any claim you had to Rain Song when you presented her to the chief and his woman. Now yield, or die!"

Dull Knife's muscles tightened, but at last he went limp and nodded.

Wind Warrior stood, gripping the branch like a weapon. "I allow you to live today because you are my brother. But I will not hesitate to kill you if you ever go near Rain Song again."

Dull Knife stood, his face red with anger. He glared at Rain Song, and then dropped his gaze—no warrior had ever beaten him before, and it brought him great shame that Rain Song had witnessed his defeat.

When Rain Song saw Dull Knife's eyes, she shivered with dread. There was no doubt in her mind he was already plotting revenge on his brother.

Without a word, Dull Knife turned and left.

Wind Warrior came to her, moving the wolf aside

and lifting her up to stand beside him. He gently touched a scratch on her face. "Did he hurt you?"

She had not meant to cry, but her shoulders shook and tears blinded her. Turning so he would not see her tears, she spoke in a tremulous voice. "No. I am not hurt. But . . . Chinook . . . is."

Strong arms went around her and Wind Warrior turned her to face him. As if it was the most natural thing in the world, her head dropped on his shoulder. Her eyes closed as his dark hair cascaded against her cheek. She relished his nearness, his warmth, and the safe feeling that enveloped her. "I was afraid for you."

"You need not have been." He tilted her chin. "Do not fear for me, little one. I can take care of myself."

"I am not a little one. I am almost a woman."

Wind Warrior did not relinquish her, and she did not try to move away from him. She could feel the beat of his heart, and she could hear the beating of hers.

"Chinook needs me."

He touched his mouth to her neck and slid it to her ear, where he whispered, "Go, my little almost-a-woman."

Wind Warrior released Rain Song and turned his attention to the wounded wolf, examining her injury. "It is little more than a flesh wound. She is going to be sore for a few days. But she will heal." He lifted Chinook in his arms. "Let us take her to the medicine man—he is adept at tending wounds."

Rain Song laid her face against Chinook, her connection to Wind Warrior. "Sweet wolf, you are hurt because of me." She knew the day would have ended quite differently if Wind Warrior had not followed Dull Knife into the woods. "I am sorry for causing you trouble yet again," she told him.

He gave her a smile that went through her like a strong wind.

"Think nothing of it," he replied, his gaze locked with hers. Then he said in a teasing tone. "It strikes me that you are always in some kind of trouble."

Rain Song nodded. "That does seem to be my nature. And it seems to be your nature to save me from the trouble I get myself into."

Wind Warrior gave her a look she did not understand. "It is no more than I would have done for any Blackfoot maiden who suffered my brother's torment."

Blackfoot maiden?

Yes, that was the way Rain Song was beginning to think of herself. For so long she had fought against being absorbed into the tribe, but she no longer belonged to the white world. She thought of Tall Woman—not even Aunt Cora had been more of a mother to her than her Blackfoot mother.

As she stared into Wind Warrior's eyes, she felt as if a flame had torched her heart. He stirred emotions in her that she had never felt before, but they were strong and consuming.

Those she loved and cherished most were Blackfoot, and so was she in spirit.

Chapter Seventeen

Two Years Later, Blackfoot Rendezvous

A feeling of festivity was in the air as the Blood Blackfoot welcomed their brothers from other Blackfoot tribes: the Piegan and the Siksika had come together for their yearly gathering. It had rained the night before and a continuous muggy breeze swept across the nearby Porcupine Hills.

The sun poked through a smoke-colored sky, promising a fine day for the gathering. The whole area was covered with wild lilies and lupine, and the wind carried the sweet aroma of spring flowers. The Milk River was running full to its banks, and children splashed happily in the shallow parts.

There were even French trappers and fur traders among the people gathered—some who had taken Blackfoot wives.

Tall Woman, with Fire Wolf on her hip, entered the tipi, laughing. "Daughter, you would not believe your eyes if you saw all the maidens fussing among themselves, putting ribbons and beads in their hair. Of course they are all wearing their best gowns, hoping to find a husband at the gathering. And you know how silly they can be when they know Wind Warrior will be attending the games."

As Tall Woman placed the child on a buffalo robe,

she noticed Rain Song was wearing an older gown with tattered fringe at the bottom. "You do know that he will be arriving at the gathering today?"

Hope blossomed in Rain Song's heart, only to be dashed a moment later. She was angry with herself for caring. She had seen Wind Warrior from a distance many times in the last two years, but not once had he spoken to her, or even looked in her direction.

"Let the others make fools of themselves. I will not." She glanced up at her mother and found Tall Woman smiling knowingly. "Is it certain he will come?"

"It is certain, my daughter. He sent word that he wants to speak to your father." Tall Woman's smile deepened. "What do you think that is about?"

Although Rain Song gave a shrug of indifference, her heart fluttered at the thought of seeing Wind Warrior, who had been away all winter. Chinook rose and padded to Rain Song, nudging her hand. Absently she reached for a chunk of dried meat and gave it to the wolf, which proceeded to curl up beside Fire Wolf.

"There is something else I think you should know." Tall Woman turned her full attention on her daughter. "Spotted Flower arrived here last night. They say she has been living with a Frenchman since she was driven from our village."

Rain Song was surprised. "I wonder why she did not return to Fort Benton."

"I suppose she does not want to go back to that life. I wanted you to know she is here, so you would not be surprised if you see her today."

"My mother, two people died in the prairie fire. One was a child, the other was an elder's wife. Why would my father allow her near our people?"

"Broken Lance does not tell the French trappers who can live among them, or who they can bring to the rendezvous."

Tall Woman poured water in a wooden bowl and placed it down for Chinook to drink. "Put her out of your mind. This is a time of great joy for the young people of the tribe."

Rain Song returned to the subject that filled her thoughts. "I wonder why Wind Warrior has not chosen a woman to share his life. He could have any maiden he wanted."

Tall Woman realized her daughter had not understood the significance of Wind Warrior asking to speak to Broken Lance. "Who can say what is in his thoughts? I suppose he must be sad since his father died this winter. He is all alone but for Dull Knife, who is worse than having no brother at all."

"Did you know his mother?"

"Yes. She was sister to my mother, and a very worthy woman. The women in my family are very strong-willed. I suspect she taught Wind Warrior much of what he believes today. Dull Knife, being the elder son, fell under his father's teachings. We know how that turned out."

Rain Song returned to her task of grinding camas bulbs, which were to be used to sweeten the flat cakes that would be served later in the day. "A warrior should choose a wife."

"Daughter, you have worked enough," Tall Woman said, removing the wooden grinder from her hand.

"Take your little brother with you and join the others of your age."

"I would rather—"

Tall Woman's hands went to her hips. "The games are meant to be enjoyed, and you must see them. But first you should change your gown."

"I refuse to make a fuss over what I wear today," Rain Song said, smoothing her hair. "There is nothing wrong with this gown."

"It has no beads and some of the fringe has fallen off. Do you not want to look your best?"

Unenthusiastically Rain Song explained, "No one will notice or care what I wear." She took Fire Wolf's hand, but then paused at the tipi opening. "I have heard there will be many couples united at the gathering. Do you suppose he has come here to select a wife?"

Tall Woman bent to fold a blanket, turning her head to hide a smile. "Of whom do you speak?" she asked, although she already knew.

"Wind Warrior," Rain Song admitted, her cheeks coloring.

Tall Woman studied her daughter. Rain Song was not even conscious that she had grown into a beautiful young woman. Her hair was a halo of gold, her eyes as green as spring grass. Her face was so lovely, warriors, upon seeing her for the first time, stopped in their tracks when she passed by them. She had a warm and loving temperament, and word that she sang beautifully had spread to other tribes.

Rain Song did not know that many young warriors had noticed her and sought to take her as their woman. She knew nothing of the many offers of marriage Broken Lance had turned away because Tall Woman had insisted on it. She was waiting for Wind Warrior to claim Rain Song.

"Some would say Wind Warrior has waited longer than most young warriors to choose his woman. There must be a reason," Tall Woman said.

Fire Wolf tugged at Rain Song's hand, and she smiled down at him. "It might be that he does not wish to marry at all."

"I believe he has already made his choice," Tall Woman said. "If we wait, no doubt we will find out who that fortunate maiden is."

Sighing, Rain Song let go of her brother's hand and quickly rebraided her honey-gold hair, placing a cluster of beads near the crown of her head.

So she did care how she looked today, her mother thought, smiling to herself. Rain Song still faced jealousy from some of the other maidens, but she was well received by the older members of the tribe. When Wind Warrior's father, White Owl, lay dying last winter, he had asked that Rain Song come to his tipi and sing to him. The old man had died with a smile on his face and the sound of Rain Song's sweet music in his ears.

Rain Song stared down at her brother, who was waiting not so patiently for her to take him outside. Lifting an empty water jug, she took Fire Wolf's hand and smiled down at him. "You can play with your friends if you do not go near the horse races. It is too dangerous."

Her brother grinned up at her, his dark eyes dancing. "You know you are the real love of my life, don't you?" she told him.

He giggled and nodded. "You do love me so much."

"Yes. So much."

Tall Woman moved past Rain Song and stepped through the tipi opening, knowing her daughter was following. "Go, join those your own age. I would have you enjoy this day."

Rain Song was lost in thought as she led Fire Wolf toward the river. Absentmindedly she watched the child pull away from her and run in the direction of his friends, who were playing beside the river. Though Rain Song would not admit it even to herself, she was every bit as aware of Wind Warrior as any of the other maidens—maybe even more so. She was just better at hiding her feelings than the others were. She hoped.

White Wing called to her and ran to catch up. Her eyes were dancing with excitement. "I have great joy. Falling Thunder has asked that I be his woman and my father has agreed."

Smiling, Rain Song pressed her friend's hand. "I know how long you have looked upon him with favor. I am happy for you."

White Wing searched Rain Song's face. "Have you heard who is arriving today?"

Cautiously Rain Song nodded, hoping her friend would not read the eagerness in her expression. Wind Warrior had been right when he had advised her to confront White Wing. Of course, it had taken two different confrontations to accomplish the feat. The very next day after Rain Song had shoved White Wing in the river, the girl had cornered her once more, yanking so hard on Rain Song's braid, it had brought tears to her eyes.

Rain Song would never forget that day: In anger and frustration she had spun around and landed a punch in White Wing's stomach that sent the girl to her knees. After that, White Wing avoided her for a time. Then one day she sought her out and asked if they could walk together. Rain Song had been struck dumb when the girl asked if they could put the past behind them. Since that day they had been friends.

"I *have* heard Wind Warrior will be arriving. It is all anyone talks about." Rain Song glanced at her friend, who was a very pretty girl with long black hair and equally black eyes. She had a broad forehead and a small nose. Today she wore a white doeskin gown and had braided her hair with beads and feathers. "You look very nice. Falling Thunder will certainly think so."

Walking beside Rain Song, White Wing sighed. "I once thought only of Wind Warrior, but he never noticed me, except the time he was furious with me for taunting you." She smiled. "Yet he is still pleasant to look upon. Do you not agree?"

"Yes," Rain Song said hesitantly.

"I have heard he has already chosen a wife. She is not likely to be anyone we know, or we would have seen him courting her."

Pain stabbed at Rain Song's heart. If Wind Warrior took a wife, she would never be allowed to talk to him. By now they had reached the river and Rain Song knelt to fill the water jug before answering. "My mother also believes he has already chosen his wife." It had been a foolish hope to think Wind Warrior would choose her.

"No one can imagine who the fortunate maiden

might be. I asked Falling Thunder if he knew, but if he does, he would not tell me. I have not seen Wind Warrior pay extra attention to any maiden in our village. Perhaps he has chosen a woman from another tribe."

Rain Song swallowed past the lump in her throat. "You are probably right."

White Wing looked worried. "I wanted to talk to you about something, but I do not know how you will take it. I do not want you to think I am mean-spirited as I was in the past."

"You are my friend. You may say anything to me."

Pausing, undecided, as if she were measuring her every word, White Wing finally said, "I want to warn you about Dull Knife."

Even after all this time, just the sound of that man's name frightened Rain Song. She had told no one except her mother about the clash between the two brothers when Dull Knife had stabbed Chinook. She might not have told Tall Woman either if her mother had not questioned her about the wolf's wound. Rain Song had said nothing, however, about Dull Knife's attack on her because Wind Warrior had allowed him to live, and her father would have demanded his death had he known.

She shivered. "I detest Dull Knife. I always have."

"With good reason. My brother told me Dull Knife is determined to have you for his woman."

Rain Song paled. "I will never allow him to come near me. There have been times when he . . . came too close to me. I will never allow him to do so again."

"You must be careful never to be alone with him,"

White Wing warned. "You must be aware that he has an ally who wants to see you suffer."

Raising an eyebrow, Rain Song replied, "At one time that could have been half the village."

White Wing grinned at her. "Not anymore. You are one of us now." Then she gripped Rain Song's arm. "Do not take this warning lightly. I believe there is someone else who wishes you harm." White Wing looked at her with a worried expression. "Spotted Flower. I saw her this morning."

Shaking her head, Rain Song frowned. "I am not afraid of her. And I believe she will be too ashamed to face me."

"She does not know what shame means—she only knows bitterness and the need for revenge. You do know she blames you for her banishment."

"She has always blamed me for everything. It is her way."

"From the first she was trying to cause you hurt. It pains me to remember that once I chose her friendship over yours."

"Do not speak of it. As for Spotted Flower, I believe she despises me because I remind her of her old life. She lost so much when she was taken away from her family, and the bitterness always ate at her."

White Wing blinked her eyes. "Why should you make excuses for her? She lost no more than you did." White Wing was quiet for a moment. "Grief sometimes twists a person's thinking, and so does jealousy. I admit there was a time I was jealous of you. But knowing you has taught me true friendship."

The two young maidens watched as several men wearing buffalo masks danced around others who waved their lances at them. The beating of the drums and the high-pitched sound of the wooden flute wound its way through Rain Song's thoughts. "My mother has said that when the heart is twisted, the mind is also twisted."

White Wing nodded in agreement. "When I saw Spotted Flower this morning, she was huddled with Dull Knife. I heard him speak your name, and I came to warn you. I do not know if they plan anything, I only know you should be careful."

"Thank you for telling me this. I will be careful."

"Dull Knife is ambitious and would like to have the chief's daughter for his woman."

Rain Song watched as a group of warriors rode through the village, with Dull Knife in the lead. "I do not want to see him," she said, moving away from the river. "I have chores I must do for my mother." With that excuse, she lost herself in the crowd of people watching a horse race.

Chapter Eighteen

It had been a difficult decision for Spotted Flower to decide on attending the rendezvous. Those of the Blood Blackfoot who knew her and knew what she had done shunned her the moment they saw her.

But there was something Spotted Flower needed to do, and to accomplish that, she must endure hatred and rejection. There were several people she hoped to avoid, such as Charging Bull and Tall Woman. She didn't care if she saw Rain Song; in fact, she hoped she would see her so she could brag that she was no longer a prisoner.

Spotted Flower's heart had almost stopped when she'd approached Dull Knife earlier. He was the one she had come to see. Her plans wouldn't work unless she could ensnare him. Failing that, she would be forced to spend the rest of her life with the French trapper, Claude Bernard. Claude wasn't a bad man, although he was not a young man. But unlike Charging Bull, who had taken what he wanted from her and gave her no pleasure, Claude had taught her many things in his bed, and she liked the things he did to her. He had given her a place to live and most of the time he was in the mountains trapping.

She slowed her footsteps, glancing over her shoulder to see if Dull Knife was following her. Earlier, she had whispered to him that she needed to meet with him in private.

She saw no sign of Dull Knife.

Maybe he wouldn't come at all.

If her plan failed, if he ignored her, then she would never find her way back to Fort Benton and home.

She didn't expect to receive a warm welcome back at Fort Benton, but from there she could join a wagon train to California. She wanted a new life, and to live where no one had ever known she had been an Indian prisoner.

Her life had been hard when she was driven out of the Blackfoot village. She was almost dead from hunger and exposure when she happened upon a French trading post. In a land where there were no white women, she became very popular. Then Claude had come into the trading post and she had left with him the very next day.

Reaching the wooded area, Spotted Flower took the left path that led to the place where she had pushed Rain Song over the cliff. It was secluded, and that would suit her purpose.

She heard footsteps behind her and knew Dull Knife had followed her. Staring into angry black eyes, she almost lost her nerve.

"What do you want of me: Speak quickly or I will drive my knife into your heart for the way you betrayed me."

"How can I make amends?" she asked him. She knew better than to try to convince him she had not planned Rain Song's death. "Ask anything of me and I will do it."

He gripped her arm and twisted it behind her back, causing pain to shoot up her shoulder. "You have nothing I want," he snarled. "You were of little help to me when you set the prairie on fire. When you allowed yourself to be caught, the shame that was supposed to fall upon my brother fell on you."

"I know."

"Did you think I would not remember how you betrayed me? Look for your death."

"Wait," Spotted Flower said, holding out her hands. "No one knows you are the one who asked me to set the fire."

Dull Knife's eyes narrowed. "But you could still tell my brother, or the council. As long as you live, you are a threat to me."

He backed her against a tree trunk and the strength went out of her legs. "I would never tell anyone." She licked her lips, watching one hand move to the handle of his knife, while the other one clamped around her throat.

"The dead cannot speak."

Spotted Flower knew she had to act quickly; she only had moments to live. Reaching out, she slid her hand down his leg and stroked between his thighs. "I have spent the last two years with a French trapper and he taught me many ways to please a man. Would you like me to show you what I have learned?"

When Dull Knife's eyes widened, she slid her hand inside his leggings. He was startled, and released his hold on her neck, so she dared to go further, sliding her hand around the swell of him.

When Spotted Flower heard his breath catch in his throat, she became even bolder. Going down on her knees, she slid his leggings aside, exposing him. When he dropped his knife, throwing his head back, she proceeded to show him what Claude had taught her.

Hearing Dull Knife's breath come out in a hiss, Spotted Flower felt joy—she had him!

Dull Knife gasped, leaning heavily against the tree.

Poor fool, she thought. *No woman has ever done to him what I am now doing.*

It pleased her to watch him shudder in release. His fingers dug into the tree and he clamped his mouth shut to keep from crying out. It didn't matter that she was no beauty like Rain Song; she could make a man remember her long after the lovemaking had ended, and leave him begging for more.

Claude had taught her well.

When Dull Knife could catch his breath, he jerked her up, shoving her gown past her waist. Spotted Flower wrapped her legs around him and bent to touch her mouth to his. She felt his surprise when she thrust her tongue into his mouth, introducing him to still another new sensation. He was breathing hard as she took his passion beyond where he had ever gone.

When it was over, he could hardly stand, or catch his breath. His hand was trembling as he reached for her. "I despise you for what you are, but I will have you do that to me again."

"Now?" She could hardly catch her breath. She

had long desired him and she had not been disappointed in the way he had made her feel.

"No. You will go to my tipi and wait for me there."

Spotted Flower smiled to herself. He had just learned something new, and she would use his growing hunger against him.

He shook her so hard, her head snapped back. "You will stay with me until I send you away."

"Someone might see me."

Dull Knife stared at her. "You are clever. Come under cover of night. I will have you do those things to me again."

She smiled, leaning toward him and pressing her mouth to his. He gasped when she jabbed her tongue inside.

Dull Knife tore his lips from hers. "Leave now. I want no one to see us together."

At that moment he wanted Spotted Flower more than he had ever wanted any woman. Breathless, he stared at her. "You are the best I have ever had," he said reluctantly.

She pulled her gown down, smiling. Testing her power over him, she rubbed her tongue along his lips, delighted when he groaned once more. "I will be waiting for you," she told him.

Spotted Flower found Claude and pulled him aside. "Dull Knife is just where I want him."

"I discreetly asked around and discovered Dull Knife brought many fine furs into the village. Will he let you near enough to take them?" the Frenchman asked.

"Of course," she said, swinging her hips. "He said to come to him after dark." She gazed up at the early afternoon sun. "But I believe I shall go to his tipi now."

Claude laughed. "You are like no other."

"And you taught me well."

He looked at her questioningly. "We will meet as we planned?"

Spotted Flower nodded. "Yes. I give you the skins and you lead me to Fort Benton."

Spotted Flower had no trouble sneaking into Dull Knife's tipi. He wasn't there, but she had not expected him to be with the games going on. She dropped to her knees and ran her hand over a very fine beaver skin. There were two huge stacks of valuable skins. Certainly there were enough to satisfy Claude, and even extra for her to keep for her own needs.

She reached for the bag at her waist, smiling. Peyote, a plant the Blackfoot used in vision quests. It would muddle the mind, and mixed with the wine Claude had given her, it would surely render Dull Knife helpless.

Dull Knife entered a moment later, surprised to find her already there, but his dark eyes immediately filled with anticipation.

"Take your clothing off."

She dropped her gown, and stood before him naked.

"Take yours off," she said, swinging her hips and walking slowly toward him.

Spotted Flower did not anticipate any trouble from Dull Knife. Her most immediate problem would be sneaking the furs out of camp without being discovered.

She would save the wine and peyote mixture until dark because it would be easier to make her escape under cover of night, especially if Dull Knife was unconscious.

There would be so many people wandering about, socializing and listening to stories of the day's contests, surely no one would notice her.

She hoped.

Chapter Nineteen

When Rain Song finally returned to her family's tipi, she stopped in her tracks. Wind Warrior was standing outside talking to Broken Lance, his expression grim.

With her heart beating faster, she ducked her head and quickly moved inside, fearing Wind Warrior would see how his presence disturbed her.

As Tall Woman watched Rain Song, she noticed the turmoil brewing inside her daughter, and knew the reason for it. Reaching for a stack of sweet cakes, she handed them to Rain Song. "Deliver these to Yellow Bird—she is expecting them."

Rain Song met Tall Woman's eyes, and mouthed the words "Thank you."

To Rain Song's surprise, Wind Warrior was still speaking to her father when she left the tipi. She moved to step around him, but his words stopped her. "I will walk with you, if you do not mind."

With her heart accelerating, Rain Song could not find her voice—she glanced at Broken Lance, expecting him to object, but he merely smiled and nodded. She made the mistake of raising her head and looking right into Wind Warrior's eyes, which were as dark and mysterious as ever.

Just seeing him made her feel that fire was running through her veins. His dark hair hung past his shoulders; two eagle feathers were tied around a thick lock of it. He wore white buckskin leggings and a heavily beaded shirt. Rain Song had never seen him dressed in such finery, and she was dismayed when she realized that he must be clothed in his wedding garments.

Wind Warrior's gaze slid to her face and lingered there for a moment. "Do you object if I walk with you?" he asked, frowning.

Rain Song could not find her voice, and apprehension tightened her stomach.

"My daughter is shy and unaccustomed to speaking with a warrior," Tall Woman said, coming to her rescue and taking the sweet cakes from Rain Song's hand. "I will deliver these for you."

Broken Lance nodded his head. "Walk beside the river. It is cooler there."

Rain Song drew an uneasy breath, more confused than ever. Why would Wind Warrior want to speak with her on his wedding day, when he had ignored her for so long?

"Yes," Wind Warrior agreed, smiling down at her. "It is cooler by the river."

Rain Song looked down at her worn gown, wishing she had not insisted on wearing it when she had a new white doeskin Tall Woman had helped her make for the rendezvous.

She moved away from the tipi, and Wind Warrior joined her, slowing his long stride to walk beside her.

"You are a woman, now," he said, his voice deep, his gaze on the swell of her breasts before he looked into her eyes.

"I . . . am."

"And I am a man."

"A warrior, yes," she said, wondering why he should make such a statement to her.

"Are you happy with your life here?"

"I . . . love my family."

"But you miss your old life?"

She looked at him. "I rarely think of the past, although I sometimes wonder about my aunt and uncle," she admitted.

"What if I asked you to change your life?"

She frowned up at him. "Why would you do that? I do not understand."

Wind Warrior stared at her, wondering if she knew her voice was low and sultry, or what effect it was having on him. His chest rose and fell when he took a steadying breath. "I do not suppose you do."

He trembled inside, anticipating how she would react to what he was about to ask her. There was always the chance she would say no.

Realizing that Chinook was racing to catch up with her, Rain Song stopped to wait for the wolf. Going down on her knees, she planted a kiss on the shaggy head. Burying her fingers in Chinook's rough coat, she glanced up at Wind Warrior to find him watching her with that intense look she had come to expect from him.

She was suddenly shy because neither of them had spoken in some time, and the silence lay heavy between them.

"Rain Song," Wind Warrior said ruefully, "I believe we have become the center of everyone's attention."

She glanced about her, noticing for the first time

that a crowd of people had gathered and were watching them with curiosity.

And who could blame them?

Rain Song was somewhat shocked and amazed to find herself with Wind Warrior on the day he should be with the woman he was to marry.

She stood up and started walking toward the river, with Wind Warrior on one side of her and Chinook on the other.

He was watching her carefully, and she felt his presence in every fiber of her body. She was also aware of every sound around her—cheering from those who participated in the games and laughter from the women who watched the contests. In a nearby pine tree a mockingbird trilled its sweet song and the wind rustled the branches. Everything was more acute, her senses more in tune, when he was nearby.

When they had gone beyond sight of the crowd, Wind Warrior took Rain Song's hand and turned her toward him. His gaze swept her face. "It pains me that you are uncomfortable with me," he said, "especially since I have something to ask you."

Rain Song gave a heavy sigh. "I know what you want to ask, and I want to say how sorry I am."

Now Wind Warrior was the one to look puzzled. "What do you think I want to know?"

They began walking again. "You were in the mountains when your father died," Rain Song said. "It must have been difficult for you because you could not be with him at such a time. Let me assure you he did not suffer. I sang to him, at his request, and he had a smile on his face when he died."

Wind Warrior studied her for a long while. "I am

grateful that you made my father's last moments peaceful, but that is not what I want to speak to you about."

She stopped to look at him. "There is something else?" She wished he would go away and leave her alone. Being with him, when she knew he had chosen another, was painful.

"Do you not suspect what I want to say to you?"

"No," she admitted. "I do not. I do not understand you at all."

"Ask me any question and I will answer it."

"Do you not realize that walking with you today will cause me trouble?"

"In what way?"

Rain Song compressed her mouth because he did not comprehend anything. "Many of the other maidens will resent me because you are walking with me."

He gave her an enigmatic smile. "Think not of them. Rather think about how alike we are. Our spirits speak to each other. Have you not realized this?"

Her eyes widened and she shook her head. "We are nothing alike. Besides my father, you are the most important man in the tribe. I am merely a white captive."

"You are much more than that. Come," he said encouragingly, "we will walk this way." Wind Warrior fell silent as he guided her down the path that led toward the forest.

Wind Warrior turned to her, lightly touching her arm, and withdrawing his hand when he saw her drop her gaze.

"Why do you fear me?" he asked.

Rain Song had seen the dangerous side of Wind

Warrior when he had fought his brother. But she had also seen gentleness in him. "I do not fear you." She could not tell him she was afraid of her own feelings for him, of the deep yearning that filled her at his touch.

"What do you want to say to me? I must soon return to my mother. She needs my help."

Wind Warrior looked at her with frustration before he spoke. "If you are willing to listen to what I have to say, it may take some time."

If she had not known better, Rain Song would have thought he was nervous. But that could not be true; Wind Warrior was never unsure of himself. Still, he couldn't seem to find a comfortable place for his hands. At last he folded them across his chest and regarded her with a serious expression.

"No matter how you may deny it, we are much alike," he insisted. "Surely you have sensed that."

She looked deeply into his warm brown eyes: Before, they had been piercing and seeking, but now they held a light of uncertainty in their dark depths. Rain Song knew her answer was important to him, although she did not know why.

"You are Blackfoot; I am from the white race. I see nothing similar about us."

"Rain Song, I have touched your spirit many times. I have felt your confusion, your restlessness, and even your fear. I have not had this connection with any other maiden."

She was more perplexed than ever. "Wind Warrior," she said hurriedly, fearing she would lose her nerve. "You must not say these things to me."

He smiled. "At last you say my name." He leaned

against the rough bark of a pine tree, watching her carefully. "I felt an affinity with you almost from the first."

Swallowing deep, Rain Song fought against the raw emotions that swamped her. "We were both young when we first met, hardly more than children. For a long time we did not speak the same language, so it was impossible for us to communicate."

His smile seemed patient. "But we are not children now." He was quiet for a moment as if he were weighing his words. "I have been waiting for you to come of age."

Chinook pressed against Rain Song's leg and she touched the wolf's head, needing comfort. Her stomach tightened in knots and her heart thundered inside her. She thought she saw where he was leading, or was she mistaken? "Wind Warrior, you never seem to notice me, and you have hardly spoken to me in two years."

He smiled as if her words amused him. "When you are near, I never take my eyes off you. I am just clever at hiding my interest."

Rain Song looked at him with dawning comprehension. Could he be telling her that she was the maiden he had chosen to take for his woman? Now she understood why he had spoken to her father. Although Rain Song had wanted to be with Wind Warrior more than anything, now that the moment was near, she was afraid. "We should not speak of such things."

Wind Warrior took Rain Song's arm, leading her to a wide stone, where he seated her. "I have your father's permission to speak to you, remember." He gazed at a hummingbird that buzzed about his head, and paused as if he were listening to something Rain Song could not hear.

"I need to tell you that Dull Knife will make an offer for you very soon. He has brought many horses to present to your father. We both knew he would come for you someday. That day has come."

Rain Song clamped her hands over her ears as if that would protect her from his words. The blood ran cold in her veins. "No!"

"It is so."

Jumping to her feet, Rain Song felt gut-wrenching terror grip her—she clamped her hand over her mouth, feeling that she was going to be ill. "I will never accept him as my husband. You do not know what he did to my friend Susan after we were captured."

"I know my brother has done bad things, and I know you fear him."

"He is a monster and I will never allow him to come near me." Her breasts were rising and falling rapidly as she fought to breathe past the fear that threatened to choke her. "I will never be a wife to him."

He spoke in a soft voice to calm her. "Dull Knife knows how you feel about him. But he is determined to have you anyway."

Anger freed Rain Song to speak her mind. "You are his brother—are you so different from him?" The moment she said the words, she wanted to call them back. Wind Warrior and Dull Knife were nothing alike.

He compressed his lips. "We have the same mother

and father, but beyond that, our similarity ends. There was a time when I admired him and wished I could be more like him. I have not admired him for many years."

Letting out her breath, Rain Song studied the tip of her moccasin. "I am sorry I made the comparison. In the past, Dull Knife has asked my father if I could be his wife. Broken Lance refused him then, and he will refuse him now."

"I spoke with your father, and he will not refuse my brother's offer this time . . . unless another makes an offer for you. He believes you have reached an age to be a wife."

Wild terror tore at Rain Song's mind. "It cannot be true! My father would not make me marry Dull Knife."

Seeing how pale she was, Wind Warrior took her arm and eased her back upon the flat rock. Then he bent down so he could look into her eyes. "There is no reason for you to fear becoming Dull Knife's woman. Someone else has made an offer for you."

Rain Song's eyes were swimming with tears, and it shamed her that Wind Warrior should witness her crying. The Blackfoot looked upon tears as a weakness. Catching her breath, she spoke slowly and distinctly, wishing her body would stop trembling. She no longer thought Wind Warrior would ask her to be his woman. It seemed he was merely trying to warn her about his brother and urge her to accept this other warrior's offer. "Do you know who he is? If you do, please tell me. Anyone would be better than Dull Knife."

Wind Warrior studied her broodingly, attempting

to gauge what her reaction would be when he told her the truth. Since he had always envisioned them together, he had thought all he would have to do was make the offer, and Rain Song would accept. This was proving more difficult than he had expected. What if she said she would not have him?

Nothing had gone the way he had imagined. He stood, full of uncertainty. "I am the one who made the offer."

Jerking to her feet, Rain Song stared at him. "Why would you do that, when you have not even been courting me? Do you think you need to rescue me again?"

Wind Warrior glanced down at her, knowing he had gone about this all wrong. "It is not like that, Rain Song. Someday I will tell you my reason. For now, you must decide, and do it quickly. I would have given you more time, but Dull Knife has forced me to act."

Unguarded tears washed down Rain Song's face. "My mother would never make me marry Dull Knife."

"Tall Woman has no say in this. Broken Lance has already decided you will marry today."

Rain Song looked at him pleadingly. "Why must this be?"

"Little one, you are of an age to be a wife. As much as you may wish it, you cannot remain forever with Tall Woman."

"I . . . I . . ."

There was sudden urgency in his voice. "Decide, Rain Song. Choose me."

Clutching her hands in desperation, she glanced around for some means of escape. Slowly she turned

back to Wind Warrior. "You could have any woman
you want."

His mouth settled in a firm line. "I have made my
choice. Your father is waiting for your answer. As
am I."

Wiping her tears on the palm of her hand, she
glanced up at him. In some ways she was more afraid
of him than his brother. Dull Knife might break her
body, but Wind Warrior could break her heart. "I do
not know how to be a . . . wife."

She was so small, so delicate, with a face so beautiful it haunted him day and night. Her green eyes
were even now drawing him in, and he wanted to
loosen her golden hair and run his fingers through
it. He wanted to find out if it was as soft as he had
imagined.

He reached for her hands but she clasped them
behind her, avoiding his touch.

His eyes hardened; his voice was deep and forceful and fierce. "My brother or me?"

Rain Song wanted nothing more than to be Wind
Warrior's woman, but not like this, not with him feeling a sense of obligation to marry her so his brother
would leave her alone. A feeling of hopelessness hit
her hard.

"I have no choice."

Chapter Twenty

"You do have a choice."

Wind Warrior wondered if he would ever be able to untangle the misunderstanding he had created.

Rain Song used the pretense of brushing dried grass from her gown to move away from him. Slumping down beside her wolf, she buried her face in Chinook's thick coat. "If I say yes, what will you expect of me?"

Kneeling down beside her, he lifted her chin. "Nothing other than what you do in your father's tipi. I will be patient until you are ready to accept me as your husband. This all happened so quickly—you are not prepared. I had meant to ask for you at this gathering, then give you more time to become accustomed to the match." Wind Warrior wiped a tear from her cheek. "But time has run out, little one."

Rain Song could hardly think past the drumming of her heart. She had almost forgotten about her old life, but now she wished she could return to the white world, where the choices were not so difficult.

Rain Song knew she must be wife to one of the brothers. She finally met Wind Warrior's gaze. "You would not expect me to do those things that Dull

Knife did to my friend Susan, and that he tried to do to me that day in the woods?"

Anger hit him hard. His brother had a lot to answer for. "Let there never be lies between us. I would hope that you would one day accept me fully as your husband."

Rain Song still looked troubled. "I do not like the custom of Blackfoot men being allowed to have more than one wife."

He touched her hair, his expression softening. "I pledge to you that I will have no other wife but you."

She searched his eyes, hoping to see the truth there. "I have known you to be a man who speaks the truth; are you speaking the truth now?"

His hand moved to her chin and he looked deeply into her eyes. "You have my word."

Rain Song nodded. "I would rather be with you than Dull Knife."

His mouth twitched—it was an acceptance, but not exactly what he wanted to hear from her. "Then it is settled," he said. "Let us go to your father and tell him."

As they moved down the well-traveled path, Chinook stayed near Rain Song as if by instinct, the wolf knew she was needed.

Rain Song hung her head, her heart beating fast. When they stepped into the clearing, Wind Warrior stopped, taking her hand and gently touching her cheek.

"It would soothe my wounded pride if you would not act like a woman who was going to her death."

Rain Song nodded, giving him a weak smile. "I

would not want my first act as your chosen wife to be one that will shame you."

He choked, trying not to laugh. "I can see you are going to be a challenge. I believe you would like to see me drop off the earth at this moment."

She tossed her head. "No. I would not like that—if anything happened to you, I would be forced to marry your brother."

In that moment Rain Song glanced up to see Dull Knife hurrying from his tipi. He was heading straight toward them with a look of rage on his face. Chinook became alert, bristling.

"What is this?" Dull Knife asked, fury dripping from each word. The veins in his forehead stood out, and anger snapped in his dark eyes. His gaze dropped to their clasped hands. "What have you done, my brother?" His voice became more intense when he said, "Rain Song belongs to me. Was it not I who found her and brought her to our village? Was it not I who made a gift of her to Broken Lance when I could have kept her for myself? Was it not I who spoke first for her?"

Wind Warrior's hand went to his knife and he pulled Rain Song back against him. "Get out of my way. She is my woman now. There is nothing you can do about it."

Rain Song knew Chinook was ready to attack, so she kept a hand on her head, murmuring low to gentle her.

Dull Knife shook with rage. Glancing about, he noticed a crowd had gathered, watching them with interest. He remembered that their last confrontation had ended in defeat for him. "You may think you have won today," he hissed. "But tomorrow will be mine."

Wind Warrior moved around Dull Knife, keeping Rain Song on the other side of him, his hand never leaving the hilt of his knife. "Rain Song has agreed to be my woman, and Broken Lance has accepted my gift of horses. You cannot go against Blackfoot law or you will become an outcast."

Rain Song saw the danger reflected in Wind Warrior's eyes, and Dull Knife must have seen it as well because he turned away, his angry footsteps taking him to his horse. Once he was mounted, he turned back to his brother. "This is not over."

Wind Warrior resheathed his knife. "It is over. Leave."

They both silently watched Dull Knife ride away, before Rain Song went limp and sagged against Wind Warrior. She was glad he had asked her to be his wife. Her gaze met his and she saw understanding reflected there.

"Do not think about his threats," Wind Warrior said. "This should be a happy day."

She was trembling, her face paler than usual. He wanted her, more than he had ever imagined. But not this way—not when she was forced to accept him.

Wind Warrior held out his hand to her and she hesitated before placing her small hand in his. "Trust in me." He looked as though he wanted to say more, but merely shook his head.

"I have always trusted you," she said with feeling.

"Come, I will take you to your family."

As Rain Song walked beside Wind Warrior, her

mind was in turmoil. Wind Warrior's proposal had been so unexpected, she couldn't separate the many feelings that were churning through her mind.

Little had she known when she'd awoken that her life would take such a surprising turn before the day ended.

Broken Lance had been watching the exchange between the brothers and he turned to Tall Woman. "Our daughter has captured the heart of our most honored young warrior. Surely you can now let her go."

"I would have her happy," Tall Woman said with concern. "I believe Wind Warrior will be good to her."

"I would have her safe," Broken Lance stated. "Dull Knife is still a threat. Wind Warrior knows that."

"Rain Song will be caught in the middle of the fight that will surely erupt between the brothers. Dull Knife will not take this public humiliation without retaliating."

"And our daughter will be the cause," Broken Lance stated, speaking more as a chief of his people than a father. His eyes narrowed on the couple walking toward them.

Tall Woman felt as if her heart would break. "I see no happiness on either of their faces. As for our daughter, she has always admired Wind Warrior. I do not know what he feels for her."

"He chose her over all others as his woman." Broken Lance frowned. "Women look for love, and men look for a companionable wife who will toil hard and give him children."

Tall Woman laughed. "Your mouth says the words, but your eyes have a different message."

"Yes," he admitted. "That is so." Broken Lance glanced at the crowd of people who were still enjoying food and companionship. "The match is made. Let our daughter go."

Chapter Twenty-one

By now Wind Warrior and Rain Song had reached Broken Lance and Tall Woman. Rain Song looked into her mother's eyes, searching for guidance. All her mother could manage was a half smile.

"Your daughter has honored me by accepting me as her husband," Wind Warrior said politely. "To show how much I value her, I offer you twelve fine horses, six beaver skins, and three buffalo robes."

Broken Lance's eyes widened. "It is a high price."

Wind Warrior glanced down at Rain Song, watching for a reaction. She merely stared at the ground. "It is a price to show how much I want to walk beside Rain Song."

Broken Lance held the tipi flap open and indicated they should precede him inside. "Let us sit and talk."

Tall Woman, as was the custom, sat beside the prospective husband, showing her support of him, although she said nothing. Her worried gaze was on Rain Song, who looked terribly unhappy, although she was trying to conceal it from them.

After today Tall Woman would no longer have this precious daughter in her tipi, and that thought filled her heart with sadness. She glanced at Wind Warrior.

He would be a worthy husband for any maiden. He did their family honor by choosing Rain Song. But more importantly, Tall Woman knew he loved her daughter.

He had patience.

He had wisdom.

And he would need them both.

Wind Warrior broke the silence when he said, "This happened quickly, but I would like the ceremony to take place tonight so everyone will know your daughter is under my protection."

Tall Woman's eyes met Wind Warrior's gaze and she knew he was expecting Dull Knife to make more trouble.

Broken Lance nodded his consent. "It is known you spend most of your time in the mountains. Is that where you will take my daughter?"

"We will dwell there for a time." The two men's gazes locked and they both knew Wind Warrior was taking her away where he could protect her from his brother. "I have prepared a place for her in the mountains. Know this—I will take care of Rain Song. She need never fear anyone, and she will never know a hungry day." He glanced down at her. "We will return before winter falls, and then we will dwell in the village."

Rain Song held her emotions in check—she had to if she was going to keep her sanity. She did not hear half of what was said between Wind Warrior and Broken Lance; she was considering other matters. She did not know how to be a wife. She had been taught everything a young maiden must learn to help her mother, but not how to make a home for a man such as Wind Warrior.

The rest of the day went by in a blur. Rain Song remembered Fire Wolf clinging to her hand and asking why she must go away. She was only vaguely aware that Tall Woman helped her slip into her finest gown and rebraid her hair, interweaving three white dove feathers in the golden braids.

She was still in a daze as they later stood before the chief's tipi, her hand clasped in Wind Warrior's. In a blur Rain Song saw familiar faces and felt encouraging handclasps as those gathered sanctioned the marriage.

Her one lucid moment came when White Wing approached, searching her eyes. "You did not tell me this would happen when we spoke this morning."

"I did not know at that time."

White Wing looked quizzical. "Now that I think about it, you are the right woman for such a warrior. He will make you happy." She spoke with great sincerity. "I will miss my little Rain Song." Smiling, she moved away.

Wind Warrior placed his hand on his new wife's arm and pulled her against him. Glancing at her, he gave her a smile that made her heart race. "I will wait while you say your good-byes to your family. If we leave right away, we can make it to the base of the mountains before dark."

"I am ready," she told him.

Chapter Twenty-two

In a haze of sadness, Rain Song walked inside the tipi and stood quivering before her mother, trying not to cry. Once again, she was being torn from the arms of a family she loved.

"How can I leave you, my mother?"

Tall Woman's arm slid around Rain Song's shoulders. "When you came to me that first day, I could not imagine caring for you as I had my beloved Blue Dawn. I do not know when I began to think of you as the daughter of my soul. My heart walks with you as a mother, and I will miss your busy hands working at my side."

"I feel the same. I . . . shall . . . miss all of you." Her gaze slid to Fire Wolf and she realized he had already been told she was leaving. The child was struggling to be strong. He must not see her cry or those tears glittering in his own eyes would gather on his cheeks.

She bent down beside him. "Little brother, do not be sad. We will see each other soon."

"Who will sing to me if you are not here?" He looked at his mother for answers, his chin at an obstinate angle.

"We must not be selfish and keep Rain Song to ourselves. It is time for her to have her own family."

Fire Wolf shook his head. "Do not go."

Rain Song hugged him to her. "Fire Wolf, you will hardly know I am gone before I shall be back."

Looking at her glumly, he toddled out of the tipi.

Tall Woman shook her head. "Your brother has never considered the thought of being separated from you. With the passing of time, he will understand."

"You make it sound like we shall never see each other again."

Tall Woman picked up a large doeskin bag and slipped the strap over her daughter's shoulder. "We will, and soon. Take these things that I have been preparing for you." She looked into Rain Song's eyes. "They are things you will need for your new home. Follow your husband, and be a dutiful wife."

"I . . . shall." Without a backward glance, Rain Song thrust the tipi flap aside and stepped outside into the late afternoon heat.

The sun had painted the sky in crimson. The roar of laughter met her ears and she could see that the games were still occupying many of the Blackfoot warriors.

Wind Warrior was talking with her father, and he turned to her with a smile. Walking toward her, her new husband took the heavy doeskin bag from her and hoisted it onto his own shoulder.

Glancing up at her father, Rain Song gave him a shy smile.

"You have blessed our tipi with your presence, my daughter. Now go and do the same for your husband."

She nodded. "I will, my father."

Broken Lance's hand landed on her shoulder. "You will be missed," he admitted reluctantly.

Rain Song felt tears building behind her eyes. She could take anyone's sadness but her father's. Turning away so neither man would see her tears, she walked purposefully toward the waiting horses. She watched her new husband secure her bag to the packhorse; then he turned to help her mount, his hands lingering at her waist longer than was necessary, as if offering her comfort.

Chinook sprang to life and ran toward Rain Song's horse. As they rode away from the village, Rain Song noticed that the wolf fell into step beside them.

She resisted the urge to turn and look back.

The sounds of celebration faded behind them as the sure-footed horses picked their way toward the distant mountains. Rain Song had never been in the mountains, although she had often stood gazing at them, thinking of Wind Warrior, and wondering what he did there.

She heard the rushing water and the wind rustling in the branches of the trees. Wind Warrior was silent and Rain Song had the feeling he had many things on his mind.

Suddenly he halted his mount and turned to her, pointing toward the sunset. The sky was a blend of red and gold streaks that arched like a rainbow across the western sky.

It was so beautiful it took Rain Song's breath away.

"Perhaps the glorious sunset is nature's way of blessing our joining," Wind Warrior said, smiling at her.

"It is very beautiful," she replied, meeting his

dark gaze. A knot formed in her throat and she glanced away, watching Chinook dash into the underbrush, only to reappear a short time later.

This was her land, her home, and this was her husband. As she watched Wind Warrior gracefully dismount, her heart leaped into her throat. He was like the wild untamed land—no one owned him, certainly not her.

He smiled up at her as he tightened the reins on his horse. "When I left the mountain, I prepared a place for us to camp this night. It is not too far ahead."

She looked into his eyes. How could he have known before he came to the village today that he would be bringing her back as his wife? Rain Song stared across a deep gorge that looked like a great scar on the land. Her mind was whirling, her thoughts jumbled.

Had he known before reaching the village that his brother was going to make an offer for her?

Night was closing in around them, and Rain Song had the feeling she was suffocating. What kind of life would she have living in the wilderness? No matter how it had come about, she belonged to the man who stood before her looking so silent and solemn.

Wind Warrior turned to gaze at her. "We should ride on."

A full moon shone down on the rugged countryside, helping them find their way across rocky gullies and small streams. Rain Song had a feeling her husband could find his way through these foothills blindfolded.

Wind Warrior suddenly halted, swinging off his

horse. "This is where we will camp for the night. I am sorry it is dark because I wanted you to see the beauty nature has given this land." He lifted Rain Song off her horse and set her firmly on the ground. "You will see it in the morning."

Rain Song had the strongest urge to lay her head against Wind Warrior's shoulder and feel his arms go around her. Her head drifted toward him and she caught herself just in time to jerk back.

"I will unload the packhorse," she said, turning away before he guessed what she had been thinking. Her runaway heart was thudding in her chest. Would he take her in his arms tonight and teach her how to be a woman? She did not know whether she wanted him to or not.

"I will build a fire," he told her, reaching toward a neat stack of deadwood he had cut the day before.

Untying the leather rope that secured the supplies, Rain Song removed the buffalo robes from the pack-horse. She laid them near the rough face of the cliff so they would be protected from the wind.

Working silently, Rain Song could feel Wind Warrior watching her, and she wondered what he was thinking. If his thoughts were anything like hers, he would come to her at once and take her in his arms.

When she had arranged their robes to her satisfaction, she turned to him. "Shall I prepare something to eat?"

Taking her hand, he guided her toward him. "Since the hour is late, we shall eat dried meat and berries. Will you mind?"

"I am not hungry." She could have said her stomach was in upheaval, but she did not. She backed toward one of the robes and sat down cross-legged.

Wind Warrior opened one of his packs, removing food and handing her a strip of dried buffalo meat. Then he sat quietly beside her.

For a time they ate in silence. Rain Song did not taste anything she ate—her thoughts were too jumbled, her path to the future unsure.

"I remember the day you told me you would never accept our ways because you had been torn yet again from your family. But I have watched you over the years accept Broken Lance and Tall Woman as your family."

Rain Song handed Chinook a chunk of her meat. Even now she ached to see her Blackfoot family. "Sometimes I cannot even remember the faces of my white family. Is that not strange?"

She suddenly felt nervous, wanting Wind Warrior to touch her, and at the same time, fearing he would.

Wind Warrior handed her a water skin and watched her take a drink before he answered. "It is not surprising that you no longer remember what they looked like." His voice deepened. "You now walk a difficult road, Rain Song. I have seen the strength in you, and I have watched you conquer your fear . . . until tonight."

Her head jerked up and she stared into his dark eyes. "I am just . . . it is that I do not—"

"If you have questions to ask me, now is the time."

Questions? She had hundreds. "I do not really know you, and you do not know me."

"Ah. You think I asked a stranger to be my wife?"

Her brow furrowed. "I believe you felt honor-bound to save me from your brother."

Wind Warrior's mouth twitched as he tried not to smile. "So you believe I took you as my woman out of some noble motive?"

She swallowed twice and still could not answer, so she nodded.

"Allow me to tell you how I really feel, for I want there to be no misunderstanding between the two of us."

"That is not necessary."

"I believe it is. Every time I came to the village, you were the first one I searched for, and when I saw you playing with the children or working beside the women, my heart was gladdened. I saw your wonderful spirit, and at times I felt your pain."

Wind Warrior reached out to her and then allowed his hand to fall at his side. "I wanted to hold the essence of who you are here in my hands so I could always feel you near."

Warmth spread through Rain Song's body, and she felt they were moving onto dangerous ground. Wind Warrior was making love to her without touching her. His eyes swept from her mouth to her neck and paused for a long moment on her breasts, and she blushed.

"I do not understand," she said, her voice trembling. His eyes were drawing her in, and she waited for him to take her in his arms.

"Rain Song, I did not ask you to be my woman out of nobility. I have wanted you for a long time. When I learned my brother's plans, I merely acted sooner than I had expected."

"What is it you want of me?"

Now he did smile. "I want to be the center of your world. I want you to think of me as your family. I want to fill you with sons, and place in your belly a daughter who will love life as you do."

She gasped and pulled back, afraid of the unknown relationship between husband and wife, but enticed nonetheless by the thought of intimacy with Wind Warrior.

She wanted him beside her, holding her, making her his woman.

Wind Warrior realized he had frightened Rain Song with his passionate admission. He could have said more; he could have told her he wanted to touch her hair because he had never seen hair that curled like hers. If he really wanted to frighten her, he could always tell her about the many nights he had lain awake, thinking of pressing his body against hers, of taking her heart into his keeping and hearing her moan his name while he made love to her.

Instead, he said, "This day has been hard for you. Get some sleep, Rain Song. Tomorrow we climb the mountain."

She stilled, turning her head so she could see his face and gauge his feelings. "I am weary."

He suddenly gathered her to him, and light as a whisper, his lips brushed her neck, then moved to the curve of her shoulder.

Rain Song was innocent and unprepared for the feelings that ripped through her body, heating her blood and cutting off her breathing. Her arms slid around his neck, and she pressed herself against him.

He had intended to win her slowly, but when she reacted so passionately to his touch, he almost lost his ability to think. Nuzzling the lobe of her ear, he whispered, "I ache for you."

When she gasped, he abruptly pulled back, staring into her passion-bright eyes. "I have dreamed of doing this and other things too," he said in a husky voice. "But," he said, standing, and moving away from her, "I shall give you time to get to know me, as I said I would." He looked deeply into her eyes. "Do not be troubled. I will be as patient as you need me to be."

Watching him walk away into the darkness, Rain Song wanted to call him back to her. She ached for him, but she was glad he was making no demands on her tonight.

She felt restless.

Unfilled.

Closing her eyes, Rain Song still quivered from his intimate touch.

Wind Warrior held his hands out, watching them tremble. He had almost broken his word to Rain Song. He would be more careful, take more time to win her.

He raised his face to the moon, craving that which was so near, yet so far away. The tie between them was more fragile than he had thought, and if he acted with passion, he might lose her altogether.

Rain Song.

How long had he wanted her?

Almost from the first time he had seen her, she had remained in his heart.

He had discovered that he could raise her passion, but he had also seen that she feared the feelings he stirred to life in her.

He wanted her to feel joy when he made love to her. He wanted to see her beautiful eyes light up with happiness when she saw him. He had waited a long time for her; he could wait longer.

Suddenly his senses became alert. Turning, he gazed back the way they had come. Someone was out there.

Dull Knife?

Chinook suddenly joined him and also gazed into the darkness. "You feel it too, little wolf?"

Wind Warrior knew there would be no sleep for him tonight.

Chapter Twenty-three

Ever watchful, Wind Warrior stood gazing off into the distance, alert to anything that moved across the wide ravine. He walked to the edge of the cliff, glancing across the valley. Something was stirring below. At first, it had only been a shadow in his mind; now it was clear.

It was Dull Knife.

His eyesight was keen, even in the dark shadows of night. A thought hit him and grew stronger—a thought of rage—Dull Knife's rage. His brother wanted Rain Song so much, he had decided to come after her.

Wind Warrior hurried back to camp, not wanting to upset Rain Song, but needing to make sure she was safe.

She was sitting where he had left her. Taking another robe from his pack, he handed it to her. "It is not cold enough to need a fire. Cover yourself with this."

Curiously, Rain Song watched him put out the fire.

He snapped his fingers and the wolf came to him. "Lie beside Rain Song, Chinook."

Obediently, as if the wolf had understood Wind

Warrior's words, the wolf padded back to Rain Song and dropped down at her side.

"Do not become fearful if you cannot see me to-night. I will be nearby. Chinook will warn you if danger is near."

She frowned. "Danger? Is that likely?"

He decided not to tell her about Dull Knife unless he had to. "There is nothing for you to be concerned about. Sleep, Rain Song," he told her.

He was worried about something that he did not want to share with her. She did not feel frightened, just concerned for him.

It had been an emotional day for her, so she lay back, staring at the stars twinkling in the ebony sky—she fastened her gaze on the brightest one, too weary to think clearly. Her eyes fluttered shut, and sleep claimed her.

Spotted Flower could not believe her good fortune. Not only had Dull Knife left the village, but he'd told her he would not be back for many days. He'd also told her to be gone before he returned.

The night was dark as she harnessed two of Dull Knife's horses. She heard dogs barking in the distance, and her blood froze. If anyone caught her, no explanation she could give would save her from death.

Securing the furs to the back of a packhorse, she breathed a sigh of relief. So far no one had come to investigate. She watched the sky, waiting for the moon to go behind a cloud before she mounted the horse and gathered the reins of the packhorse. Slowly she rode through the village, heading for the river.

Once she crossed, she nudged the horse forward in a gallop.

If she could make it to the prairie, where Claude would be waiting for her, he would guide her home.

She rode swiftly for over an hour and no one followed her.

With relief in her heart, she laughed aloud.

She was free!

Wind Warrior waited until Rain Song fell asleep and then slipped into the shadows, positioning himself on a cliff that jutted out over the valley, giving him a view of the surrounding foothills.

He did not underestimate Dull Knife, who was a battle-hardened warrior; if he did not want to be seen, very few could track him. Wind Warrior was reluctant to leave Rain Song even for a short time, but he had to backtrack and see if he could find Dull Knife's trail.

Wind Warrior silently moved down the hill, then slipped into the woods, every sense alert.

He found the ashes of a campfire and knew it had been his brother's. The ashes were still warm, so Dull Knife was somewhere nearby.

Melting into the shadows, Wind Warrior hurried back to his own campsite. Dull Knife would use every trick and Wind Warrior had to be ready for him when he came.

Here in the foothills, Dull Knife had a chance to track them; but he did not know the mountains as well as Wind Warrior. There were safe places Wind Warrior could take Rain Song that his brother would never find.

When he returned to camp, Chinook rose, looking at him expectantly.

"Lie down."

The wolf plopped back down beside Rain Song, resting her shaggy head on her paws, her yellow eyes on Wind Warrior.

For a long time Wind Warrior watched Rain Song sleep. Her hand rested on Chinook's head, and she sighed. He could not help notice the rise and fall of her breasts, and loneliness settled on him. She was his woman, but he could not yet become as one with her.

Soon, he hoped.

Very soon.

Chapter Twenty-four

Wind Warrior did not sleep at all, but remained on guard all night.

In the soft glow of early morning, he saw a mother bear and her two cubs amble toward a stream and proceed to catch their morning meal of fish. Warmth filled him as he watched a family of beavers frolic in the water. What had always been a place of peace and pleasure for him was now a place of danger, where he and his brother would play out their deadly game. A game he must not lose.

Dull Knife was out there somewhere, hiding, maybe watching them at this very moment. His brother would bide his time and wait for the perfect chance to take his revenge. Wind Warrior just had to make certain he did not get that chance.

Knowing her fear of Dull Knife, Wind Warrior was more determined than ever to keep Rain Song from suspecting his brother was stalking them. As soon as they reached the high country, she would be safe.

Rain Song had slept soundly, and awoke feeling refreshed. She spread her arms wide, yawning. The twittering of birds was like music to her soul, and the smell of mountain air was like a tonic.

It took only a moment for her to remember where she was, and why she was there. The day before she had become Wind Warrior's woman. Glancing around, she saw no sign of her new husband. She looked down at the buffalo robes and noticed he had not lain beside her the night before.

Chinook came out of a thicket, bounding toward Rain Song, who laughed, going up on her knees to ruffle the wolf's shaggy fur. "Where have you been?" she asked as Chinook licked her hand.

"Your wolf was out hunting for her morning meal," Wind Warrior said, emerging from the thicket. "Remember I once told you she was a wild animal. You must be prepared if she leaves us one day, if the call of her true life bids her go."

"I know that might happen. I hope it will not."

He smiled. "The voice of nature calls its own." He watched Rain Song's elegant movements, and swelled with need for her. "Have you never heard the call?"

Rain Song realized she must look disheveled, and quickly raked her hands through her hair, shoving loose tresses back in place.

Deciding he was not going to get an answer, he commented, "The weather is sweltering here, but the higher we climb, the cooler it will be."

Rain Song noticed that everything but the robes she slept on had already been loaded onto the pack-horse. Rising, she folded the buffalo robes and secured them with the other supplies.

Last night had been her wedding night, and she had spent it with Chinook. It was her fault, though. She was the one who had made Wind Warrior promise not to touch her.

She set about braiding her hair, unaware that Wind Warrior was watching her. When she turned and caught his eye, she saw a yearning reflected there that she had not seen before. "My hair gets tangled if I do not keep it braided," she said self-consciously.

Wind Warrior's gaze swept across her hair. "I like it flowing free."

She unbraided it, and smiled. "As you wish, but it will get tangled."

He stepped close, allowing his hand to run down the silken strands. "I have never seen anything so beautiful."

She smiled at him mischievously. "I like your hair."

He tilted her chin up, his tone soft. "Did you rest well?"

Not having the courage to look into his eye, she lowered hers. "Yes. I did."

He handed her dried meat and his water skin. "After you have eaten, we will leave."

Nodding in agreement, Rain Song took a bite of dried meat and washed it down with water. "Will we reach our destination today?"

Wind Warrior studied her closely. "Not for three sunrises. A bit longer," he added evasively, "if I need to backtrack."

"Why would you need to do that?"

He was only partially honest with her. He still did not want to tell her Dull Knife was tracking them. "To make certain no one is following. Now, if you are ready, we should leave."

He tightened her horse's reins and said with his back to her. "I have so many wonderful sights I want to show you."

There was an excitement in his voice she had not heard before.

"What kind of sights?"

"You have not seen beauty until you stand on a mountain peak and stare down below, viewing the earth as the eagle sees it."

"I would like that," she told him nervously, not wanting him to know she was afraid of heights—a result of Spotted Flower pushing her off the cliff.

Wind Warrior turned her to face him, finding he had no defense against her beautiful green eyes. He took a breath and said, "Your feelings are open and honest and much of the time I can see clearly what you are thinking."

Rain Song looked at him questioningly.

"I have known for a long time that you did not fall off that cliff—Spotted Flower pushed you."

Her mouth opened in astonishment. Although her mother knew, she had told no one else that Spotted Flower had pushed her. "How did you know that?"

Wind Warrior watched her face carefully. "Tall Woman told me, when she sought my help in rescuing you. I waited for you to accuse Spotted Flower. It would have been a good opportunity to shame her before the whole tribe, but you never did."

"I dealt with her in my own way."

"When you did not shame her, as many would have, it gave me a great insight into who you are."

"Well, know this about me, and you may not think so highly of my motives—I went to Spotted Flower's tipi that night and knocked her down!"

She watched his beautiful mouth curve into a

smile. "That I did not know, but I approve. It was well done."

She met his gaze and had the feeling she was drowning in the dark depths. "It seems very few things escape your attention."

"That is true where you are concerned," he agreed.

Her heart was beating so fast, she was sure he would notice. Ducking her head, she started to turn away.

As if he could not help himself, Wind Warrior took her by the shoulders and brought her body against his. She went stark still as he rubbed his face against hers. "All the same, you are a mystery to me. I want to know everything about you. But," he said, dropping his hands and stepping back, "we have a lifetime to discover each other."

Warmth spread through her and she resisted the urge to walk right back into his arms. "What wonderful sight will you show me today?"

He turned away. Happiness such as he had never known poured through him like water rushing over a cliff. Rain Song gave meaning to his days—he ached for the time when she would bring passion to his nights.

"I will show you a place where you can sing with yourself."

"How can such a thing be?" She laughed.

He grinned. "You will just have to wait and see."

Chapter Twenty-five

It was their second day in the foothills, and they moved through the shadows cast by an enormous mountain. Graceful spruce trees twisted in the wind, dominating the smaller cedars. The air was clean, the land washed in vivid colors of green, incredibly beautiful against the flow of a stunningly blue sky.

Rain Song drew the knot tight on the packhorse, looking downward at the lacy patterns made by the sun shining through a pine tree. Her gaze moved on to a clump of scrub oaks that clung to the side of the hill. Gazing upward, she wondered if they would ever make it to the top. Down below were dark shadows in a deep canyon.

She watched a small rabbit emerge from a thicket, take one look at Chinook, and dart right back.

She followed Wind Warrior as he led the horses to a nearby stream and let them satisfy their thirst.

"Why have you always spent most of your time in the mountains?" she asked.

He glanced at Rain Song with an expression she could not read. "I was not aware you noticed my absence."

She felt color climb her cheeks. "Everyone knew you preferred to dwell in the mountains."

Wind Warrior loved it when she blushed; it painted her face with a beautiful rose color. "I am not sure I know why I felt the need to come here. But I will be spending more time in the village now that you are my woman."

Rain Song's heart lurched.

His woman.

How right that sounds.

She had dreamed of him last night, and in that dream he had slept next to her, and she had curled up in his arms. Again she blushed, hoping he could not read what she was thinking this time.

"You were not in camp last night. Each time I awoke, you were not there." She had not been concerned because she had known he would not leave her in danger, and she always had Chinook at her side, but she wondered why he left each night.

"I was nearby," he replied.

Sometimes he could be maddening—especially when he did not fully answer her questions. Rain Song bent down and filled their water skins, hoping they would soon reach their destination.

Wind Warrior watched her lithe young body as she moved gracefully toward her horse. He loved the way the sunlight fell on her golden hair. He wished he knew what she was thinking as she paused to look back the way they had come. Perhaps she was wishing for Tall Woman and the life she could never go back to.

Being alone with her caused his mind to run wild. He could imagine taking her to his body, holding her against him until she felt the same passion for him that he felt for her. In many ways she had been protected, and knew very little of life and probably nothing about what went on between a man and his woman, other than what Dull Knife had subjected her to.

"You are not the only one who has insight," she said, glancing at him with a serious expression. "I know why you have not been sleeping."

His voice came out in a whisper. "Why is that?"

"You watch for Dull Knife, lest he come upon us unobserved."

She was no fool. "Do not trouble yourself about my brother. I would not allow him to hurt you—you must know that by now."

She did know it. "How long can you go without sleep before it affects your judgment?"

Wind Warrior's eyes narrowed as he glanced down a deep gully, watching an elk dash out of the greenery. "As long as it takes."

The sun set early in the mountains, and it was almost dark when Wind Warrior announced that they would stop for the night.

Wearily, she dismounted, taking the reins of her horse and following Wind Warrior up the steep path. When the path narrowed, he turned to her. "We will leave the horses down here for the night—they cannot climb any farther."

Rain Song watched him hobble the horses; then she helped him unload the packhorse, and he slung the supplies they needed onto his back.

"Chinook, stay and guard the horses," he said, nodding at the wolf.

Chinook lapped at his hand and hunched down on guard.

Was it possible Wind Warrior had mystical powers as many of the Blackfoot believed? "How do you get Chinook to do what you want her to?" she asked, slinging her own pack over her shoulder.

He paused thoughtfully. "She is a very obedient wolf, as I am sure you have discovered." Wind Warrior took her hand and helped her over a wide boulder. "I believe you will find comfort in our campsite tonight."

She glanced about her, unable to see much in the darkness. Wind Warrior led her up a steep incline. When they came to another huge boulder, he lifted her as if she weighed nothing. He slid her against his body, holding her there for a long moment.

Looking into his expressive brown eyes, she felt a jolt go through her and pushed his hands away, struggling to stand on her own. He looked pained when she stepped away from him, as if he thought she did not want him to touch her. Rain Song could have told him the opposite was true—she was afraid she would press herself against his body and throw her arms about his shoulders as she longed to do.

"How far to the campsite?" she asked to break the awkward silence. It had been a long day and she was very weary.

"We are there," he replied, sliding her pack off her shoulder and then dropping both his and hers to the ground. "Can you not see?"

By now it was completely dark and Rain Song could see nothing. It amazed her that Wind Warrior had no trouble finding his way. "Where?"

He took her hand, leading her forward. "We are in a cave, Rain Song. Actually, it is not deep enough to be called a real cave, it is more of an overhang."

She reached out until her hand came in contact with a solid rock wall. "It will be nice to sleep inside," she remarked.

Wind Warrior bent to light the campfire he had laid before going down into the village.

When the flames ignited and grew, their glow danced against the walls of the cave. Rain Song turned around, taking in the sight. He was right; it was not a deep cavern, so she did not have to worry that wild animals might be living in the space. Fur robes had been placed on dried grass to make a comfortable bed. There was a supply of drinking water in jugs.

She glanced up at Wind Warrior. "Is this your home in the mountains? Is this where we will be staying?"

He added more wood to the fire. "This is but a stopover. I hope you will like it here."

"I do." Rain Song bent down to her pack and begun taking out the supplies they would need.

Wind Warrior went outside the cave and covered the entrance with branches until he was satisfied the light of their campfire could not be seen.

Wearily, Rain Song sat down on the fur robe and her eyes widened when she felt its smoothness. "This was made of beaver skins," she said delightedly, bending to bury her face against the softness.

"I had White Wing's mother make it for you. It is my gift to you."

She rose up, looking quizzical. "Then you must have—"

"I must have known I would be bringing you here?" His eyes darkened. "I hoped I would. You are so much a part of me, I feel every breath you take and contemplate your every thought." He came to her, dropping down in front of her, taking her hand. "You now know my secret; this place was finished for you only last winter. I dreamed of you here, and now my dream has come true."

"But I—"

He placed his hand over her mouth. "Let me say what I must before I lose my nerve. I have known almost from the first time I saw you that you were the one who would walk through life with me." His expressive eyes searched hers. "Did you not suspect how I felt about you?"

Tears were building behind her eyes. She could not believe that he had loved her for so long. "No, I never dared consider you might care for me."

"Everyone else noticed. My friends teased me mercilessly for the way my gaze followed you when you were not looking."

Rain Song's mind was whirling—all she remembered was how he ignored her. She was too stunned to speak.

Wind Warrior raised her hand, touched his mouth to her fingers and closed his eyes. "How could you not know?"

She swallowed hard, understanding what he was telling her. Her hand seemed to move of its own volition, touching his face, sliding into his thick black hair. "All those years I felt alone, you were watching over me?"

His voice thickened. "You were hardly out of my sight. I made a bad mistake when I left you on the prairie where Spotted Flower set the fire." His eyes softened. "I would never have forgiven myself if anything had happened to you."

"Why did you think I was your responsibility?"

He paused as though deep in thought. He was silent so long she was sure he was not going to answer her. Then he gently pulled her into his arms. "Because you were mine. I knew it in my heart—you must have felt it too." He raised his head, looking at the top of the cave. "You cannot know the torture I lived through because you were so young, and I had to wait to claim you." He glanced down at her, his finger sliding across her lips. "You have not said how you feel about me."

She sighed, laying her cheek against his. His confession shook her world. "I . . . love you. I have for a very long time."

Wind Warrior's eyes glowed as he pulled her into his arms, bringing her close to his body. She felt him tremble, or was it she who quaked with the pain of need?

The hunger began slowly and built as his hands slid down her back, circling, soothing, then unsettling. Rain Song's overburdened heart thudded against the wall of her chest and she wanted him as a woman wants the man she loves.

Wind Warrior laid her down on the soft robe.

"Make me your woman," she pleaded.

She watched his head dip, as if he was experiencing emotions too difficult to control. Afraid she had been too bold, she started to sit up, but he came down beside her, those beautiful eyes telling her what he was feeling. He desired her, yet he would not take what he wanted until she gave him permission.

Taking his hand, Rain Song laid it against her breast. She felt him tense, and then she felt the dam break inside him.

Chapter Twenty-six

It was hard to believe a man of such power and strength could be so gentle. Wind Warrior's hand stroked down her neck and he nuzzled the hollow there.

Quivering, Rain Song turned her head, her mouth brushing against his. For a moment they both froze as unbridled passion ripped through them at the unexpected contact.

Again she tested the move that had sent shivers through them both. Wind Warrior could not breathe as she brushed her mouth across his.

He moaned, his body shook.

She cried out passionately.

His breath hissed through his teeth.

She was taken by surprise when he gripped her shoulders, taking command of the kiss. Her mouth quivered beneath his as he explored this new territory. He had not known the mouth could be so sensual. Just the feel of her mouth, her breath teasing his lips, made him want more.

Wind Warrior stilled, trying to catch his breath. His need for her was driving him out of his mind. "Do you want me to stop?" he asked, hoping she wanted him as much as he wanted her.

Breathlessly, she touched his face. "I belong to you."

He took a deep swallow. "Not yet."

He nudged her doeskin gown aside and buried his face in the cleavage of her breasts. Needing her was the worst pain he had ever experienced. She surprised him when her fingers tangled in his hair and she held him closer.

"I want . . . to belong to you. I want you."

Wind Warrior did not need to be asked twice. Moving back, he pulled her to a sitting position and lifted her gown over her head. His gaze moved from her slender neck down over her firm young breasts. He groaned when he saw the pink nipples and bent forward, touching his mouth to one tempting bud.

Rain Song jerked, her eyes widening.

He raised his head, exhaling shakily. "Did I hurt you?"

"No." The cry was torn from her throat.

He understood better than she did what she needed. "Come to me," he said, holding his arms out. "You will receive me into your body and we will be one," he said huskily.

She was trembling so hard, she could not stop. Her gaze followed him as he stood, stripping down to his breechcloth. When he came down beside her, he took her in his arms and she melted against him. Her gaze sought his, and there were questions in her eyes.

"What must I do?"

The catch in her voice and Rain Song's innocent question were almost Wind Warrior's undoing. He had been born for this night. No matter what he accomplished in his life, nothing would be more important than this moment.

Realizing how innocent she was, he had to hold back his own passion and introduce her gently to the bond that would make her his woman in deed as well as word.

Wind Warrior knelt before her, and his gaze moved down her breasts to her stomach. He placed his hand on her hips as his gaze moved lower, and what he saw sent tremors through his body; he had never imagined that the hair between her thighs would be the same color as the hair on her golden head.

Rain Song's silken body was the most beautiful sight he had ever beheld. So deep was his need for her, he fought the overwhelming urge to pull her beneath him and drive into the sweetness of her body.

"I will teach you," he said in a choked voice that he did not recognize as his own.

Her simple nod went straight to his heart.

Had any man ever loved a woman as much as he loved her?

She filled his life and gave purpose and meaning to his world. She made him think of the future, of sons and daughters—of growing old beside her. He wanted to give her everything she wanted in life, and he wanted to take from her only what she would give him.

Gently, Wind Warrior pulled her to him, absorbing the quakes that shook her virginal body. "You were created for me," he whispered, his tongue darting to the lobe of her ear. "Even though your world was far from mine, we found a way to be together."

Rain Song's arms slid around his shoulders and

she pressed her breasts against his bare chest. The moan that escaped her lips stirred his blood even more.

She reached for his hand and raised it to her lips. Her gesture made him pause to think, to harness his passion and look to her pleasure.

Wind Warrior eased her onto her back, and lay beside her. His hand trailed over her breasts, down her stomach to her thighs. With gentle pressure he pushed her thighs apart, gently caressing her until she was mindless, desperately needing something to fill the emptiness inside her.

As if he knew what she was feeling, he gently eased his finger inside her warmth. Circling, nudging, withdrawing, and plunging forward again. He touched the barrier that proclaimed no other man had touched her.

She was whimpering, and moving restlessly, and he could wait no longer.

As he pressed his mouth against hers, it seemed they both gasped for breath at the same time. His feelings were so strong he could not give them voice; he did not even try.

He nuzzled her breasts, taking each into his hot mouth and suckling, all the while nudging her thighs apart.

"Ohhh," she murmured.

He nuzzled her face, wanting all of her. He watched her eyes widen with uncertainty, then close in pure ecstasy when he blew against her mouth.

Removing his breechcloth, he tossed it aside, watching her stare at his nakedness. He could read the confusion in her eyes, and then the understanding of how they would be joined together.

Slowly, Wind Warrior eased himself inside her. She was hot, wet. "You are ready for me," he whispered in a rugged voice.

He was past ready for her.

Rain Song watched his eyes, wondering what would happen next. Already he had made her body come alive as she had never expected, but she was sure there was more.

She could hear him breathing hard, and when he eased farther inside her, she gasped. Then forcefully he drove deeper and she arched her back, trying to throw him off. She had not expected pain.

"My soul, the pain is all but over," Wind Warrior said in a deep voice that grew even deeper when he said, "Look at me. I want to see everything you feel."

She stared into tender brown eyes, and knew if she lived a hundred years, she would never be able to recapture this moment.

And then the pleasure hit.

As Wind Warrior thrust deeper, her hips bucked and she gasped. He slid out and then in again, finding the spot that made her go still. Then her hips came off the robe, twisting and turning as she tried to ease the ache inside her.

Throwing her head back, she bit her lips while he set a rhythm that thrilled her to the core. She slammed her lower body upward against his and saw his passion-dark eyes widen. She was inexperienced, but instinct guided her in the way to give him the greatest pleasure.

Wind Warrior attempted to go slow, to be gentle with Rain Song but never had a woman stirred his blood so. He knew he should carefully guide her through her first time, but the softness of her skin and the sweetness of her body broke his resolve. Although his woman was innocent, it seemed at times she was guiding him.

Her body quaked and she dug her fingernails into his muscled back. Groaning, she buried her fingers into his black hair, holding his face to hers while she ran her tongue over his lips.

That simple action set him on fire and his body quivered and shook in release. He fell forward, crushing her beneath his weight.

For a long moment neither spoke.

She was shy after what had passed between them.

He could not catch his breath.

Rain Song held him close, loving the feel of his naked body pressed against her.

At last she said shyly, "I did not expect what happened."

He levered himself off her and turned to his side; unwilling to move away from her, he held her close. "It took me by surprise too." His hand moved down her back to clasp her tighter. "My life—that is what you are to me."

"Do you look at love the same way I do?" Rain Song asked innocently, not knowing how to put a name to what had happened to her. Before, she had wanted him as a young girl wants the attentions of a handsome man; now she felt she was a part of him, and love for him burst through her mind.

He rose on his elbow, smiling down at her. "What way is that?"

She frowned. "I cannot imagine how I lived before this night. I always thought you were handsome." She smiled at him. "You know all the maidens in our village looked at you with . . . yearning."

"Did they?"

"Yes."

"I never saw them. My eyes were always on you."

She nestled her head against his shoulder and he drew her to him. He touched her intimately. "Are you sore?"

She shook her head, hoping he was going to make love to her again. "No. I am not."

He took her hand and placed it on him, and her eyes widened. "Already I want you."

She turned to her back and pulled him toward her.

Wind Warrior laughed delightedly. She filled him with joy, and he wanted to do the same for her.

Although he knew he should take her carefully, her movements, her reaction to him, heated his blood.

He was not gentle as he drove into her, and she was not gentle when she clawed his back. This time, she reached ecstasy along with him.

In the aftermath, they both lay with hearts thundering, gasping for breath. Their fingers intertwined and she nestled close to him.

Long after Rain Song had fallen asleep, Wind Warrior lay thinking. Their fingers were still entwined and he raised them toward the campfire, where the light fell on them—his hand was bronze, hers was white. He touched her golden hair and allowed it to sift through his fingers. Her hair was golden, his was black.

And yet none of that mattered. The two of them had reached across the divide separating the Indian and the white world, finding something so rare he dared not speak of it for fear it was but a dream and he would awake to find it gone.

"Sweet one," he whispered, touching his mouth to her brow. "How you torture me." He saw her eyes open.

"I do not mean . . . I never expected—" She shook her head. "What did I do?"

Wind Warrior smiled. "You made me want you more than anything I have ever wanted in my life."

"Oh," she said. "I thought I had done something wrong."

Laughing softly, he shook his head. "You do everything right, sweet one. I hope I can survive the night."

Brushing his mouth against hers, he trembled and so did she.

"I never dreamed I would be here with you like this," she admitted.

"I have."

She heard the quaver in his voice and touched his face. "I want to make you happy."

His eyes drifted shut. No one had ever said that to him before. His woman was a rare jewel, and he would treasure her all the days of their lives.

Chapter Twenty-seven

Wind Warrior felt something soft brush against his face. Becoming immediately alert, he opened his eyes and then, remembering the night before, smiled. A lock of Rain Song's hair had fallen across his face, and she was curled up in his arms.

Turning his head, he studied his sleeping woman. Long lashes rested against the pale cheeks of the most beautiful woman he had ever known, and she was his.

He could not help himself; he had to gather her close. She had just given him a night he would never forget. In her sleep, she sighed and snuggled closer to him.

Staring at the ceiling of the cave, he said a silent prayer of thanks to the Great One for giving him such a woman.

He felt himself swell, and he wanted her. But she was not yet accustomed to his demands, and he must not give in to his deepest urges. Touching his mouth to her brow, he gently untangled her from his body. When he pulled the fur robe aside, the sight of her beautifully curved body almost caused him to change his mind.

Taking a steadying breath, he covered her with the

fur and rose. Quickly dressing, he shoved his knife in the sheath and walked out into the cool morning air. The sun had not made its appearance for the day, but the eastern sky was painted with a pink glow. It was quiet—as if the earth had taken a breath and was waiting for the sun's appearance.

The wind touched him, whispering against his skin. Raising his arms, he allowed the essence of the coming day to fill his whole being.

Today he was completely happy.

Hearing movement behind him, Wind Warrior looked over his shoulder at his woman. She came up behind him, sliding her arms around his waist, pressing her face against his back.

"How do you feel this morning?" he asked.

"Like I belong to you."

Wind Warrior pulled her around in front of him. "And so you do."

Clasping her to him, he rested his chin on top of her head. "It will rain today." He nodded at the clouds gathering in the north. "But it will be only showers and we can still continue our journey."

"How do you know it will rain?"

He smiled down at her. "Do not tell me you are one of those who believe I can see into the future."

"I have heard you can."

"If that were true, I would have known you would be here with me, and would not have suffered so many doubts when I asked you to become my woman."

"But you said you prepared this cave for me?"

He placed his hands on both sides of her face, raising it and brushing her mouth with his. "I lived in hope."

"Where do we go today, my husband?" she asked.

Wind Warrior moved away from her and reached into a leather bag to give her a handful of nuts and berries. "It will be colder where we are going. You should change into warmer clothing. From here on, we travel on foot and must release the horses. Do you feel up to it?"

Rain Song nodded. "I want to see the place you call home when you are in these mountains."

He took her hand and led her back down the path. He made her a light pack, and himself the heavier one. Removing the blankets and bridles from the horses, he spoke to them, "Go home."

To Rain Song's surprise, the horses galloped down the hill and were soon lost from sight.

Wind Warrior turned to Rain Song, and when he saw her raised eyebrows, he merely smiled.

They had been climbing steadily for hours. Often Wind Warrior would stop and let Rain Song rest before resuming the climb. In some places there were paths leading upward, and other times they had to pick their way up steep inclines.

Just when Rain Song thought they would never reach their destination, Wind Warrior took her hand and led her up a rock-face cliff. What she saw took her breath away. One mountain rolled into another, and then another, as far as the eye could see. The sky was so blue, the fluffy white clouds seemed like chunks of cotton.

Her gaze feasted on the wondrous sight. "Some of the peaks look like pictures of cathedrals I have seen in one of Aunt Cora's books."

Wind Warrior looked at her with interest. "What is a . . . cathedral?"

"It is a place, a building where we worship God. Of course, I have never actually seen one. At Fort Benton we had a small chapel."

Wind Warrior nodded in understanding. "Then your place of worship is similar to this place, where I seek the Great Spirit."

Rain Song gazed into his eyes. "Wind Warrior, do you believe your Great Spirit and my God are the same?"

He looked pensive for a moment. "How could our Gods not be the same? There is only one Creator of man. It matters not where you worship him, or by what name he is called, he is God, the Creator of all living things."

Her heart melted as she gazed into his soft brown eyes. "When you say it like that, I believe you."

He took her hand and assisted her to the top of the mountain, where he slid his arms around her waist, holding her against his body. "There is much you can teach me about your people. I want to know who they are and where they came from."

"And I want to learn what your connection is to these mountains. What were your thoughts when you were up here alone?"

His mouth curved into a smile. "Many of my thoughts were of you. I imagined you here with me, like this. I was sure in my heart you would love this place as much as I do."

She was filled with joy. Had he really thought of her? "It is so beautiful, it takes my breath away."

"There is a curious quality about in this place that might please you."

"Show me."

"Stand right here, and speak as loudly as you are able."

She looked puzzled.

"Go ahead," he urged. "Call out a greeting to the mountains and they will answer you."

She nodded, wetting her lips and wrinkling her brow in seriousness. "Hello . . . hello . . . hello . . . hello . . . hello."

Her eyes widened. "Is that an echo?"

"It is."

Wind Warrior took her hand. "Let us continue. It is not far to our home."

She laced her fingers through Wind Warrior's, feeling so full of happiness she could not speak.

Wind Warrior's mind was on other matters. He knew Dull Knife would have heard the echo, but the reverberating sounds were deceptive. Although his brother was one of the tribe's best trackers, he would not have been able to discern from which direction the sound came.

Although he was pushing Rain Song hard so she would be safe, she did not complain. At the end of the day, he noticed the tired lines under her eyes and decided to stop early.

As the sun went down, Rain Song fell upon her robe, exhausted. She was so weary she fell asleep with the uneaten meat still clutched in her hand.

Wind Warrior knelt beside her, taking the meat from her fist. Brushing a tress of hair from her face, he was lost in wonder that such a marvelous woman belonged to him. "Rest, my soul," he murmured, lowering his head to brush his mouth against her forehead.

Tonight he would be on guard, for Dull Knife must know this would be his last chance to track them. Tomorrow they would be walking on stone and leaving no footprints.

Chinook came up to him and dropped down beside him. He rubbed her furry coat and then pointed to Rain Song. "Chinook, lie beside her. Guard her with your life."

The wolf rose and trotted toward Rain Song, then dropped down to curl up beside her.

Wind Warrior walked a little way back down the incline, ever watchful. He heard an owl on the wing, searching for some night creature to feed on. He heard the wind whispering against his ears.

Glancing across the darkened woods below, he saw a small flicker of light. Dull Knife was no more than an hour behind. But if he had built a campfire, he was resting for the night. And after tomorrow, Rain Song would be safe from pursuit.

Chapter Twenty-eight

In anger and frustration Dull Knife moved slowly forward, stopping often to examine the area for an overturned stone, a bent grass blade, or even a footprint.

The countryside looked familiar to him.

He was certain he had passed the bent pine tree earlier in the day. And he thought he recognized the cliffs. But then again, everything here looked the same.

Give him the wide-open prairie and he could track anyone. But it was impossible to find footprints in this mountain of rock and stone.

Wind Warrior knew every tree and stump in these mountains, and he had no doubt cleverly backtracked to make certain he left no sign of his passing.

Dull Knife was lost.

Dropping his pack and leaning against the tree, he was disgusted with his own inability to track his brother. If he gave up, Wind Warrior would have won.

Again.

Glancing toward the west, he saw that the sun had dropped behind the tree line. Darkness fell early in the mountains. It was unnatural to Dull Knife. He liked the land along the Milk River, or even the prairie beside the Sweet Grass Hills. Only mountain goats, and his brother, could survive in a place like this.

As he fed off a roasted rabbit he'd killed earlier, Dull Knife leaned against a boulder, allowing his mind to wander. He would not give up. Wind Warrior would have to leave the high country before the threat of winter settled over the land.

He would force himself to be patient, although patience was not in his character. When he wanted something, he did not like to wait for it. It infuriated him that he had waited years for Rain Song, to no avail.

Tossing a clean rabbit bone into the campfire, Dull Knife thought of Spotted Flower. She had drawn him in with her wicked tricks and he shuddered when he remembered what she had done to him. Even now his body hungered for her, while his mind rejected her.

Rain Song was pure, Spotted Flower was evil, and yet his body craved the evil one.

Why, then, did he want Rain Song?

Because in his own way he loved her—loved her goodness, her purity, and her beauty. He remembered the first time he had heard her sing—the sound had gone through him like a strong wind. He admitted to himself that he was a selfish being and thought only of his own needs, and he needed Rain Song.

Hate ate at him when he thought of his brother touching her.

Rage would be the knife he drove into his brother's heart when they at last faced each other in combat and Dull Knife took the prize.

When they finally reached Wind Warrior's mountain home, it was dark. Clouds covered the moon and Rain Song had to rely on his guiding hand for each step she took. She could hear a stream gurgling nearby and wished she could see the beauty Wind Warrior had described to her.

Wind Warrior led her into a cave, where she collapsed on a pile of fur skins while he lit the campfire. Warmth soon surrounded her as she burrowed into the soft skins.

She had not meant to fall asleep, but the furs were so comfortable and her body craved rest. When she awoke, a wonderful scent wafted through the air. Meat was roasting over a spit.

Wind Warrior smiled at her and she thought her heart would burst with joy.

"I am hungry for fresh meat," she said.

He came over to her, dropping down beside her. "The meat is almost cooked."

She shyly touched his hand, lacing her fingers through his. "I am glad we have arrived."

His eyes darkened. "As am I." He touched her hair, releasing it from the braids. "So long have I imagined myself doing this."

She touched his face, and he gripped her hand.

"I want to be all things to you, Rain Song—when you are hurt, I want to heal you—when you are sad, I want to cheer you. Walk beside me in this life and we will find joy together."

"If I thought you were sad, I would hurt for you," she admitted as new emotions tumbled through her mind. Love was a wondrous emotion, and it came in many forms. She thought of how she loved her mother and father, and Fire Wolf. But that love did not compare with what she felt for this man beside her.

Wind Warrior rubbed his mouth across hers. "I believe you can keep me happy."

She touched her lips to his cheek. "Really?"

He eased her back on the furs. "Let me show you." He slowly pushed her gown upward and touched her intimately. He stared into her eyes and saw the look he had always wanted to see shining there. "You are my heart and soul."

Rain Song could hardly believe she had won the heart of this magnificent warrior.

He yanked off his leggings and settled his naked flesh against hers. Slowly he pulled her to him. "Show me how much you love me."

Breathless, Rain Song closed her eyes, giving herself over to her husband.

Wind Warrior's hands moved across her body and she tossed her head feverishly. Her hands were fisted at her sides, until he loosened them, brushing each with his lips. He was skillfully seducing Rain Song, making her whimper with need.

"Now," she pleaded, trying to catch his elusive mouth with hers. At last she succeeded pressing her lips against his.

Wind Warrior groaned as she became the seductress.

He arched over her, eased forward, and did not disappoint.

The next morning when she awoke, Rain Song found Wind Warrior still asleep. Boldly, her gaze traveled across his long, muscled body and she marveled at the beauty of him. His ebony hair spilled across the soft robe he lay upon and she touched it lovingly. His face intrigued her—it too was beautiful.

She touched his forehead, then traced a finger lightly down his cheekbone to the corner of his jaw. Her gaze moved to his beautifully sculpted mouth.

She pulled away when that mouth curved into a smile.

Wind Warrior rolled her over, his eyes intense. "So you want to play?"

He dipped his head, tracing the arch of her eyebrows with his lips, and she melted inside.

When he moved his hand down her neck and gently covered her breast, her eyes widened.

Wind Warrior touched his mouth between her breasts and Rain Song moaned with pleasure.

She ached and tossed when his hand slid from one breast to the other—cupping, torturing, teasing. Desire poured through her as his hand swept lower. Rain Song's reaction was instinctive, and she raised her hips in invitation.

Wetting her lips, she met his gaze. "You win, I surrender." Then she proceeded to torment him. She raised her lower body, rubbing against the swell of him.

He tried to hide his smile—she was flirting with

him, and she took his breath away. Touching his cheek to hers, he slid inside her.

Rain Song's body sang to his tune.

Spotted Flower could hardly believe she had escaped.

True to his word, Claude had guided her in the direction of Fort Benton. She was weary, but happy, when they finally reached the Missouri River.

"I will leave you here," he said in broken English.

Spotted Flower watched him remove seven of the beaver skins from the packhorse and tie them to the back of her horse.

"You gave me your word you would take me home."

"I am French, and would not be welcomed into the American fort. All you have to do is cross the river here where it is shallow, and then follow it to Fort Benton."

"Must you take so many of the skins? I'll need money."

Claude smiled at her. "*Oui*. I must."

"Then go," she said angrily. "I don't need you anyway."

He touched his fingers to his cap. "It has been a pleasure knowing you, Spotted Flower."

She glared at him. "That is no longer my name— I am Lillian," she said, entering the shallows and swimming her horse across the river.

Lillian did not know what she would find when she reached Fort Benton, but anything would be better than the life she had been forced to live. She hoped her pa was still alive and running the outpost so she would have a place to stay.

Glancing back over her shoulder, she watched Claude ride away and frowned. He had nothing to fear from Dull Knife; the risk had been all hers.

Thinking of Dull Knife made her shiver. He would search for her when he discovered what she had done—he would want his revenge.

But she would be safe as soon as she was inside the fort.

Lillian kept following the river as Claude had told her to. A day and a fearful night passed, and still she saw no sign of Fort Benton.

Doubt gnawed at her mind—what if she had become confused in the dark and was riding in the wrong direction?

Just when she had given up hope, she saw the Missouri widen and there was Fort Benton.

She was home.

Life beside the stream, nestled in the mountains, was good.

Spring moved into summer and before long autumn beckoned with a splash of glorious reds and yellows as the trees changed colors.

Each day Rain Song discovered more about her husband. He taught her how to trace the flight of an eagle, to watch the bear cubs playing with their mother. He taught her how to track wild game, and to discern the difference between the hoofprints of a deer and an elk.

At night, after they had feasted on fresh game and she curled up in his arms, she told him about her life before she had been taken captive. Wind Warrior would ask her to sing to him, and he would listen with his heart in his eyes.

"I could live here forever," she told him one night as she lay in his arms. "I would not care if we never returned to the village." She paused. "Except I would miss my mother and father, and Fire Wolf."

His arms slid around her, drawing her close. "Sadly, we will be leaving in two days. I fear I have already lingered too long. For a week now, I have seen frost on the plants and trees."

"I suppose the winters are too harsh to remain here through the season?"

He closed his eyes, loving her in the very depths of his heart. "You will want your mother when it is time for the baby to be born."

Her eyes widening, Rain Song was amazed. "A baby?"

Smiling at her innocence in the ways of the world, he bent to kiss her slightly swollen stomach. "Have you not noticed you have had only one blood flow since we came to the mountains?"

"I . . . did not think it meant anything." Her eyes widened in amazement, and a feeling so sweet and strong hit her, it stole her breath. She was going to have Wind Warrior's baby.

"I planted my seed in you," he said past the lump in his throat. "You are with child."

He laid his cheek against her thundering heart and closed his eyes. "Are you happy about what we have created out of our love?" he asked, not knowing how she felt about having a child. He raised his head and watched closely for her reaction. "Are you?"

The wonder of having Wind Warrior's child

washed through Rain Song, and she laid her hand on her stomach. "A child," she whispered. When she looked at him, there were tears in her eyes. "My husband, my heart cannot contain my joy," she admitted brokenly.

Wind Warrior held her to his heart. He had a sudden fear that he could not hold on to such happiness. It now filled his being, but would it one day slip through his fingers like sifting sand?

Were his thoughts a dire premonition? he wondered.

I do not know.

Nothing lasts forever.

Chapter Twenty-nine

Wind Warrior was fighting his way out of a thick fog, his heart beating, his throat dry. He caught glimpses of fire, destruction—women, bloody and dying, children crying out in pain. For a moment he thought he was glimpsing the great prairie fire. But no, the horror that was unfolding before him was happening in the Blackfoot village along the Milk River.

His eyes snapped open and he lay gasping for breath. He had been dreaming, and yet it was more than a dream—it was very real.

Danger!

Rain Song still slept beside him. Not wanting to disturb her, he eased away from her body and stood.

With his heart pounding, he made his way to the edge of the stream, splashing water in his face. Standing, he made his way to the edge of the cliff and stared down below.

Something was stirring in his mind, something terrible. Panic rose inside him and he had the strongest feeling he had to get back to the tribe as quickly as possible. He had to warn his people about approaching devastation.

Hearing a noise, he turned to find Rain Song behind him, a troubled look in her eyes.

"What is wrong, my husband?"

He took both her hands in his and gazed deeply into her eyes, trying to rid himself of the horrible vision that had come upon him.

"Wind Warrior?"

"What I say to you now is nothing I can prove; I can only feel."

Rain Song was confused. "I do not understand."

He slid his arms around her. "Of course you do not, when I do not understand myself. Sometimes dreams come to me. I cannot see the future: as some believe. But when I have a vision, I must act."

"Tell me," she urged, sensing the unrest in him.

Explaining his vision to her, Wind Warrior wondered if she would dismiss it as merely a dream. He needed her to believe in him, for he knew what he saw was something that would come to pass if he did not act quickly.

"I must go to warn our people, and I must go alone."

"What is it you think you must do?"

"I must get to the village as soon as possible."

She frowned, taking his trembling hand in hers, wishing she could comfort him. "Then you must go at once and you must go alone. I would only slow you down," she said with a catch in her voice.

He closed his eyes so she would not see the pain he was experiencing at the thought of leaving her. "I must."

"Then I will help gather supplies."

In that moment he loved her more than he'd thought possible. She did not question his need to save their people, even if it meant she had to stay in the mountains alone. She trusted him to keep their people safe . . . to keep her and their child safe.

"I cannot leave you here. Winter will sweep over this land before I can return. I must take you to a lower elevation, the cave we stayed in on our way up the mountain. There are supplies there, and I will make certain you have everything you will need until I return." Wind Warrior laid his face against hers. "You will have Chinook to protect you," he said, as if he were trying to convince himself. "I would not leave you if there was any other way."

Rain Song was frightened at the thought of being left alone in the mountains, but she knew this was the time to be brave for her husband's sake, and for their people. "You must not fear for me. As you said, Chinook will be my guard."

Urgency struck him like a blow. "Pack all the dried meat and all the warm furs. We must leave at once."

He grabbed her to him and held her for a moment. Reluctantly, he released her. "Do not fear that Dull Knife will find you. I will build campfires each night, and he will see them and follow me, thinking we are together."

That thought struck fear in her heart. "You think he still hunts us?"

He gazed into the distance, feeling urgency building inside him. "I know he does."

Three days later, they had reached the lower campsite.

"I must leave you now," Wind Warrior said regretfully. "Do as I said, and remain hidden."

"I will," she said, her voice breaking. "Promise me you will stay safe."

Wind Warrior placed his hand on her stomach with a look of helplessness. "I place you and our child in the hands of our God."

"And I will pray that He will walk beside you in this time of trouble."

Wind Warrior pulled her to him and held her for a long moment. Then reluctantly, he dropped his arms and turned away, walking swiftly toward the trail that led downward.

"I will be waiting for you," Rain Song whispered.

She stood with her hand resting on Chinook's head, watching Wind Warrior disappear into the thick forest. Her real fear was that in trying to lead Dull Knife away from her, Wind Warrior would bring danger upon himself.

Loneliness settled heavily on her shoulders and Rain Song walked into the cave. Sitting on a soft fur, she closed her eyes. The silence was so deep it unnerved her. Wind Warrior would soon return for her, she reminded herself, and they would leave the mountain together.

Chinook looked at her, then burrowed down beside her. She wasn't really afraid because her wolf would protect her, and she had a knife if she needed to use it. Bears and mountain lions roamed the mountains, but the creatures had never come near their camp, so she should be safe from them.

Wind Warrior had instructed her not to light a fire, although it was growing colder. She gave Chinook a chunk of dried meat and took a handful of dried berries to munch on.

Rain Song was weary, and her stomach had been upset lately. She remembered when Tall Woman had had the same symptoms before she gave birth to Fire Wolf. Taking a sip of water, she lay down, thinking if she slept, she would feel better when she awoke. She wanted time to pass quickly. She had never felt as alone as she did now.

Chinook stood, shook herself, and went to the cave opening, where she dropped down.

Rain Song fell asleep, knowing her faithful wolf was on guard.

Wind Warrior ran.

He was torn between protecting Rain Song and his unborn child, and ensuring the safety of the whole Blackfoot village. He would gladly give his life to keep his wife and baby safe, but he could not sacrifice his people for them, no matter how much he would wish it.

He leaped over a tall boulder, not stopping even to catch his breath. He was taking the steepest way down the mountain, certainly not the safest way, but urgency pushed him onward.

It was long after dark and still Wind Warrior did not slow his pace. Finally, he was so weary he tripped over a fallen log and hit the ground hard. Taking a quick drink from his water skin, he leaped to his feet and continued to run.

When he reached the foothills, he could go no farther. He felt sure he was far enough from the cave where he had left Rain Song to draw his brother's attention to him.

He built a campfire, knowing Dull Knife would eventually see it. He would not remain there long because when Dull Knife came to investigate, he must not discover that Rain Song was not with her husband.

He must draw his brother out of the mountains!

Chapter Thirty

The troops from Fort Benton were making camp for the night. Susan's husband, or widower, Major Cullen Worthington, was in command of the patrol that was heading into Blackfoot country.

Just looking at the major made Lillian's heart race. He was a handsome man, tall, with blond hair and sideburns, and real pretty gray eyes. He had been a bit cold and standoffish to her at first, and he still was, but she had won men over before.

The patrol was bivouacked beside the Milk River. Sentries on high alert were posted every hundred feet because they were in the heart of Blackfoot country.

Lillian sat on her cot, her chin resting on her folded hands. Going home had not turned out as she had expected.

She was glad to hear her father was still alive, even if he had remarried and moved to California. Some of the army wives she'd known before were still there. Though they had offered her sympathy and felt sorry for all she had endured, they stared at her as if she were an abomination. It had not escaped her notice that they sent their children from the room when she went to call on them.

Well, let them think what they wanted to—she didn't care.

After she had told her story, and she had of course deviated a bit from the truth about herself, the commanding officer had agreed that a rescue should be mounted to recover Marianna Bryant.

Lillian was left to wonder if they would have made such a fuss to rescue her. She doubted they would.

Of course, Marianna's uncle was now a high-ranking officer attached to the White House, and her aunt had once again taken up her career as an opera singer. Lillian learned that Marianna's aunt and uncle now had a son and daughter of their own. She couldn't understand why they would want to recover Marianna if they had their own children. They had sent a telegram asking the army for help and said they were coming as soon as they could.

Frowning in disgust, Lillian wished she'd told everyone Marianna was dead. No one had welcomed *her* home. Ike Everett, who had bought the trading post from her pa, had even shunned her. He'd been a friend of her family at one time, but was no friend to her.

Lillian was sorry now she had told the commander of the post that she could find her way back to the Blackfoot village. She had never wanted to see the place of her greatest humiliations again. Not that she was afraid to go near the Blackfoot, even though Broken Lance had banished her and Dull Knife would want to kill her. She had a full patrol of soldiers and two cannons to guard her.

Once she'd come past the Great Falls, and across the wide prairie, she had had little trouble finding her way. She hoped the Blackfoot resisted when they saw the army patrol. Then they would be wiped out, every last man, woman, and child.

Hatred was a bitter pill, and Lillian almost choked on it.

Dull Knife dropped to his knees, sifting through the ashes. Puzzled, he saw that no meat had been roasted at this campsite. Why, then, light a fire? Wind Warrior must have known he would see it and track him.

It made no sense.

Looking about, he could tell that his brother had swept the site with tree branches. Wind Warrior was in a hurry—he was getting careless.

But no, he would not be careless. Something was wrong.

Heading into the woods, he found his brother's footprints. Wind Warrior was moving fast—running. Dull Knife found no second set of tracks.

Wind Warrior was alone.

Dull Knife turned back to look at the mountains, a frown on his face. Rain Song was not with his brother. He could not imagine Wind Warrior being so careless as to leave her behind.

Wind Warrior would not have left her unguarded.

What if she was dead?

If that were so, Wind Warrior would not be trying so hard to get Dull Knife to follow him away from the mountain.

"You made a big mistake, my brother. Did you really think you could outsmart me?"

Shouldering his pack, Dull Knife headed back toward the mountain, a smile twisting his lips.

He had her now.

He was almost disappointed he would not have to fight his brother for her.

That would come later.

After Rain Song was his.

Wind Warrior stumbled and fell. He had been running for most of the day, even when he thought he could not take another step. His chest burned and he heaved, trying to catch his breath.

He was very near the village now—he could see the campfires.

As he stumbled into camp, he fell hard and everything went black.

Wind Warrior did not know how long he had been unconscious, but when he woke, he found a frantic Tall Woman holding his head and trying to get him to drink.

"Where is my daughter?" she demanded.

"Why is Rain Song not with you?" Broken Lance wanted to know.

The closer the soldiers got to the Blackfoot village, the more hatred Lillian felt for the Indians who had held her captive for so many years and then kicked her out with nowhere to go. She could have died for all they cared.

She wanted to see Charging Bull with a bullet through his heart. And she would be glad to hold Yellow Bird down while they shot her. She thought about her daughter and shrugged. She'd never liked her; the girl looked too much like Charging Bull. And there wasn't any way she'd be saddled with the brat now that she was back in civilization.

They would all pay for what had been done to her—Broken Lance, Tall Woman, even Wind Warrior. If she was lucky, the soldiers would mistake Rain Song for an Indian squaw and kill her before they realized what they'd done. Lillian's eyes gleamed with anticipation at that thought.

Last of all, she considered Dull Knife. If the soldiers killed him, she wouldn't ever have to worry about him coming after her because she'd stolen furs and horses from him.

The years she had lived among the Blackfoot as Spotted Flower gave her the knowledge to destroy them.

The countryside was very familiar to her now. The Milk River could not be many miles ahead. There she would find the village where Broken Lance's Blackfoot people would dwell for the winter months.

Wearing a green gown one of the women at the fort had given her, Lillian had twisted her hair up in green ribbons, hoping to attract the handsome major's notice tonight. Even if he wasn't interested, several of his soldiers had certainly noticed her.

Lillian found Major Worthington seated on a stool inside his tent, with a map spread out before him on a camp table.

He glanced up at her. "Tell me what you can about this particular tribe of Blackfoot."

She leaned over him, pretending to study the map

and brushing her breasts against his arm. She felt him stiffen before he stood and walked a few paces away from her.

"Major," she said in an annoyed tone, "the Blackfoot are fierce fighters. It would be best if you hit them at night, and hit them with all you got. Don't give them time to fight back."

Major Worthington looked disgusted and turned to his second-in-command, who had just entered the tent. "You might explain to Miss Baskin here that we did not come to slaughter the Blackfoot. Our orders are to bring Miss Bryant out safely. Peacefully."

"That's right, miss," Sergeant Sanderson agreed. "If we start shooting, no telling who we'll hit." Then he addressed the major. "If you have nothing for me, sir, I think I'll turn in."

"Dismissed, Sergeant," Major Worthington said. "And thank you."

Standing a safe distance from Lillian, the major said, "Tell me again what you know about Miss Bryant."

Lillian sighed. "It's like I told you before—she's the reason your wife was killed. She told Susan to run and hide, and 'course Dull Knife went after her, and I told you what he did."

Major Worthington turned his back on her, closing his eyes. "Miss Bryant was but thirteen when she was captured. How can you say it was her fault my wife was killed by one of the savages who took her captive?"

"Well, it *was* her fault. She's always telling everybody what to do."

"A prisoner telling her captors what to do," the major said disbelievingly. "She must have been a fearsome thirteen-year-old."

"You don't know her or you wouldn't defend her," Lillian said sulkily.

"Let's move on from that," the major said icily, remembering Susan had once told him she liked Marianna Bryant. Maybe that was part of the reason he'd volunteered to lead this mission, and why he wanted to rescue the girl and return her safely to her aunt and uncle.

"I suffered more than she did," Lillian said bitterly. "With my ma and brother dead, and my pa pulling up stakes and moving to California, I don't have anyone."

"Miss Baskin, I am sorry for your loss," the major said a bit more gently. "But you are already safe. If we can rescue Miss Bryant, maybe my wife will rest in peace, and so can I."

"I'll tell you what I do know of Marianna, or Rain Song, as the Blackfoot renamed her. Chief Broken Lance and his wife, Tall Woman, adopted her. They treated her good, which is more than I can say for those who took me."

"You were adopted by another family?"

"Uh, yeah, that's right." She saw no reason to tell anyone that she'd been taken as a wife and borne one child, then lost another. "Those Blackfoot need killing for what they did to us—for what they did to Susan."

Major Worthington waved her aside, unwilling to listen to any more of her venom. "That's all I need from you. The hour is late, seek your bed."

"Major," she said, sidling up to him. "Is there anything else I can do for you?"

His head snapped up and he glared at her. "There is nothing you have that I want, Miss Baskin."

She tossed her head. "You don't know what you're missin'."

Lillian cringed inside when she saw the look of distaste on his face. No one had ever looked at her that way.

"Good night," he said stiffly.

She whirled around and stomped off to her tent. "It's California for you, gal," she told herself. "Maybe I'll find Pa." And even if she didn't, no one would know about her past in California and she could start a new life.

Removing her gown, she folded it neatly before climbing onto the cot. She would pass herself off as a widow, destitute and in need of a good husband. It was said there was a shortage of women in California.

She smiled. Yes, she would be a very respectable widow.

After Lillian had gone, Major Worthington took a cleansing breath. He didn't know how much truth Lillian Baskin had told him, but she didn't seem to mind expressing her opinion.

He had served in the war, not caring if he lived or died. It did not even matter to him when he had been promoted to the rank of major. Susan had been his only love and her capture had left him bereft. He had hunted for months to find her, and he did finally find her body. He had known the skeletal remains had been hers, because he recognized the scraps of her gown.

After the war, he had felt compelled to take the assignment at Fort Benton. It had been painful at first to return to the place where he and Susan had been so happy.

Everyone told him to go forward and forget the past, but something kept holding him back. He had been in love with Susan since they had been mere children back in Philadelphia.

Now he had the strangest feeling he needed to rescue Marianna Bryant. He owed it to Susan to try.

The raid had happened over six years earlier. He would rescue Marianna Bryant, without bloodshed if possible. If not possible, he would do whatever he deemed necessary to return her to her family.

The major glanced back down at his map and studied it for a moment. If the Baskin woman was telling the truth, they were no more than two days from the Blackfoot village.

Wearily he rubbed the back of his neck. In the morning they would head out again, and there was every reason to believe they would meet up with the Blackfoot, who might very well object to the intrusion into their territory.

No one knew much about this particular tribe, so there was no telling if he would be offered the hand of friendship, or the war lance.

Chapter Thirty-one

In a hastily assembled council meeting, Wind Warrior explained to the elders and Broken Lance that he felt they should move the village as soon as possible.

"I do not understand your reason," Running Elk stated, taking a draw on a pipe and watching the smoke circle above him. "You have said nothing that convinces me we should leave when we are already settled for the winter."

Wind Warrior shook his head. "I cannot give you a reason, except to say I feel it in my mind, in my head. I feel it so strongly I left my wife, who is with child, to bring you this warning."

Broken Lance took a puff on the pipe Running Elk handed him, and nodded. "Each time we have followed Wind Warrior's advice, it has been proven sound. But to move the women and children this late in the year is a major undertaking."

"That is so," one of the other elders agreed. "It will cause hardship for many."

Wind Warrior placed his hand on his father-in-law's shoulder. "You know I would not be here if I did not feel great need. I sense danger. Where it will come from, I do not know. I only know it is real, and it is imminent."

Broken Lance nodded. "Then let us have our women make ready to leave. It will take at least two days for that."

"Two days," Wind Warrior said, frowning. "I press you to make ready in one day. Leave behind that which you cannot take. Lives are more precious than possessions."

Broken Lance looked into the young warrior's eyes and knew there was danger for those who did not follow his advice. "Let us call everyone together. We will be ready to leave in one day."

The elders finally nodded in agreement.

"Let us see it done," Broken Lance said. "I trust in Wind Warrior's words."

At that moment raised voices were heard in the village and Falling Thunder rode to the council lodge, jumping from his horse and rushing inside. "I saw many soldiers camped not more than a day's ride from here! They are heavily armed and it looks like they are coming this way."

Those who had not been convinced by Wind Warrior's warning now stared at him in wonder. Everyone quickly scattered to their own tipis to help get their families out of the village and into the foothills.

Wind Warrior followed Broken Lance outside. "I must leave at once and return to Rain Song. We will join you in the foothills." When Wind Warrior took a step, he stumbled, catching Broken Lance's arm to keep from falling.

"You are ill, my son?"

"I am but weary. I have not slept. I ran all the way."

The chief's eyes were troubled. "Then you must rest."

"I dare not. Dull Knife searches for Rain Song. You understand I did not want to leave her."

Broken Lance nodded, seeing for the first time the torment Wind Warrior suffered because of his spiritual gift. "Take my swiftest horse. Tall Woman will see that you have food to sustain you."

A short time later Wind Warrior raced out of the village on a spirited mare. He had done all he could to help his people. Now he would return to Rain Song.

Suddenly a feeling of dread touched his mind and tears choked him. Something was wrong.

He would not make it back to her in time.

Chapter Thirty-two

In the chill of the early autumn afternoon, Rain Song listened to the lonesome call of the elk that echoed down the valley. Draped in a fur robe, she shivered.

She had awakened to frosty air, and as the day progressed, it had grown colder. It was now late afternoon and dark clouds rolled across the horizon. It looked as though it might snow before morning.

Gazing across the small valley toward the stream, Rain Song tried to spot Chinook. The wolf had left hours ago and had not yet returned. It was unusual for Chinook to stay away so long.

If only she could light a fire to warm herself. But Wind Warrior had warned her against it, so she dared not.

Gazing across the valley, she watched a mother bear leading her two cubs up the side of a mountain, no doubt going into hibernation. The sound of a howling wolf filled the chilled air, while an eagle patrolled the air in search of prey. A mountain goat, with its majestic curved horns, fleetly bounded up a seemingly impassable rock slope and disappeared over the top.

Wind Warrior had taught her to observe everything around her, and she had done so to fill the long days he had been gone. Life abounded here in this place, and yet Rain Song felt the heavy hand of loneliness. She noticed the way the swaying pines dappled the ground around them and then turned her gaze upward to a weak sun whose light barely pierced the gathering clouds.

Wind Warrior had been gone for five days, and she doubted that was enough time for him to reach the village, much less make it back to her.

Smiling, she touched her stomach. She carried a part of her husband with her. If the baby was a boy, she would want him to have Wind Warrior's coloring and his beautiful brown eyes.

With a heavy sigh, she entered the cave, pulling another robe over herself. She blew on her frozen fingers. She heard a familiar yelp, and Chinook came bounding into the cave. Rain Song cheered up as the wolf dropped down in front of her and stared into her eyes.

"Are you trying to tell me something, or are you trying to avoid a scolding for leaving me alone all day?"

Chinook whined.

"I know," she said, rubbing a huge paw. "I miss him too."

Rain Song laid out a chunk of dried meat for Chinook, but since the wolf showed no interest in it, she assumed the animal had been hunting on her own. "You probably had fresh meat, while I will have to make do with this."

It was growing colder. She had to do something to block the wind that was sweeping through the cave. After finding several branches, she dragged them forward and braced them against the entrance as she had seen Wind Warrior do that night when he had first brought her to the mountain.

The branches helped a little, but the wind still managed to find its way through the wide cracks. Tomorrow she would look for more branches.

Shadows stretched across the cave, darkening the corners. Rain Song lay down on a soft robe and covered herself with two others. Chinook curled up against her, sharing her warmth. Thinking of Wind Warrior, Rain Song finally fell into a fretful sleep.

Dull Knife climbed higher as the sun rose on a new morning.

Rain Song was somewhere ahead and he would find her. A blast of cold air struck and he reeled under the impact. It was reasonable that Wind Warrior would not have left her without some protection from the cold.

He should be looking for a cave.

Raising his head, he searched the cliffs. If he found no cave in this valley, he would go on to the next one. He would not give up until he found Rain Song.

Suddenly he spied something out of place. It might be a cave, but it was high up the steep cliff. It looked strange, as if someone had propped tree branches against the rock wall.

He struggled upward. Gripping the side of the mountain and hoisting his body forward, he found the climb harder than it looked. Just a little farther and he would be able to see if what he'd spotted was an encampment.

He hunkered down, gauging the situation. He saw nothing out of the ordinary, except the branches. His eyes gleamed. It was a cave. Animals did not drag branches and block cave entrances—only humans did that.

He clamped his jaws together tightly, feeling great satisfaction.

He had found her.

Chinook leaped to her feet, alert. The wolf quivered, her eyes piercing the darkness of the cave, picking up the smell of man. Nudging Rain Song, Chinook made no sound, instinctively knowing there was a need for silence.

Sleepily, Rain Song pushed Chinook away.

Chinook continued nudging Rain Song's hand, then licking her chin.

"Go away, Chinook. Let me sleep."

The wolf persisted, and Rain Song opened her eyes. Chinook was in an attack stance, quivering, alert. Quietly easing to her feet, Rain Song reached for the knife, gripping the handle and trying to remember what Wind Warrior had told her about using it. He had warned against allowing the adversary to get too close. He'd told her to keep her wrist stiff or the knife would not fly true when she threw it. He'd taught her that the knife would rotate before it hit the target. She had practiced with him, but she had not mastered the knife well enough to be a threat to anyone or anything.

If it was a predatory animal, Rain Song certainly did not want to get too close.

A sound brought a rumble to the wolf's throat.

Rain Song watched as someone removed several of the branches at the cave entrance. She knew who it was even before he called out to her.

Dull Knife!

Knowing she would be no match for him, she slid the knife into her bag and waited for him to enter. "Stay beside me," she warned Chinook. Dull Knife would not hesitate to kill her wolf, and she could not live with that. She placed a calming hand on the wolf's head. "Stay."

It took Dull Knife a moment for his eyes to become accustomed to the darkness inside the cave. "Order the wolf to attack and I will kill it," he warned, seeing only the shadowy outline of the woman and the glowing yellow eyes of the animal.

"What do you want?" Rain Song was surprised how steady her voice sounded. She was terrified. "There is nothing for you here. My husband will be back any moment and he will not like finding you with me."

"You lie," Dull Knife snarled. "My brother has left you, although I cannot imagine why he would abandon such a prize." He stepped closer. "Do you fear me?"

The hackles rose on Chinook's neck, but Rain Song kept a calming hand on her head.

"What do you want?" she asked.

He stepped even closer, although it was still too dark to make out her face. "I want you."

"You do not want me as much as you want to cause Wind Warrior pain."

"That much is true. So I advise you to come with me peaceably or I will kill the wolf, and then when he returns, which he surely will, I will kill my brother."

In wild terror, Rain Song took a step back, coming against the cave wall. "I will not go with you." Now her voice did tremble. "Go away! Leave me alone!"

"I cannot do that. I have wanted you, ached for you, but you never looked my way."

"You raped and killed my friend Susan. Do you think I could ever want a man who committed such an atrocity?"

He was quiet for a moment. Now he understood why she had always despised him. It had been a mistake for him to kill the young white woman, but he could not change what was already done. Dull Knife decided that if Rain Song would obey him, he would treat her gently until she learned to trust him. But have her he would, eventually.

"You have no choice. Come with me now."

The first streaks of daylight had penetrated the inside of the cave and Rain Song cringed when she looked into Dull Knife's cold, black eyes. There was no doubt he would kill Chinook if she did not do just what he said.

She thought of the baby she carried within her, and she was afraid he would kill her too if he learned of the child.

Taking a deep breath and lowering her head, she said, "I will go with you."

A look of satisfaction flashed across Dull Knife's countenance. "A wise decision. Dress warmly. I will gather supplies for our journey."

Rain Song bent to retrieve the bag she had slipped the knife into. She could feel her wolf quiver beneath her hand, waiting for her to give the order to attack. "You will not harm Chinook?"

"I will not if you command her to remain here."

"I do not know if that is possible. She will eventually follow me. Perhaps if I tie her to a tree," Rain Song said hopefully.

He pointed to the wolf. "Then do it. I'll watch you," Dull Knife said. "I want to make sure you tie the rope tight." He smiled, as if he had just thought of something humorous. "Chinook can welcome my brother when he returns."

A short time later Chinook pulled and jerked on the rope that Rain Song had used to secure her to the trunk of a pine tree. Going down on her knees, she slid her arms around the wolf. "Forgive me. You have to stay here. I do not want you to be hurt."

As Rain Song stood and hurried away, Chinook threw back her head and gave a mournful cry.

Rain Song wanted to weep and wail too—she wanted to drive her blade into Dull Knife's heart. But she could do none of that. She stood stiffly before Dull Knife. "I am ready."

He slung the bag of supplies he had gathered over his shoulder and motioned Rain Song forward. "Stay in front of me until we reach the steep part of the mountain."

With a last glance at Chinook, Rain Song walked slowly away, once more Dull Knife's captive.

Chapter Thirty-three

Major Worthington held up his hand as a signal for the troops to halt. Across the river was what remained of an abandoned Indian camp. "Sergeant, take two men and check around. See what you can find."

Moments later the three men rode back across the river.

"There was a large village there, all right, sir," the sergeant reported. "And it hasn't been more than a day or so since they pulled up stakes."

"They knew we were coming," the major said. He motioned for Lillian, who had been riding at the back of the column, to come forward.

Lillian stared openmouthed at the remains of the Blackfoot village. Some tipis still stood, although most of them had been taken down. There was broken pottery scattered everywhere. "They left in a hurry," she told the major. "It's unheard of for them to leave anything behind."

"Let's ride across, soldiers. Look sharp," Major Worthington ordered. "I don't want any surprises."

"The woman's right, sir," Sergeant Sanderson observed, cocking his rifle. "These Blackfoot left in a mighty big rush."

"Why do you suppose that is, Miss Baskin?" the major asked.

She shook her head, frowning. "There doesn't seem to have been a battle. The only thing I can think is that Wind Warrior sensed you were on the way and warned them. He's made them move the village before, and they listen to him."

The major turned in his saddle and stared at her incredulously. "What do you mean he sensed we were coming?"

Lillian raised her hands in a hopeless gesture. "Wind Warrior sees things. The Blackfoot think he's some kind of mystical warrior. They say he sees the future and animals talk to him."

The officer stared at her. "That's nonsense. I have heard of this Wind Warrior, but I don't believe the stories they tell about him."

"I'm not saying I believe it, I'm saying the Blackfoot do." Lillian looked at the scattered remnants of the village and shivered. "But to be truthful with you, I've seen him look into the mist and save his people. Believe me, anything you heard about him is probably true. He's the one who took Marianna as his woman."

"We will camp here tonight," Major Worthington said, urging his horse into the Milk River. "Send out a scout in each direction, Sergeant. I want to know where this tribe of Blackfoot have disappeared to."

Lillian rode to the other side of the river and dismounted. Dull Knife's tipi was still standing. That meant he had not been in the village when the others left. Curious, she moved through what should have been a thriving village.

There was trouble here. Possibly between Dull

Knife and Wind Warrior. She frowned. The mystery eluded her. Glancing toward the mountains, she wondered if the two brothers had at last met in a final battle. If so, which one had survived, and where was Rain Song?

Heavy snow swirled down the mountain pass and whipped through gullies with punishing force.

Unable to see what was in front of her, Rain Song clung to Dull Knife's hand. Each step she took was torture. The wind tore at her hair; particles of ice and snow stung her face and eyes. Wind Warrior would never find her in this storm.

"Can we not stop?" she called loudly so Dull Knife would hear her above the roar of the wind. "I am weary."

Dull Knife pulled her forward. "No. To stop now could mean our deaths. We have to get off this mountain."

Taking a painful breath, Rain Song faltered, too tired to take another step. Seeing her exhaustion, Dull Knife pulled her to the sheltered side of a huge bolder, allowing her to rest.

"I am sorry to push you so hard," he said, pulling the fur wrap about her head, "but this storm is only going to get worse."

Rain Song blinked her eyes. She had never known Dull Knife to apologize, and she did not trust his motives. "I cannot go on."

His grip tightened on her arm. "You will, even if I have to carry you," he threatened.

"It will soon be dark. There is danger if we continue without being able to see where we are going."

He pulled her against him. "I know you are stalling so Wind Warrior can catch up, but you would do well to forget about him. You will never again be with my brother in this lifetime."

Rain Song swallowed a sob. She felt sick to her stomach, and her legs and arms ached painfully. But Dull Knife pulled her forward and she had no choice but to follow.

In this nightmare world of swirling white, she felt as if she were dying inside. She had to survive for her baby . . . and for Wind Warrior.

Her feet were so frozen she could no longer feel them. She took one painful step after another, each carrying her farther away from her beloved. Yet when Rain Song closed her eyes, she could see him.

He would grieve when he found her gone, and he would blame himself for leaving her.

Would he know what had happened?

Her heart cried out to him in despair.

Frantic, Wind Warrior searched first the cave and then the surrounding area. He dropped down by a tree, picking up the leather rope that had been gnawed in two. Reading the signs, he realized Chinook had been tied up there, but had managed to escape.

He raised his head to the sky and a cry of anguish echoed against the mountains. His woman, his heart was . . . gone.

He could not feel her. He did not know if she still lived.

Anger and grief swamped him. "Dull Knife," he whispered in a pain-filled voice, "for this you die!"

The snow was falling heavily. It would not be easy to pick up Dull Knife's tracks, and since his brother did not know his way around the mountains, Wind Warrior could not predict which way he might have taken.

Grabbing his lance, he started running. It was his fault Dull Knife had found Rain Song. He should not have left her, but what else could he have done?

He felt as if an arrow had pierced his heart. He thought about his unborn child and stopped, placing his hands on the rough bark of a tree, dropping his head.

"I will find you, my soul," he vowed. "I will not stop until you are with me again."

Chapter Thirty-four

Dull Knife had built a fire where the rocky path widened a bit and seated Rain Song nearby. She was listless and kept falling asleep.

"I pushed you hard, but we had to leave the high mountain or we both would have died."

She closed her eyes, her head falling forward. He touched her face and it was feverish. Worried about her, he bent and rubbed her hands.

"Let me die," she moaned past the burning in her throat.

"I will not. When you are warm enough, we will continue, even if I have to carry you." This time his voice held concern, not a threat.

Shaking her head wearily, Rain Song looked at him. "I despise you. Must you always destroy my life?"

Anger fueled his actions. He grabbed her hand and yanked her up. "We resume our journey."

Rain Song didn't know where her strength came from, but she struggled, trying to pry his hand away. "Leave me alone!"

Twisting around, she found herself staring over a deep crevice. If she fell, it would kill her baby. The cliff edge was iced over and slick. She felt her feet sliding out from under her, taking her nearer the drop-off.

Two things happened at once—Dull Knife grabbed her hand to keep her from slipping over the cliff, and Chinook came flying through the air, her teeth bared as she went for Dull Knife's throat.

Stepping back in surprise, Dull Knife tottered on the edge of the cliff. He grabbed for Rain Song's hand, and she began to slide with him. In one brief moment, Dull Knife looked into her eyes and let go of her hand.

Reaching out to him, Rain Song watched him tumble downward, bouncing off boulders as he fell. Far down below, she saw his dead body lying like a broken doll.

Sobbing, and covering her face, she was shaken by the horror of what had occurred. Dull Knife could have taken her with him when he fell, and she had been looking into his eyes when he'd decided to let her live. For whatever reason, he had spared her life.

She was crying and Chinook licked her face. Throwing her arms around the wolf, she shuddered. "You saved my life." She couldn't stop crying. "You wonderful wolf—you saved me!"

Then it hit her. Dull Knife was dead. She need no longer fear him. She was not sorry, because of what he had done to Susan.

Gathering her robe about her, she stood. "I am lost, Chinook. I do not know my way back to the cave. But I do know if I follow that stream, it will eventually take me to the Milk River and home."

Chinook turned her shaggy head and looked at Rain Song, as if waiting for her to make a move.

Although she was exhausted, Rain Song stepped lightly as she started down the steep path, holding on to Chinook so she would not fall.

"Come on," she said, joy filling her heart. "Wind Warrior will find us in the village."

Sergeant Sanderson had just returned from patrol. He dismounted and hurried to the major's tent. "Sir," he said, working his hands out of his gloves, "we spotted a group of Indians from a distance, but when we gave chase, they disbursed through the woods, and we saw nary hide nor hair of 'em."

"It was hopeless from the start," Major Worthington said, pacing the crowded boundaries of his tent. "A chance in a million we would find her. No more than that."

"What do we do, sir?"

Major Worthington's eyes widened and he pointed in amazement at the animal that had just entered the tent. "Isn't that a wolf?" he asked, unsnapping the flap of his holster.

"I believe it is, sir." The sergeant placed his hand on his commander's arm. "But it doesn't seem dangerous."

Lillian came into the tent, her eyes wide with wonder. "This, gentlemen, is Chinook. She belongs to Marianna. Since the wolf is here, Marianna will not be far behind."

Chinook turned around, heading out of the tent, and then returned. "Why, I believe she wants us to follow her," Major Worthington said, resnapping his holster.

Chinook looked into the major's eyes, and it was as if the animal had spoken to him. "Lead on, Chinook," he said.

Rain Song tossed on the small cot as fever wracked her body.

Major Worthington sat next to her, forcing her to drink from his canteen. "Just a little more, Miss Bryant."

She pushed his hand away, saying words he could not understand. Probably Blackfoot, he reasoned.

Marianna Bryant was no longer the carefree young girl he remembered, who had raised her voice in church and delighted everyone with her sweet song. She was a beautiful woman, and he didn't know what to do with her.

"Major," Lillian called out. "Can I see Marianna?"

"Yes. Please come in. Maybe you can tell me what she is saying."

Lillian gazed down on the person she hated most in the world. "Sure I will, Major." She bent down to Rain Song. "Where does it hurt?" she asked in Blackfoot.

"Spotted Flower? What are you doing here? I must find Wind Warrior . . . Please help me," she whispered, so tired she could barely get the words out.

"Why should I?"

"He . . . probably believes I'm dead. Find him . . . tell him I am fine . . . and so is our baby." Her words trailed off as she fell into a deep sleep.

Lillian's eyes narrowed. "She wants to be taken back to Fort Benton, Major. She hopes you will leave before the Blackfoot come for her." Lillian stood. "She's afraid they will keep her captive."

"Then assure her we will leave at first light in the morning." He glanced down at the golden-haired woman. "She is the loveliest creature I have ever seen."

Lillian drew in a disgusted breath. "So everyone thinks. I believe even Susan thought she was pretty," she said, spitefully reminding the major of his dead wife.

"Susan thought everyone was pretty, Miss Baskin—she even trusted people and believed in their goodness," he said angrily. "Get some sleep. We leave early."

The troops moved out the next morning. They had rigged a litter for Rain Song, who kept going in and out of consciousness.

"No," she moaned in Blackfoot. "Do not take me away from my people. I want my mother."

"There, there," Sergeant Sanderson assured her. "We'll have you home in no time, miss."

Chapter Thirty-five

Rain Song felt despondent, disconnected.

She wanted Wind Warrior—she wanted her Blackfoot mother and father—wanted to see her little brother and sing him to sleep.

Pacing the room, she wrung her hands. "Wind Warrior, find me," she cried in the Blackfoot language. "Please find me."

"Poor thing," she heard Mrs. Pierce, who was housing her, remark to her husband. "She's quite lost her mind. They say this happens to white women when they're captured by Indians."

"Likely she won't live long, feeling the way she does," her husband observed.

"It might be a blessing if she died before the child is born. Imagine bringing such an—"

Rain Song whirled on Captain and Mrs. Pierce. "Stop talking about me as if I have no feelings," she said in English, "and as if I don't understand what you are saying. And how dare you think my baby would be better off if he died before he is born just because his father is a Blackfoot."

"Well, well," Mrs. Pierce said, ducking her head in shame. "It's just that—well, you know, you will never fit in with white folks after you've been—"

Rain Song held up her hand. "After I've been given love and respect. After I was shown kindness and humanity by the Blackfoot people. My Indian mother would never treat anyone the way you have treated me. Why will you not let me go home?"

Captain Pierce cleared his throat. "We . . . ll, your aunt and uncle will be arriving from Washington within the month. Surely you will want to go home with them."

Rain Song thought for a moment. She had loved her aunt and uncle, but she could not remember their faces. She would like to see them again, but her home was no longer with them.

Rain Song forced herself to sit in a rocking chair and fold her hands in her lap. She felt suffocated in the small parlor with lace curtains at the windows. She yearned to go outside, to breathe the air and walk free.

Mrs. Pierce was looking at her strangely, as if she didn't want to say the wrong thing again.

Rain Song thought back to the white woman who had been taken captive by the Indians and returned to her white family. Everyone, including Rain Song, had pitied the woman, but thought she was crazed, with her pacing and not being able to communicate. For the first time Rain Song realized what that poor woman had suffered, with no one to understand that she probably just wanted to go back to her Indian family.

Most people at Fort Benton seemed to think Rain Song had lost her mind.

"Please tell Major Worthington I would like to speak to him, Mrs. Pierce."

"He's been here every day, asking about you, while you were ill. Such a nice young man."

"Thank you." Was she acting properly? she wondered. Had she given them any more reasons to think she had lost her mind?

"This is your first day out of the sickbed," Mrs. Pierce said kindly. "Don't you think you should rest? You are pale and look all tuckered out."

Rain Song gripped her hands tighter. "I feel perfectly fine, thanks to your care. But there are some things I would like to speak to the major about. I want to tell him about his wife."

"Well, sure, honey." Mrs. Pierce looked doubtful. "You aren't going to tell him how Susan died, are you?"

"I will never tell anyone about that. I promised Susan I would give her husband a message if I ever got the chance. I believe he would want to know what she told me."

Rain Song stood. "I do think I'll lie down. Please call me when the major arrives."

"Of course, dear," the older woman assured her.

Major Worthington arrived early in the afternoon. As he stood straight and tall in the Pierces' parlor, he looked every bit the proper officer in his blue uniform and highly polished boots.

"I suggest, if you are feeling up to it, Miss Bryant, that we take a walk about the fort. I am sure you are weary of being shut in and would enjoy a nice outing."

Rain Song grabbed the shawl Mrs. Pierce had given her, and the major helped her place it about her shoulders.

"I promise not to tire you. We won't walk too far."

She smiled. "I can see why Susan felt the way she did about you, Major. You have been very kind to me. This is my first chance to thank you."

Mrs. Pierce nodded in approval as they left. "Do not take her as far as the parade ground. She is still weak."

"I won't, ma'am," he said, holding the door for Rain Song. When they were out of hearing, he laughed. "Mrs. Pierce is kindness itself, but she is a bit of a mother hen, don't you think?"

"I am grateful to her for taking care of me while I was ill."

He turned to look at her. "I have never been one to beat around the bush, as they say. I know you have heard some unkind remarks and I want to tell you how sorry I am."

"I don't really care what the people of Fort Benton think about me. I do not belong here, and everyone knows it."

"But you will have a new life when your aunt and uncle arrive. They will take you back to Washington with them, and you can leave the past behind, Miss Bryant."

"I don't want to leave the past behind. I want to go back to my husband. And, Major, please call me Rain Song. It is the name that is familiar to me."

"If you would like. And will you call me Cullen?"

Rain Song smiled. "Susan was my friend." She met his gaze. "She did what she could to take care of me, and even today . . . I miss her."

Cullen stared down at his boots. "As do I."

"Susan was extraordinary. She saw only the good in people. I liked that about her."

"If you recognized that about her, you knew her very well."

Rain Song stopped, pulling the shawl tighter about her shoulders in a nervous gesture. "Susan knew . . . they . . . would not be taking her to the Blackfoot village." She swallowed a lump. "If I am completely honest with you, it may be my fault she is dead."

"Miss Baskin said much the same thing to me. But I do not believe it."

"It's true. Susan realized . . . Dull Knife was not acting properly toward her. I encouraged her to run." Tears were falling down Rain Song's cheeks. "I told her to try to get away."

Cullen shook his head. "It was not your fault. Any friend would have done the same."

"You are generous."

"Be generous with yourself, Rain Song. If my Susan liked you, then so do I."

"Thank you," she choked out. "You don't know how relieved I am to have you tell me that."

Cullen glanced toward the parade ground and touched her elbow, guiding her toward a small grassy area. "I get the impression you and Miss Baskin were not such good friends."

"You are very astute."

"And your ability to speak both Blackfoot and English is beyond anything I expected," he said, looking at her with wonder.

"My aunt Cora was a world-traveled singer. She was also my teacher."

"So I understand."

They had been walking down a path lined with flowers and Rain Song stopped. "I have a message to you from Susan."

He waited breathlessly.

"She said if I ever saw you, I should say this to you. I was to tell you she was not afraid." Rain Song lowered her head, unable to look into his eyes, for they were shining with tears. "She wanted me to tell you she was taking your love with her wherever she went." Her voice faltered and she had to clear her throat. "She said you should find another woman to love. She did not want you to live in loneliness."

He turned his back, and she walked away, giving him privacy. He was a man who loved his wife, just as Wind Warrior loved her.

After a while, Cullen rejoined her. "Thank you for that. I don't know if I will ever love anyone the way I loved her."

"No. You won't. But you are a wonderful man, and Susan wanted you to be happy. Take her love with you, but let her go."

"If only . . ."

"I know. I want my husband. I love him with every bit of the intensity you feel for Susan. At the moment, he believes I am dead. I can only imagine the anguish he is suffering. I am sure you felt the same anguish."

"You speak of the legendary Wind Warrior?"

"He is my husband. I carry his child. I believe you would like him."

"Would Susan have liked him?"

"Yes. If they had ever met." She touched his hand.

"I don't know if this will give you comfort, but Dull Knife is dead."

His jaw settled in a hard line. "I hope it was a long, painful death."

"He was attacked by Chinook, and fell over a cliff—a very high cliff."

For the first time, Cullen smiled. "I was ordered to pen the wolf that insisted on following you. I believe I will let her out and take her to my quarters, Rain Song."

"I think Chinook will like that."

Chapter Thirty-six

Lillian had come by the Pierces' house to see Rain Song. Mrs. Pierce excused herself and went into the kitchen. It seemed most people in Fort Benton tried to avoid Lillian.

"Wish me luck," she told Rain Song, swinging around to show off her new green gown and matching bonnet.

"I do wish you luck, but what for?"

"Tomorrow, I'll be taking the paddlewheel down to St. Louis. I'm getting married."

"Married! To whom?"

"Horace Mangers. He's a whisky drummer out of St. Louis, and he's crazy about me. We've only known each other a week, but he popped the question last night."

"I'm happy for you, Lillian." Strangely Rain Song found she meant it.

"He's a lot older than me, in his forties, but he's got money and we're moving to California, come spring."

"I wish you everything you want out of life, Lillian. You have lived through some hard times. Put that all behind you and look forward."

"I never used to like you much. But you're not so bad now."

Rain Song smiled. "I never used to like you much either. But you're not so bad now."

They laughed, and a look of understanding passed between them. They had both been through heartache and sadness, and they would always bear the scars.

Lillian looked smug. "I heard tell that handsome Major Worthington rode out a few days ago to find Wind Warrior."

Rain Song shot out of her chair. "He did?"

"That's what they're saying."

"He'll never find him. Wind Warrior will not talk to a white man he doesn't know. Especially not one in uniform."

"Oh, I think he'll find him, all right. He took Chinook with him."

Cullen knew he was back in Blackfoot country, but he did not dare approach the village. Even though he was not dressed in his uniform, he would find no welcome there. He glanced down at the wolf, which was on alert. "Go find Wind Warrior," he said, knowing the wolf did not understand him. He was amazed when the animal shot forward, toward the pine forest.

Cullen waited a moment, until the wolf disappeared, then turned his horse back toward the fort. He had done all he could to help Susan's little friend. He did not know if the wolf would lead Wind Warrior to Rain Song, but he hoped she would.

"Land sakes," Mrs. Pierce said, pulling the lace curtains aside. "There's some kind of commotion going on at the front gate. Looks like the guards are arguing with a bunch of Indians. Wonder what that's all about."

Tall Woman sat astride her horse, with her arms crossed over her breasts. "Tell that white man to get out of my way. I want to see my daughter."

Mule Deer, whom they had brought with them as translator, spoke English to the guard.

"We don't have no Blackfoot girl inside the fort," the young corporal said, taking a step back.

"Then I will speak to your chief," Tall Woman demanded.

Rain Song was running as fast as her legs would carry her. "My mother," she cried. "My mother!"

Tall Woman slid off her horse and ran toward Rain Song.

Throwing herself into her mother's arms, Rain Song wept. "I thought I would never see you again. How is my father, and Fire Wolf, how is he? I know he has grown."

"What about me?" a deep, beloved voice asked.

Rain Song flew into the arms of her husband. He held her tightly to him, pressing his cheek to hers. "I did not know what had happened to you." He pulled back and touched her face. "I found Dull Knife's body, and I feared . . ."

He grabbed her to him, unable to go on.

"I wanted you. I needed you," she said brokenly.

A crowd was gathering inside the fort, watching the unusual reunion. Cullen walked across the parade ground to the gate, a smile on his face.

"Will you introduce me to your husband?" Cullen asked. "The colonel would like to speak to the legendary Wind Warrior."

Rain Song quickly told Wind Warrior about Cullen. The two men sized each other up.

"Rain Song," Wind Warrior said, "thank the major for releasing Chinook, so we could follow her here, but tell him I will not speak to his colonel. Also tell him that if at any time he would like to visit our village, he will find a welcome there."

Rain Song turned to Cullen, and after she told him what Wind Warrior had said, she made her own request. "Please, I want to go home now. I want to have my baby with my mother beside me. When my aunt and uncle come, bring them to the village. I want them to know my husband and my family."

Cullen smiled. To be invited into the Blood Blackfoot village was an invitation no white soldier had ever received. "Will the village be located beside the Milk River?"

Rain Song asked Wind Warrior, and he nodded.

"Come home with me, Rain Song," Wind Warrior said. "Come with me now."

Joy spread over her face. "Yes. Let us leave right away."

They camped the first night beside the Missouri River. Tall Woman had a small tent of her own, with three of her husband's braves sleeping nearby. Farther into the woods Rain Song shared a tipi with her husband, while Chinook lay just outside. Curled up in Wind Warrior's arms, Rain Song had never known such happiness. "I will not be parted from you again."

Suddenly Wind Warrior gripped her arm, holding her tightly, his gaze searching hers. "Did my brother . . . did Dull Knife . . . hurt you?"

"No. Put that fear out of your mind. You might even like to know that at the last moment he could have pulled me to my death, but he let me go."

Wind Warrior trembled with pent-up emotions. "I knew he had taken his revenge on me through you. I feared you were dead and I wanted to die too."

Rain Song touched his face, smoothing her hand over the frown there. "I had to live. You made me keeper of your child."

He brushed his mouth against hers. "Forgive me."

"Why?" she asked, although she knew what was bothering him.

"I left you alone and defenseless, and at the mercy of my brother. How will you ever trust me to watch over you and our child?"

"Husband, it is a hard task you have been given in life. You are somehow responsible for the well-being of all our people. I know this and I accept it, as you must. I would not have you any other way."

His hand trembled as he placed it on her swollen stomach. "I am nothing without you."

"I know," she answered with the confidence of a woman who realized how much she was loved.

His hand moved higher and he cupped her breasts. "These are bigger."

"Yes."

He nuzzled his mouth between her breasts and she smiled. "Will I hurt the baby if I have you?"

"I am told it will not harm the child."

He let out a long breath. "I need you."

"I know."

He shook her playfully. "Why is it you know everything about me?"

"I do not. There are many mysteries surrounding this man I love. It will take me a lifetime to untangle them."

She realized he had shed his doeskin shirt because she felt his muscled back beneath her fingers. He pulled away so he could raise her gown over her head. Then he stopped, puzzled. "How does this white woman's gown come off?"

She laughed as she unhooked it down the front. He watched, his breathing heavy. When she was naked, he picked her up in his arms and held her for a long, silent moment.

"I will tell you something. When I saw you at the white man's fort, I did not know if you would come home with me."

She arched her brow. "You do not know how seductive your powers are, my husband." She placed her hands on either side of his beloved face. "Make love to me."

He dropped to his knees, as if his legs had gone out from under him. Laying her on the buffalo robe, he touched her breasts, nuzzled her neck, and ran his tongue over her lips. "I cannot wait to be inside you," he said in a hoarse voice.

Rain Song quaked when he hovered above her, and moaned when he pushed into her. Clutching him to her, she closed her eyes. He filled her heart, and took her loneliness away.

"My soul," he whispered.

"My love," she said.

Rain Song had come home.

Epilogue

Spring had come at last to Blackfoot country. Gentle breezes blew off the Milk River, where happy children frolicked and played in the sun.

Wind Warrior stood with his arms folded across his broad chest, feeling at peace as he watched the serene scene around him.

Rain Song had given him a son, and he raised his head to the wind with pride in the child that carried both their races in his small body. He watched Tall Woman scolding Fire Wolf, and Broken Lance looked on, his brow arched. Wind Warrior knew by his look that Broken Lance was thinking it was time he took over the rearing of his son.

Wind Warrior's heart swelled as Rain Song came out of her mother's tipi, with his son strapped to a cradle board. The Blackfoot people no longer saw his woman as one of the white race; they saw her for the exceptional person she was.

At that moment, Rain Song's lullaby floated on the wings of the wind and he closed his eyes, absorbing the sound of it.

Rain Song's aunt and uncle had come to visit earlier in the year. At first they tried to convince their niece to return to Washington with them. But after a few days, they admitted she had a good life and a family that loved her.

The best part of their visit had been when Rain Song and her aunt sang a song together, their voices blending so sweetly, many cried when they heard them. The beauty of that song would stay with Wind Warrior's people for many years to come, and was often retold around the campfires.

He watched Rain Song move gracefully in his direction, and saw her dip her head to place a kiss on his son's face.

"Our son has no name," she reminded Wind Warrior as she drew close to him. "When will you name him?"

He smiled, pulling her into his arms. "For now, you may pick his name. But our son will not wait for his father to name him, as I had to wait. He will go on his own vision quest when he is of an age."

"My father has been calling him Wolf Runner, because his eyes already follow Chinook."

Wind Warrior laughed. "Broken Lance's act of revenge against me because I chose your name."

"Speaking of my wolf, have you seen her? She has not come home since her latest adventure."

Wind Warrior touched his child's hand and the baby curled his fingers around his father's. "Remember when I told you Chinook might one day leave us."

Her mouth flew open. "I do not want to lose her."

He took the cradle board and smiled down at his son. He wondered if every father thought his child was perfect. "Fear not, Chinook will return, for she is attached to you. But do not be surprised if she brings a mate with her, and even cubs."

A smile lit Rain Song's face. "It would be wonderful if Chinook could have a family of her own. She has spent so much time taking care of me."

Wind Warrior touched his son's smile and it lit his heart. "Wolf Runner. It is a worthy name." In that moment a fleeting impression of a young Blackfoot boy, running with a wolf pack, touched his mind. Before he could examine the thought, it was gone.

"My father told me Cullen would be coming to the village, and he promised to take him hunting for elk."

"I never thought I would say this about any white man, but Cullen has become a good friend. Broken Lance has accepted him as a friend as well."

Rain Song looked into the eyes of her husband, and saw love reflected in the shimmering depths. He was a man of honor and duty toward those he loved. Later in the summer they would take the baby and climb up the mountain. It was a place she wanted her son to love as much as she and Wind Warrior did.

Raising her head, she watched an eagle floating on the currents of the wind. Because of Wind Warrior's teachings, she was able to envision the world through its eyes. Because of Chinook, she could look at the world through the eyes of a wolf.

Life was good beside the Milk River.

✂ ☐ **YES!**

Sign me up for the Historical Romance Book Club and send my FREE BOOKS! If I choose to stay in the club, I will pay only $8.50* each month, a savings of $6.48!

NAME: _____

ADDRESS: _____

TELEPHONE: _____

EMAIL: _____

☐ I want to pay by credit card.

☐ **VISA**　　☐ **MasterCard.**　　☐ **DISCOVER**

ACCOUNT #: _____

EXPIRATION DATE: _____

SIGNATURE: _____

Mail this page along with $2.00 shipping and handling to:
Historical Romance Book Club
PO Box 6640
Wayne, PA 19087
Or fax (must include credit card information) to:
610-995-9274
You can also sign up online at **www.dorchesterpub.com**.
*Plus $2.00 for shipping. Offer open to residents of the U.S. and Canada only.
Canadian residents please call 1-800-481-9191 for pricing information.
If under 18, a parent or guardian must sign. Terms, prices and conditions subject to change. Subscription subject to acceptance. Dorchester Publishing reserves the right to reject any order or cancel any subscription.